"Careful, Simone. Baiting me will only make me do something you'll regret."

"Like what?" She crossed her arms ~~~~~~~~~~~ chest and inched up ~~~~~~~~~~~~~~~~~~~~~

"Well? I'm wai~~~~~~~

"Yes, you are, ~~~~~~~~~~~~~~~~~~~~~~~ed the back of her he~~~~~~~~~~~~~~~~~~~~~ hers. He wasn't cert~~~~~~~~~~~~~~ surprised.

There was only one thing more invigorating than kissing an expectant Simone and that was kissing an angry one. He drew her so tightly against him he wasn't certain whose heart was beating double time.

She nipped at his lip gently. He grinned even as he pulled back and opened his eyes to stare into hers.

"Anytime you want to add sex to the deal, you let me know."

She lifted a hand to his face, stroked gentle fingers down his cheek before she curled her fingers under his chin. "I hope you got that out of your system, because it's not going to happen again."

* * *

Be sure to check out the next stories in this exciting miniseries!

Honor Bound—Seeking justice...and falling in love

* * *

If you're on Twitter, tell us what you think of Harlequin Romantic Suspense! #harlequinromsuspense

Dear Reader,

I've often wondered at what age we are most vulnerable as children. At what point can something happen that's so devastating that we are changed from whatever fate meant us to be? For me, I was nine and the event was my parents' divorce. I can trace so much of what makes me who I am directly to that event.

When the idea of the Honor Bound trilogy first took hold, I knew: three friends had survived something tragic, their childhood friend's murder. From a psychological and writing perspective, the idea that Simone, Allie and Eden would deal with Chloe's murder in entirely different ways made writing these stories even more exciting.

When Simone Armstrong first appeared in *More Than a Lawman*, I realized she would do whatever it takes to protect those she considers "hers." As a prosecutor, her dedication gives her what she needs: the opportunity to put dangerous criminals behind bars. But at what cost to herself? I could find only one answer: her marriage. Can you hear me cackling with glee at the discovery of who her hero had to be?

You guessed it. Her ex-husband.

Vince Sutton fell hard for Simone from the moment they met, but as a former soldier who continues to fight his own personal battles, he wasn't a man used to taking second place. And that opened up a lot of those "conflict" doors.

I'm a fan of reunion stories and as soon as I'd found these two characters, I knew I'd struck gold. It's a serious battle of wills and one I hope you enjoy reading.

Anna J.

REUNITED WITH THE P.I.

Anna J. Stewart

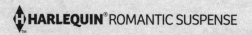

HARLEQUIN®ROMANTIC SUSPENSE

Recycling programs
for this product may
not exist in your area.

ISBN-13: 978-0-373-40212-0

Reunited with the P.I.

Printed in U.S.A.

Anna J. Stewart, a *USA TODAY* and national bestselling author, loves to spend a free weekend curled up in her favorite chair with Snickers, her cat, remote in hand, flipping through whatever streaming service her Wi-Fi will connect to. A geek at heart, she loves blow-'em-up action and sci-fi movies and has rarely met a superhero she didn't like. Anna writes both sweet contemporary and romantic suspense for Harlequin and believes that, when all is said and done, there's nothing better than writing about falling in love, with a little action thrown in for good measure.

Books by Anna J. Stewart

Harlequin Romantic Suspense

More than A Lawman
Reunited with the P.I.

Harlequin Heartwarming

Christmas, Actually
"The Christmas Wish"

The Bad Boy of Butterfly Harbor

Make Me a Match
"Suddenly Sophie"

Recipe for Redemption

Visit the Author Profile page at Harlequin.com for more titles.

For Brenda Novak
who never let me forget this was the dream.

Chapter 1

"Miss Armstrong, is the state ready to proceed with opening statements?"

Simone gripped the gold-tipped fountain pen her father had given her for law school graduation, a graduation he couldn't be bothered to attend. An unfamiliar rush of uncertainty flooded her body and pulled her to her feet. She ignored the not-so-subtle murmurs of the packed courtroom along with the amused gleam of challenge in high-priced defense attorney Silvio Poltanic's beady-eyed stare.

"Respectfully, Your Honor…" Thanks to the five years she'd spent in the Sacramento County DA's office, none of the unease in her belly eked out in her practiced, determined voice. "The district attorney's office would like to request a week's postponement."

"Your Honor!" Poltanic pushed his significant bulk

out of the wooden chair. His nasal voice made Simone dig her manicured nails deep into her palm. "The jury has been chosen. My client has been waiting for over four months for his day in court. We are ready to proceed immediately."

"And we will. In one week. I apologize, Your Honor. I take full responsibility for my lack of preparedness." The words nearly sliced through her. There hadn't been a day in all of Simone's twenty-nine years that she hadn't been prepared for whatever life threw at her, but even she hadn't expected the call from Mara Orlov's protective detail this morning letting her know that sometime in the last twelve hours her star witness had vanished.

"I do see where the original trial date was set for next month." Judge Buford glanced over his wire-rim glasses from Simone to the files on his desk. The tension in Simone's chest eased even as she sensed Poltanic's blood pressure rise from across the aisle. "I also understand the district attorney recently let three of his full-time investigators go."

"One of whom was assisting me on the case, Your Honor." It wasn't a lie…exactly. She had been assigned an investigator when the fraud investigation into Denton and his business practices first landed on her desk. Before Christmas. Last year.

"As it is a Thursday and there's no court tomorrow, I'm inclined to grant the prosecution's request," Judge Buford said.

"But—"

"In light of that, Judge." Poltanic held out a hand to calm his protesting, panicking and suddenly pale client. "I would like to revisit the issue of bail for Mr. Denton.

As I've previously argued, he has a wife, children." He motioned to Marilyn Denton and their two teenage sons sitting in the gallery behind their father. The older boy had a defiant, controlled expression on his face while his brother looked...lost. "Along with a business that needs tending, not to mention Mr. Denton has strong ties to the community."

"The charges levied against Mr. Denton certainly constitute strong ties to *some* in the community." Simone shifted her focus to the judge. She couldn't allow herself the luxury of sympathy when it came to the Denton family. It wasn't their fault who they'd been saddled with. Well, his sons at least. After a few run-ins with Marilyn Denton, Simone had little doubt his wife knew exactly the type of man she'd married. "I would remind the court the business Mr. Denton is so concerned with would be the same one we believe he established specifically to launder illicit funds." Simone took a deep breath. She hated having to lay even one card on the table, let alone half her hand, but she needed time to find Mara. "Our ongoing investigation has uncovered multiple criminal connections that would make Mr. Denton's fleeing the jurisdiction a definite possibility."

"Then might I suggest you get on with presenting your case instead of trying new stalling tactics?" Poltanic sneered.

Simone didn't react. She kept her eyes on the judge, with his wrinkled grandfatherly face and kind eyes. Judge Buford was, above all, a civil man. He appreciated patience and respect. Only the law itself ranked higher on the acceptable scale than professionalism.

"Will one week give you the time to complete your preparedness, Miss Armstrong?" Judge Buford leaned his arms on his desk. The skepticism she saw in his gaze told her he didn't buy the "I'm not prepared" argument for a second.

"I certainly hope so, Your Honor." Before she crushed the fountain pen and sent ink exploding all over the table and her white silk suit, she set it down. "You have my word."

Poltanic's derisive snort was the last bit of ammunition needed as Judge Buford slid a disapproving glance the defense attorney's way.

"Well, let's be certain, shall we." The judge offered a tight smile. "I'll give you until a week from Monday to get your case in order."

Simone's lips twitched. "Thank you very much, Your Honor."

"Your Honor!" Poltanic puffed up to the point Simone worried the buttons on his strained vest would become lethal weapons.

Judge Buford held up his hand, gestured for his court clerk to approach. Simone curled her toes in her shoes, not an easy feat given the sharp points on the designer pumps.

"We will reconvene in ten days ready for opening statements. If," Judge Buford said with a pointed look at Simone, "at that time the DA requests another delay, I'm going to give serious consideration to Mr. Poltanic's request for bail. Get it together, Miss Armstrong. That's all for today." He banged his gavel and brought an end to Simone's overly crappy morning. "Court dismissed."

"Care to comment for the *Sacramento Journal*, Simone?" Benedict Russell, recently promoted feature crime reporter held out his cell phone like a recorder. His hawk-like brown eyes and sallow skin reminded her of a bird of prey swooping in on yet another one of its victims.

"On the record?" She waited until a flare of hope flashed in his gaze before she arched a brow and snapped her case shut. "I'm just an ineffectual, pedantic political pawn, Russell. Those were your words last year, weren't they?" She hoisted her briefcase off the table and offered him her best "I could kill you with my pinky finger" smile. "I can't imagine your readers are interested in anything I have to say."

"They'll be quite interested in what the valley's own Avenging Angel has to say, actually." He smirked at the moniker he'd tagged her with.

"Don't call me that." She might approach every case with her eye aimed on justice, but that didn't mean she had anything resembling an angel's wings. Far from it. She did whatever she could to balance the scale for victims. She wasn't vengeful. Just…determined.

"Hey, it's not my fault it's caught on." But didn't he look proud of himself. "And you're wrong. Our readers are more than interested in what someone who's thinking about running for district attorney has to say."

Had Simone not spent most of her life keeping a mask of impassiveness in place, she might have tripped over her stiletto heels. How had The Troll found out when she hadn't even made up her mind?

"No comment." She pushed through the gate, unable to avoid the tear-filled accusatory glare Marilyn Denton aimed at her as she headed from the courtroom. She couldn't matter, Simone told herself. Denton was a criminal. His so-called businesses had helped other, more dangerous criminals. She was certain of it. He belonged behind bars. End of story.

Russell's scurrying footsteps behind her called to mind a rat targeting a particularly nice pile of garbage. Before she reached the stairs, she spun around and held up her hand. Russell skidded to a stop and nearly plowed into her.

"Did I stutter? No comment, Russell." She needed to remind her assistant Kyla to be extra vigilant in manning her phone. She wouldn't put it past the reporter to get someone else to do his dirty work by trying to scam a statement.

"So this delay isn't the DA's means of stalling for a deal with Paul Denton?" Russell demanded.

Anger washed over her as the last trace of humor faded from her face. What was it with everyone thinking there was a deal to be made? First the DA, then his political advisor, now Russell? "There will be no deal." Shoot. She'd just given a statement. She glanced around the slick, tiled hallway, through the crowd of overworked public defenders and disgruntled potential jurors. May as well make her morning a complete loss. She motioned to Russell's phone and waited for him to click the recorder back on. "It is my intention to see Mr. Denton pay for his crimes by serving a significant prison sentence. The *maximum* sentence. If he chooses to try to mitigate that time by offering evidence against those he's worked for and with, we will be more than happy to take that into consideration after his trial. But again, there will be no deal."

"And if I called DA Lawson and asked him to comment?" Russell was practically salivating at the idea.

"He'll tell you the same thing." The chances of Benedict Russell making it past Ward Lawson's gargoyle of a receptionist were slim to none. "If you'll excuse me, I have an appointment." Beginning with finding out how the hell her witness had managed to disappear despite two experienced deputies sitting outside her apartment.

She was downstairs and outside in record time, listening to a stream of messages through her earpiece. Days like this, when the DA himself left a terse "we need to talk" message on her voice mail, Simone would give anything for her office not to be less than a few feet away from the courthouse. They'd already discussed deal options for Denton, none of which sat well with Simone. While the DA hadn't pushed—exactly—she knew Lawson would be happy to make this case go away as quickly as possible. She'd offered to step down, publicly of course. But the obvious discord in the DA's office signified it was something the beleaguered Lawson couldn't afford, with his stagnant approval ratings. The Denton case remained hers.

For now.

Despite Poltanic's accusation making perfect sense, Simone wasn't interested in stalling.

Unless of course said stalling included stopping for a triple-shot latte from her favorite coffee cart on the corner.

Simone might, as Dr. Allie Hollister—one of her best friends—often accused, live life as part rabbit with her penchant for salads, nuts and an inordinate amount of blended juices, but that didn't mean she didn't have a weakness. Especially on a day like today.

Simone looked forlornly at the chocolate croissant peeking out at her from the pastry case. Okay, two weaknesses.

Coffee in one hand and warm, gooey croissant in the other, she slowed her pace and crossed the street, detouring to the underground parking lot for one of those quick, private pull-it-together sessions she'd started holding in her car during law school. Between the adrenaline rush of getting her delay and the dawning realization that Mara Orlov had turned her case upside down, she needed a few minutes to decompress before tackling whatever her boss—and fellow prosecutors in the office—were going to lay on her.

She couldn't shake the feeling her time as the office's rising star was about to come to a screeching halt.

She dumped her briefcase in the passenger seat, stashed her cup in the holder and leaned her head back. One, two, three deep breaths later, she finally felt the calm descend...

Ah. There. Now she could savor the combination of chocolate and caffeine.

She sipped. And nibbled. And just about swooned.

Her phone rang. Simone groaned. Leave it to the DA's office to make sure reception was crystal-clear in their parking lot.

Seeing Allie's grinning face pop up in caller ID had Simone smiling in spite of herself. She tapped her ear. "What's up, Al? I've got about five minutes before I have to face a firing squad."

"I tried to catch you at the courthouse, but you didn't hear me."

"Sorry." Simone sank her teeth into the pastry and moaned. Wow, this was better than sex. "Bad morning in court. My brain's a mess."

"Must have been. Eden's never going to believe you gave Benedict Russell five seconds let alone two and a half minutes."

Simone could envision Allie's trademark pixie smile

shining from under her cap of dark hair. "Eden's not up to believing anything until she gets back from her honeymoon."

Allie laughed. "It's just like Eden St. Claire to celebrate catching a pair of serial killers by getting married."

The residual tension in Simone's spine eased. "Our friend has always prided herself on being unpredictable. Why else would she leave journalism and have accepted that new job as a police consultant in their cold case division?" Eden and Allie. Simone smiled. Sometimes she swore her life began that first day in kindergarten when they'd found each other on the playground. Sisters from the start. Simone, Eden, Allie and...

Simone squeezed her eyes shut against the unwanted image of a freckle-faced, redheaded little girl with mismatched sneakers. *Chloe*. Simone brushed her finger against the heart pendant at her throat.

"You have a court case today?"

Allie sighed that exhausted sigh that normally took her weeks to build up to. "I've been consulting on a custody battle that's getting nasty. This poor kid. Hearing her parents fight over her and their failures as human beings is taking its toll. She's a sad little thing. Hard to believe her name is Hope."

"How old is she?" Simone sipped her coffee and settled into BFF mode. Whatever was lurking upstairs could wait a few more minutes.

"Nine," Allie said after a slight hesitation. "The age when everything changes." Simone dug her manicured fingernails into the hem of her skirt. How well they knew. After twenty years of trying to put the murder of her childhood friend Chloe Evans behind her, behind *them*, Chloe's killer had resurfaced and begun bestowing special "gifts" on her, Allie and Eden. The gifts she could handle, for the most part. It was the psychopath's attention to their professional—and personal—lives that got to her. He'd wedged himself into Eden's case, nearly costing an FBI agent his life. It was all Simone could do not to think about what Chloe's killer might be planning next. As much as Simone agreed Chloe Evans's case should be readdressed, the wounds that came with it weren't ones Simone was in any hurry to revisit.

The pastry and coffee churned in her stomach as the image of wilted violets and pink stationery came to mind. *Push it aside. Focus on the case. On Mara. On what you* can *control.*

"You sound stressed. I take it you can't do lunch today?" Allie asked.

"Any other day, Al, I swear. My case is circling the drain and I have massive damage control ahead of me. Ah, how about dinner tonight or tomorrow?"

"I'm leaving tonight for a conference in Los Angeles. How about next week after Eden and Cole get back?"

So it wasn't a one-on-one she needed, but a community confab? "It does for me if it does for you. Allie..." she trailed off, almost afraid to ask. "You haven't gotten any more notes, have you? This doesn't have anything to do with Chloe's killer, does it?"

"There's been nothing since Chloe's missing shoe was mailed to the police last month. And no, it doesn't have anything to do with that. Well, not directly. Just something that's come up I need to talk out."

"You know what?" Simone knew how much it took for Allie to ask for help. Their stalwart "take on anything" friend was one of the most logical, stable people

Simone had ever known. She was also a terrible liar. "How about a late lunch? I can probably get out of the office around two—"

"It can wait, Simone," Allie cut her off. "Honestly, it's not that big of a deal. You have enough on your plate without adding my sudden insecurities to the mix."

Since when did Allie feel insecure about anything? "I'm a phone call away, or a text." Simone looked down at her phone as a second call came in—another from her boss. A headache pounded against the side of her head as if asking permission to be admitted. "Chin up, Al. The world isn't used to seeing you frown."

"How do you know I'm frowning?"

"Because I know you and Eden better than you know yourselves." She hadn't earned her mother hen reputation by accident. "I'll talk to you later."

"Yeah. Good luck with the boss."

"I'm going to need it." Simone disconnected and tested her stomach by plucking off another flaky bite of chocolaty goodness. She heaved an Allie-worthy sigh and leaned her arm on the door, rubbing her temple as she willed the caffeine to take her away.

The sharp knock on her window had her yelping. Coffee sloshed over the back of her hand, spattering the side of her white shirt, and left her seeing red. "Son of a—"

Simone leaned back and stared out at the familiar, slightly pudgy middle-aged face. "Russo?" The senior deputy who had been assigned to watch Mara stepped away as she shoved open the door. "What do you think you're doing sneaking up on me like that?"

"I needed to talk to you." He motioned her into the shadows. "Alone."

"Well, nothing gets the attention of a single woman faster than stalking her in a parking garage." Simone planted her hands on her hips and dipped her chin. After a calming breath, she looked at him, only then noticing he wasn't in uniform. But he was wearing his sidearm. "Is there any news on Mara? Tell me you found her."

"Can't say that." Russo's eyes narrowed. "And I won't be getting any updates since Ernie and I have been advised by our union rep not to discuss the investigation."

"What investigation?" Simone crossed her arms as alarm bells clanged in her head. "It's not your fault she's rabbited."

"Apparently that's not how the higher-ups see it. Dereliction of duty was one of the phrases my boss and one of your lot from the DA's office were throwing around. Dereliction, yeah, right."

One of her lot? The hostility in his voice shoved her off-kilter. Russo was as easygoing as anyone she'd ever known. It was one reason she'd specifically asked for him where Mara was concerned.

"Ernie and I did everything by the book," Russo continued. "From the time we parked in front of her apartment at six p.m. We did the routine checks, confirmed arrangements for this morning to bring her to court. She even made us a big thermos of coffee before she turned in around midnight."

"Sounds like Mara," Simone said. "Then what happened?"

Exhaustion crept over the deputy's face as his anger seemed to abate. "One second we're drinking coffee and eating oatmeal cookies, and the next, the sun's streaming through our windshield and Mara's gone. We didn't even have a chance to get our bearings before we're called into the station and put on indefinite administrative leave effective immediately."

"You're suggesting Mara drugged you." There wasn't any way to keep the disbelief out of her voice. "That doesn't make any sense."

"Show me one thing that's made sense with this case from the get-go," Russo said. "That's not even the weirdest part. As we started asking questions about this morning and tried to explain ourselves, our captain informs us the orders for our suspension came from a higher-up. We're off the case."

"And the higher-up he's referring to is someone in my office?" Could this day really get any worse?

"My only other guess would be the Feds stuck their nose into the Denton case, but I haven't heard one word about them sniffing around, have you?"

"No, I haven't. Who was it you spoke with from the DA's office?"

"Didn't get his name but I've seen him around the last few months. I don't know what happened last night with Mara, but in all my twenty years on the job, I've never once fallen asleep. I can only hope it was Mara who drugged us."

"But what would she—"

"She's gone, isn't she? Our best guess is she wanted out. Maybe she came to it on her own, maybe she had help." Concern and suspicion shone in his dark eyes. "I hate to think of anything happening to her, Simone. Especially when she was under our watch."

Not just under their watch; Mara was *her* responsibility. Not that it had taken much convincing to get the young woman to testify against her former boss. Other than last-minute panic a couple of weeks ago, the recent college graduate had seen her involvement in the case as a grand adventure. How many times had Simone wished all her witnesses were as eager to help? "Wait. Back up a second. Did you say your boss called you to the station *before* you could report Mara as missing?"

"Now do you see why I wanted to talk to you away from your office?" Russo asked. "Whatever's going on with your witness, with this case, someone's putting their thumb on the scale. It's like we're five steps behind. It's bad for Mara, she's either out there alone getting into trouble, or…"

Simone held up her hand in defiance as guilt and fear rose. "We're going to assume it was her choice to run until we have evidence to the contrary." Simone had been distracted lately. Maybe she'd missed something with Mara. Maybe she hadn't been as convincing as she'd thought. But the more Simone digested it, the more it didn't make sense. How many times had Mara told her she was still running and crunching numbers, that she was determined to lock down every penny of money Paul Denton had funneled through his companies, both legitimate and shell? Simone had told her there was enough data already. But she hadn't specifically warned her off.

Simone's arms began to tremble and only then did she realize she'd clenched her fists so hard her muscles were rebelling. "You're sure she didn't give any indication she was going to bolt?"

"I've guarded my share of witnesses, Simone. She was nervous, sure, but she was solid. Besides—" He hesitated and winced.

"Besides what?"

"She didn't want to let you down. She looks up to you, Simone. You're a bit of a hero to her."

A new layer of guilt overtook the sense of responsibility she'd felt. "Tell me about this guy from the DA's office." She needed to put all this into some kind of order before she talked to her boss.

"I snapped this before I left the station." He pulled out his cell phone and tapped on the screen. "I'm assuming you know who he is."

Simone looked at the thirty-something, impeccably dressed blond man. The icy blue eyes were all too familiar even from the far distance. Simone's world tipped. "That's Cal Hobard, special assistant to the DA. He came to work in this office about six months—" *Six months ago.* The same time she'd officially filed charges against Paul Denton.

If Simone was the type of person who believed in them, she'd think this was a coincidence. She and the DA had always had a cordial relationship despite his belief the Denton case was a no-win situation, one that could even put his political future in jeopardy. Whereas everyone else in the office seemed to understand Denton's conviction could be a career maker.

Simone gnawed on the inside of her cheek. Still, there was no telling what anyone's agenda might be.

"We need to find Mara," Simone said. Not only because the case hinged on the young woman's testimony, but because Simone had promised to keep her safe. "Can you get me copies of all your notes? Anything you might have kept track of since you've been watching her?"

"Absolutely. You want me to deliver them to your office?"

"No." She couldn't risk it—someone in the office was working against her. Right now, she couldn't shake the sensation that returning to the DA's office three floors above would be tantamount to walking into the enemy's camp. "No. Get everything together and deliver it to Jack McTavish in Major Crimes. Do you know him?"

"Sure. Jack's good people. Excellent cop."

That Simone had been dating him off and on for the last few weeks should help. Apart from Jack's partner, Cole Delaney, there wasn't anyone she trusted more in the police. Jack would never betray her. "I'll give him a heads-up to expect something. I also want to know what you were dosed with. I don't suppose you kept the thermos—"

"We had to turn it in to confirm our story," Russo said as he reached into his pocket. He pulled out a small vial in an evidence bag and handed it over. "But to be safe."

She'd definitely brought the right cops on board. "I'll get this tested." One of the reasons she kept up good relations with her former expert witnesses. "You might mention to Jack that you turned in the thermos to your superiors, to get that information out there and on the record. Meanwhile, if you need to get in touch with me, contact me through this email address." She ripped off a piece of paper out of his notebook and scribbled the backup email she, Eden and Allie shared on Eden's private server. And here she'd called Eden paranoid when she'd first set up the arrangement. "Have the subject line say 'A Bert and Ernie update.'"

Russo smirked. "Gee, that's a new one."

"Blame your partner's parents for naming him Ernest," Simone said. "You good now?"

"I won't be good until Mara turns up." Russo shook his head, his concern palpable. "I've dumped a huge mess in your lap, Simone. You can't do this alone. There has to be someone you can trust to help you."

"There is." Simone's throat tightened in dread. "But he's not going to be happy to see me."

Chapter 2

"Now that's not something you see every day."

The dazed wonder in his most recent hire's voice had Vince Sutton glancing up from where he'd been filling a third pitcher of beer. It was a Thursday night and the regulars were in The Brass Eagle. "What's that?"

Since he'd hired Travis Fielding all of three months ago, Vince had found there was little that didn't amuse the college senior. Tall and gangly with an odd penchant for retro seventies' paisley and sideburns, the computer science major seemed to be off in his own world most of the time.

"Tell me that's not an angel who just walked in." Travis suddenly jumped back as he'd over-poured the line of tequila shots. The pungent liquid dribbled over the lip of the bar and onto the kid's pristine white sneakers.

Despite hearing the distinct *cha-ching* of lost cash,

Vince tossed Travis a towel. When he glanced over again, he found his employee's "angel" standing directly across from him. "Simone."

Vince went numb as he took in the familiar lush waves of thick hair, her startling sapphire-blue eyes that, despite every attempt, couldn't hide her emotions. Not from him, at least. Had it really been three years since he'd touched her face, those cheekbones? Trailed his finger down that pointed nose that only hinted at the stubbornness he knew she possessed? Traced that small tattoo on the base of her—

"Hello, Vince."

Her voice washed over him, sultry, intoxicating. How two words could hold so much—a greeting, a promise, a reminder—was beyond him. Then again, he'd stopped trying to figure out Simone Armstrong around the time he'd served her with divorce papers.

As if by rote, he reached for a bottle of Riesling. He poured her a glass before her tempting smile captured him completely. "You're looking good." As if Simone could ever look bad.

Beside him, Travis guffawed and blinked wide eyes at Vince as if he'd become his idol.

Simone still had that classic Hollywood blond bombshell thing going for her. But beyond the seductive touch of Veronica Lake and the fulsomeness of Marilyn's curves, there was more than a fair share of the smart spitfire combo of Hepburn and Bacall.

"So are you." With a slight nod, she accepted the wine he offered. "Hello." She offered her other hand to Travis, who scrubbed both his palms hard against his chest before taking her hand. "I'm Simone Armstrong."

"She means Deputy District Attorney Armstrong.

The Avenging Angel," Vince added with enough venom in his voice to make Simone's eye twitch. "And this, Simone, is Mr. Travis Fielding. I'm betting he'll find his voice once he picks it up off the floor along with his tongue." His gaze skimmed her as low as he dared. "I see you haven't exhausted the fashion industry's supply of white fabric yet." His eyes stopped on the tiny pearl button between her full breasts, and then on the pendant at the base of her throat. The open collar of her tailored silk shirt dipped respectfully enough for office attire, but allowed a peek at those luscious curves of hers. Did she still invest in that barely there underwear? His fingers itched to discover whether she wore lace or silk. Or anything at all.

"Why change what works?" Simone flicked an annoyed expression at him before offering a warm smile to Travis. "It's a pleasure to meet you, Travis. Do you mind if I have a word with your boss for a few minutes?"

"N-no." Travis's breath came out in a shudder.

Vince walked around the kid to move beyond the bar. "Don't forget those shots for your customers. And take two pitchers to the back table for me. The construction workers are getting restless."

Travis nodded and blinked himself out of whatever hormonal trance Simone had put him in.

"Do you mind?" Simone stopped him when he led her to a booth by the front window. "Back there?" She gestured to the cubby beside the bar where he normally did the daily books. The stubble of hair on the back of his neck prickled as he noticed the tight grip she had on her briefcase. Simone was nothing if not professional, but now he saw something he wasn't quite used to.

His ex-wife was nervous.

Whatever pleasure he might have taken in causing her some temporary discomfort vanished as every ounce of training—from his service in the Marines to his subsequent years as a private investigator—put him on guard. Whatever was going on had to be bad for Simone to turn up on his doorstep.

"Sit wherever you'd like." He maneuvered her ahead of him, getting her situated before he sat facing the room. He kept one leg out and braced in his usual "just in case" posture. "What's going on, Simone? You don't do social calls on a whim." Or ever. "And certainly not after this much time had gone by."

She cringed, her knuckles going white around her glass as she drank half its contents. "I want to hire you."

If she'd come in here saying she wanted to reconcile she couldn't have surprised him more. "You need a bartender for a private party?"

"I need an investigator I can trust."

For an instant, the desire for a beer overtook his power of speech. He shook his head and shifted his attention to the bar, keeping the memories—and the nightmares—at bay. "I'm out of that business."

The brief flash of sympathy that crossed her face had him gnashing his teeth. Of course she knew what had happened. Everyone in the whole valley knew what happened.

"I heard about the Walker case. That you'd taken a break after…" Her soft voice hit his heart like a sledgehammer. "I didn't realize you'd decided to make it permanent."

"Now you know." Vince had made it permanent because it was the only way to save his sanity. A man could only witness the sickening things people did to one another for so long before he started to expect the worst. Not that anything would change the endless nights he spent wondering if he'd missed something, if anything he could have done might have stopped a young girl's murder. If he'd been a day, hours, even minutes faster. "This is my focus now." He indicated the polished wood paneling and brass fixtures, the tables he'd refinished himself. "The building's mine free and clear. I've got a steady clientele, one that doesn't expect anything other than a topped-up glass and a full plate. Best of all? I don't answer to anyone other than myself and my employees."

"I really don't want to be difficult about this," Simone said.

"Since when?"

"I can't take no for an answer, Vince."

He smirked. "Want to bet?"

"Oh, for…"

She scrubbed a hand across her forehead and only then did he notice the tired, dark circles under her eyes. He'd always worried that her job would eventually get to her. Clearly he'd been right.

"If this is about Jason—" she began.

"It's not."

Her eyebrow arched so high it almost disappeared into her hairline.

"It's not *just* about Jason, Simone. But since you brought it up." He rested his arms on the table and leaned toward her. "You sent my brother to prison." It took all his effort to keep his voice down. "Without a second thought. You never once allowed yourself to consider the extenuating circumstances that happened during that robbery. To top it all off, you and I were barely back from our honeymoon when you advised the prosecuting attorney to throw the book at him, at a kid who'd gotten in with the wrong crowd."

"First." Simone leaned far enough in that he could feel the warmth of her breath on his face. "Jason *always* ran with the wrong crowd. Second, I can't believe you're still blaming me for doing my job. And, not to repeat myself, but at the time I had no idea what specific case they were asking about. I read the notes and gave them my *opinion*. I didn't realize they'd use the strategy I came up with to prosecute your brother."

"Nor did you step in and try to stop it when they did. He's family, Simone. He was *your* family."

"I can't believe we're still having this conversation." She pressed her fingers into her temple and squeezed her eyes shut. She was trying to hide it under all that fancy makeup, but she looked as if she was doing more than burning the candle at both ends. It looked like she'd torched an entire candle shop. She took a deep breath and released it. "There was more to the case against Jason and you know it. He could have taken the deal he was offered and testified. And I'm sorry, but you've never been objective where your brother is concerned. You know this. You've told me so yourself."

"The line between good and bad gets blurred when your father beats the crap out of you and your mother lets it happen."

"And yet *you* turned out fine. It all comes down to choices. You made good ones. Jason didn't. Funny how you're all about consequences except in this scenario."

That Simone was right—had always been right about his kid brother—never did sit well with him. It didn't matter how many times he'd gone to bat for Jason, tried to help him, detour him or get him a job, the kid was a wreck. If he didn't have bad luck, he'd have no luck at all. Part of Vince had begun to believe he had to choose: his brother or his wife. And the more he dwelled on it, the more he resented it. And her. That the press had dubbed her an avenging angel hadn't surprised him. What had taken them so long? "Okay, fine, but I'm making another choice now. Find yourself another investigator, Simone. I'm not your man."

He hadn't meant to sound taunting, or cold, but he'd always seemed to say the wrong thing around his former wife.

"Are you so determined to punish me for something that happened years ago you won't even hear me out?"

"You should have asked whose file it was." And here he thought he'd set the resentment aside when he'd filed for divorce. He braced himself as she looked at him in silence. "You should have paid closer attention to whose life you were about to destroy."

"You're right." She drank the rest of her wine and cringed as if the admission burned. "I should have. If I'd known it was Jason, maybe I would have done things differently." She hesitated. "If that's worth anything now."

"It's not," he lied. Her personal learning curve was one of the qualities he admired most about her. Simone wasn't one to make the same mistake twice. But she'd made one that put his brother behind bars for ten years for a crime he hadn't technically committed, and it wasn't something Vince would get past anytime soon.

"Good to know you've moved beyond it." She toasted him with her empty glass. "At least let me tell you about this case before you shut me down. Please."

"Nothing you say will change my mind."

"So long as you're keeping an open mind."

There it was. The sarcasm. The passive aggressive mind games she excelled at. "Why me?" He sat back and kept a steady gaze on hers. "Those expensive investigators at the DA's office not cutting it? You need to slum it with us mere mortals?"

"If you must know I'm having some trust issues with the people I work with, and by the way, I never thought of you as a mere anything, Vince. Not once."

If she meant the statement as a peace offering, it was a pretty good one. Hating himself, fighting that stomach-clenching dread that his world was about to open up under his feet again, he gave in to her. "I assume this has something to do with Paul Denton?"

Her brow furrowed. "You've been following things?"

More like he'd been following her. Just because he'd ended it between them didn't mean he wasn't proud of Simone's accomplishments. He knew she'd blown through college and law school in record time, landed at the DA's office weeks after graduation and won her first case a month after that. Her ambition and determination were what had attracted him to her in the first place. Until he'd realized that same ambition and dedication to the letter of the law didn't leave much room for him.

"It's been difficult not to," Vince told her. "Front page headlines for the past few weeks. Corporate kickbacks, shell companies, money laundering. Sexy stuff."

"I'm convinced it's the tip of an iceberg," Simone added as she pulled out a file folder and set it on the table. She flipped it open to show a small photograph stapled to the top of a report. A pretty, dark-haired young woman. Green eyes. *Green eyes…* Vince forced himself to look. Did they always have to have green eyes?

"Mara Orlov was fresh out of college when she started in Paul Denton's private office as his record keeper," Simone continued. "She's smart, Vince. Like supersmart, with an eidetic memory, and she picks up on everything. So when she came across a pattern in his books, she dug deeper and uncovered Denton's fraud. Money that should have been dispersed was getting moved from business to business and then it would vanish. She wrote out a detailed report, photocopied all the records and brought everything she had to a friend of hers in my office who brought it to me."

"Why you?"

"The DA was in the hospital. Gall bladder surgery and then complications," she explained. "Luck of the draw meant he was out of the office for weeks."

Vince smirked. "Luck? You never take a day off and were there, ready and able, to assume control."

"She'll be a star in the witness box." Simone's eyes narrowed as she plowed on. "She's unshakable, actually. Or so I thought. We hit a rough patch a little while ago and she got spooked. She thought someone was following her. So after some convincing, I assigned two deputies to watch her. She was back on board, until this morning." She was staring at him, hard. "She took off, Vince. Poof. The deputies guarding her were drugged and when they went up to her apartment to get her, they found she was gone—her car, too. Now they've been suspended pending an investigation that shouldn't even be open. I need someone completely unconnected to law enforcement. This could be good for you, Vince. Maybe you need this. *I* need you."

If only that were true. "You're certain she took off?" Vince purposely flipped the pages over to obscure the photograph. The facts and details blurred, got lost behind the past, locked away by sheer will. "You sure she wasn't bought off?"

Simone inclined her head and frowned; he recognized the move. "Bought off? You mean bribed?"

"You didn't think of that?" he asked. Could his ex be that naive? He wouldn't have thought so.

"No." She sagged in her seat to the point he wanted to reach over and gently erase the lines of concern between her brows. "No, honestly, it never crossed my mind. She's not that kind of person, Vince. But you thought it immediately, which proves I've come to the right person. Maybe she got scared again, or..."

"Or maybe someone got to her."

"I can't let myself think that." He heard a hint of desperation in her voice, one that had slipped through her defenses. "Not yet."

Whatever sharp retort Vince considered throwing at her became stuck in his throat. He might know what buttons to push when it came to Simone and her devotion to protecting people—especially women. But he wasn't so callous as to use the unsolved murder of her childhood friend as a verbal weapon against her.

"Will you please take the case?" she pleaded.

"Based on what you've told me?" Despite his instincts, his mind was already ticking off avenues to pursue: the girl's address, her friends, family. He still had contacts at various phone companies to trace the girl's cell phone. Wouldn't take much to get a feel for things. "No."

"If it's money—" His eyes narrowed and she held up her hands in surrender. "Sorry. I know. Touchy subject."

"Only where you're concerned." Never in his wildest dreams had he imagined he'd end up marrying a woman with a trust fund larger than a small country's national budget. She hadn't lorded it over him, but her too-generous offer of spousal support had left a giant hole in his ego. As if he needed or wanted anything from Simone other than…Simone. "There has to be more to this than a simple missing witness, Simone. What aren't you telling me?"

"A lot." Her lips were pinched. "But nothing I can prove. Yet. I only have ten days before I'm back in court. If we can find her by then—"

"What do you mean *we*? You hire me, I do the job and report to you. I don't play well with others. And you definitely don't play well with me."

"Right. It said that on the divorce decree."

"Simone—"

"If you take the job, you work for me," she said. "My terms. Not the DA's office. And not officially. I'm paying you. Off the books. In cash. Up front if you want. But I need to be involved, Vince. Especially when you find her. I need her to verify on the stand where those books of Denton's came from. Without her, my case falls apart and Denton—and whoever he might be connected to—will get off."

When he found Mara, not if. Did she honestly expect to find…no! He couldn't go down this road again. Except that deep chasm opening moments before hadn't been despair, he realized; it had been Simone's rabbit hole of a conscience. Mara was one of Simone's crusades; one of those "I'm going to save her and fix her" situations his ex kept getting involved in.

When was she going to accept that no matter what, she couldn't go back and save Chloe Evans?

Vince tapped his fingers against the file. It didn't matter how long Simone spent in the criminal justice system, she clung to that optimism of hers like a life preserver. In Vince's experience, cases like this rarely ended well. But he also knew Simone well enough to admit that telling her would only make her dig her heels in.

He honestly didn't know what she'd do if he didn't take the case.

"Well?" Simone asked. "Are you going to help me?"

"Depends."

"Depends on what?"

Vince's eyebrows shot up. Did she just whine? "Depends if you're honest with me about when was the last time you ate."

"What's that got to do with—?" There it was again, that tightness in her voice, as if it was a rubber band about to snap. When she pushed her hair behind her ear—her telltale sign of nerves—her hand trembled. "All right. I ate part of a croissant after court this morning."

Vince chuckled. She might excel at taking care of other people, but when it came to taking care of herself, she was last in line. "That's what I thought. Stay here. Decompress for a few minutes. I'll fix you something in the kitchen. And no," he added when she opened her mouth. "It won't be anything you'd usually have. You need some protein. I'll have Travis bring you coffee since we know what happens when you've had too much wine on an empty stomach. We'll eat, we'll catch up a bit and then maybe discuss Mara's situation."

She grabbed his wrist as he stood and squeezed

hard enough to make his heart skip a beat. "Thank you, Vince."

"Don't thank me yet. I haven't said yes."

But even before he left the table, he knew he would.

Chapter 3

He'd help her.

Simone saw it in his eyes, beyond the reluctance, the suspicion. The grief. The distrust and betrayal that had come between them years ago wouldn't matter. When all was said and done, Vince Sutton was too honorable a man to say no when he could do something to help someone. Even her.

With Vince in play, with her feet on more solid ground, she called her boss.

"Would you like to guess how many times I've thought about firing you today, Simone?" Ward's tense voice made her cringe. "It's not like you to run and hide, not to mention dodge my calls."

"Damage control takes concentration." She dug her fingernail into a groove on the table. After her Deep Throat conversation with Russo, the last thing she felt comfortable doing was confiding in people she wasn't sure of. And if whoever was behind this was going after Russo and his partner, she had to be on someone's hit list, too. "I needed to regroup and I couldn't do that surrounded by a dozen voices yelling at me."

"No one was going to yell at you," Ward said. "I run a civilized office."

"Tell me you didn't have at least half the office offering to replace me on the Denton case?"

"A little less than that, actually," Ward replied. "Look, Simone, we can both agree that your hinging the Denton case on one witness seriously backfired. I'm sure the pressure got to Mara, but without her and now this postponement—"

"The postponement is so I can find her," Simone interrupted in the hopes of derailing any deal-making he might be considering with the defendant. "Please issue a material witness warrant for her, Ward." The more people they had looking for Mara, the better. "At least give me until Monday before you concede. You know me. If I say I'm going to do something, I do it."

Vince was an exceptional investigator. Sure, he'd had some bad luck and she could understand his reticence about opening closed doors, but this could end up being good for him. He needed to come to terms with what had happened with the Walker case.

Her boss's silence pressed in on her. She counted off the seconds, half expecting to be updating her résumé before the end of the day. "Are you still there?" she asked the DA.

"You really think you can find her?"

"I do." Simone bit her tongue to avoid admitting out loud to having a secret weapon. "If you genuinely believe the case is already lost, Ward, there's no more damage I can do, right?"

"There's always more damage that can be done." He sighed. "But, okay. However, I'm only giving you until Monday to make some progress. Cal'll be unhappy about this. He's already pushing me to settle this Denton business now on your behalf."

Simone's stomach clenched. Cal Hobard again. "I don't get this obsession he has with my case." She couldn't repress the concern any longer. In fact, she should press for more information about Ward's newest employee. "He has no vested interest in Denton, right? Besides, I thought *he* worked for *you*."

"I have to let him have a say in some things, especially where public perception is concerned."

So Ward had definitely decided to run for AG, which put Hobard in charge of damage control if this case spiraled out of control. Was that what he'd been doing at the police station with Russo and his partner when they were being questioned? Protecting his candidate? Or was there more to it? "I appreciate the extra time. I'll see you on Monday."

"First thing, Simone. Don't make me hunt you down. I'll get that warrant issued before I turn in for the night. Should be processed by the time you get up. As if you're going to sleep."

Truer words were never spoken. "Thank you." She turned off her phone and dumped it into her bag.

When she ran her hands through her hair, she felt shaky. When she'd gotten out of bed this morning, she'd had little to worry about other than her usual before-court butterflies.

That she'd ended the day sitting across from her ex-military ex-husband was something she couldn't have fathomed if it had been written by a bestselling novelist.

Vince. Simone groaned.

Why couldn't he have acquired a beer gut, grown a Santa beard or at the very least developed an attitude worthy of a hermit who'd been done wrong by his woman? Because he was Vince.

Six feet and more of solid muscle with arms she'd bet could wrap around the world as easily as they'd wrapped around her. A face that was a cross between chiseled perfection and stony acceptance. Vince had taken the buzz cut to the extreme, his barely there hair making her fingers itch to explore. That he hadn't shaved in what she guessed was almost a week should have put her off, but instead the stubble boosted her estrogen levels. He could still melt her with that steely, blue-eyed stare of his. She'd never met someone who could read her so easily, someone she couldn't hide from. That had been intoxicating and more than a bit scary. Whatever mask she attempted to don, whatever attitude she cloaked her insecurities in, it always fell away around him.

It also didn't hurt that he could turn her on as easily as one struck a match. Their first kiss was the best she'd ever had. Their second? She blew out a long breath. Until Vince, every minute of her life had been meticulously scheduled, keeping her on the road she'd sworn to walk twenty years before. Until Vince, she'd never considered another path. She should have known the one impulsive move she'd made in her life—marrying him in less than three months of meeting him—would end in disaster.

What unsettled her more than anything, however,

was the fact that now that she'd seen him again, she realized how much she'd missed him.

She murmured her thanks to Travis as he delivered an oversize mug of steaming coffee. She'd always thought Vince owning a bar was a bit of a pipe dream, one of those "maybe someday" goals that she'd encouraged. Sure that was when he was thriving as an investigator and turning away clients by the carload. Part of her had expected a run-down hole in the wall, not this polished, welcoming pub that she'd bet did exceedingly well during sports seasons.

Located in downtown Sacramento, and close enough to the new arena and entertainment complex to ensure a steady customer base, this place appeared to have given Vince everything he'd ever wanted. At thirty-five, and after having served in Afghanistan, he'd been out of the military a good six years. No doubt he still valued the Corps, given the name of the bar. He'd be smart to turn away from this mess she'd brought him. Their marriage might have gone down in flames, but aside from Allie and Eden, and perhaps Cole Delaney and Jack McTavish, there wasn't anyone else she could trust. Vince had not only refused any spousal support when they'd separated, he'd walked out of their marriage with the same military duffel bag he'd arrived with.

Simone squeezed her eyes shut and leaned her chin on her hand. What was she doing here? Asking for his help and taking a dangerous stroll down memory lane? She inhaled the aroma of frying burgers, hot oil fries, fresh brewed beer and…she sniffed and opened her eyes as Vince deposited a large plate in front of her. "You made me a steak?"

"I was fresh out of lawn."

Despite the joke, he barely cracked a smile. What she wouldn't give to hear that laugh of his. That unexpected and infrequent burst of humor never failed to lighten her heart. "You sound like Allie." Her stomach growled as she unwound the napkin-wrapped fork and knife. He'd acquiesced to her vegetable preference by loading half her plate with steamed broccoli. Memory like a steel trap, that's for sure. If only they could both forget certain personal things as easily. "I wasn't complaining. It looks great."

"Don't tell me you've ditched that menu app that tells you when you can have your one-red-meat-a-month meal?"

"I kicked it up to two a month," she said, smiling. The baked potato swimming in butter could very well throw her into a carb panic, but it would be worth every glorious calorie.

He set his own steak dinner on the table—sans broccoli—and reclaimed his seat. "I did consider throwing it all in a blender so you could drink it."

"That would have been a crime." She cut off and stuck a rather large piece of fillet in her mouth. "Thank you." When she looked at him, she found him watching her, tight gaze on her mouth. Out of nerves—or maybe to test the waters—she licked her lips and tasted tiny droplets of butter.

"Don't, Simone."

She swallowed and wished she had another glass of wine. "Don't what?"

"You know what. You've always made me as hot and ready as a teenager. Trust me when I say nothing has changed."

She bit back a gasp when his leg brushed against hers.

"And you should know, turnabout is fair play. Thanks to that skirt you're wearing, I bet it wouldn't take much to find that spot on the back of your knee—"

"Sex isn't part of the deal." She grabbed her coffee, drank down enough to scald her throat. The last thing she needed in her life right now was Vince Sutton in her bed.

Vince grinned, displaying that stunning smile she'd first seen from across a ballroom at a charity event for the military one Fourth of July. The memory of him in his dress uniform and that granite-strong jaw of his, how his lips quirked and stretched into a promise of so much more than she'd ever expected came back to her. Even the medals on his chest hadn't distracted her that night. Or the next night. Or the next.

"Then you'd best stop looking at me like that," he said. When he switched his attention easily to his dinner, she realized what he'd been doing.

"You're distracting me."

"Never took much," he said. "Except that one time during the Tasher case. Do you still have that dining room table?"

"Yes." The steak was rare enough to bleed, so she stabbed it. Again. "Despite your best efforts to break it."

"*Our* efforts. Okay, truce. Let's talk about something neutral. How are Eden and Allie? Other than unavailable?"

"What makes you say that?" She cut her broccoli into tiny florets.

"Because you're sitting across the table from me and not having one of your wine-and-pizza confabs with them."

"It's kind of creepy how you remember everything about me."

"You're a difficult person to forget."

Great. Something else to dwell on when she couldn't sleep tonight. "You're right. Normally I'd have talked to them, but Allie left town tonight on business and Eden's on her honeymoon—"

"Eden got married?" He held up a hand. "Sorry." She grinned at his laugh, which she'd wished for only moments before. The sound didn't disappoint. "That came out far ruder than I'd planned. Who had the nerve to take her on?"

"Remember Cole Delaney?"

"Detective for major crimes?" She tried to recall Vince ever looking so shocked. "Eden St. Claire married a *cop*? How did I miss the headline? I didn't think she had any time for them."

Simone relaxed, happy to shift to a topic she couldn't resist. There might be conflicts between them that they'd never resolve, but one thing she'd always loved about Vince was how much he'd liked her friends. He'd also understood how important they were to her. Never once did he appear to resent them or ask her to choose between him and them. He got the importance of family. All the more reason to regret her actions when it came to his brother. "You heard Eden had a hand in catching the Iceman a few weeks back?"

"That I did read. Sounded as if she had a close call."

"Mmm." Simone nodded. "A wake-up call, too. She decided to…shift her priorities. Good thing given what's coming down the road." A chill shot up her spine as she thought about Chloe's killer rearing his head after two decades. Vicious monsters should stay locked in basements where they belonged.

Vince shrugged and then tilted his head, a silent urging for more details that she quickly detoured away from. Chloe's murderer didn't have any bearing on the Denton trial, and besides, it wasn't any of Vince's business.

"What about Allie?" he asked.

"Flitting about like the goodwill fairy she is. Still a child and criminal psychologist, and still doing family counseling when she's not consulting for the police or the FBI. Speaking of goodwill, I talked to my boss while you were in the kitchen. There's been a change in plan."

"That's a good trick considering there isn't any plan yet. But let me guess." Vince carved up the rest of his steak before gesturing to Travis for another coffee. "He doesn't approve of you attempting to hire your ex-husband."

"I didn't tell him about you." She focused on her dinner again.

"Why not?" His tone sounded as if he was suspicious.

"Because I don't want anyone knowing what I'm— what we're doing. It's tricky."

"I can solve that, I'm not taking the case."

"Yes, you are."

"Really?" Did he have to make it sound as if she'd issued a personal challenge? "No, wait. First things first. Before I turn you down again, what's this change you're talking about?"

"I need to find Mara by Monday."

"Three days." He stopped eating, set his fork and knife down, and picked up his napkin. He stared at her while he wiped his mouth, then pushed his plate aside and leaned his forearms on the table. "You want me to find this girl in seventy-two hours and she's got what—almost a twenty-four-hour head start?"

"You're good, Vince. If I didn't think you could do it—"

"You said you had over a week before you had to be in court again."

"I do. But I need to have information to give him on Monday morning if I'm going to keep my job."

"So this is a bait and switch. Lure me in with promises of a cash payout and no sex and hope I'll come through. Yeah, not real tempting, honey."

How did he manage to make that endearment sound so inviting? "What if I sweeten the offer?"

"Clearly you overestimate how far my goodwill will stretch."

Simone reached for the blue file in her briefcase. "If you won't help me because of the demons nipping at your heels or because it's the right thing to do, how about you do it to help your brother?" She set the file down and waited for him to read the name *Jason Sutton* scrawled across the top.

She'd considered every angle, spent the day thinking this through. As much as she hated the idea of dangling his brother's case over his head, she couldn't take the chance he'd turn her down. She was betting big here and not only with her career. She was gambling with Mara's life.

"It's been enough time for me to gain some power in the DA's office," she said, dropping into the rehearsed explanation. "I can justify taking a second look at Jason's case without raising suspicions. Help me find

Mara Orlov by Monday morning and I'll take that second look."

She couldn't remember ever seeing his hands shake, but they did now as he brushed his fingers over the file before he asked, "What are the odds you'll find something to get him out?"

"Slim." She sat back and crossed her arms. "I told you, I've been over the files before. He could have flipped on his accomplices for a lenient sentence, he could have done a lot to help himself, but instead, he played martyr and threw himself on his sword. I could have missed something," she lied, shoving the guilt aside as she kept an image of Mara in her mind. "Something that might lessen or end his sentence."

"This case, your job, they're that important to you?"

"Mara is that important to me." This was what she'd been dreading, what she'd hoped to avoid. Admitting the truth to anyone, that whatever trouble Mara was in could very well be her fault. "I told her I'd take care of her, Vince. I promised she'd be okay."

He shook his head in that slow, disbelieving manner he had. "You're a smart woman, Simone. You know finding her, saving her, fixing her life, none of that will change what happened to you and your friends all those years ago."

"I am well aware." She flinched and swallowed the tears that threatened to form. That he refrained from mentioning Chloe's name touched her heart. "Mara's a starry-eyed kid trying to do the right thing, Vince. Partly because she loves the excitement, but also because I talked her into it. This can't go bad for her. I can't let it."

He winced as he shifted his gaze to her empty wineglass before he took hold of her coffee cup and downed the last of its contents. "I can't promise you the outcome you want."

"I know that, too." But she'd cling to hope as long as she could. "Does this mean you'll do it?"

"You're asking me to trust you with my brother's life. Again. You want me to believe you won't put your job, your career above Jason or even me. You've shown me before you're incapable of doing that."

His words, however softly spoken, felt like arrows to the chest. "You're right. I have."

"There's only one thing you can say to me to convince me you're worth taking a risk on."

"What's that?"

"You swear to me on Allie's and Eden's lives that you'll do your best by my brother. You'll come with me to see him, you'll talk to him, reexamine every file, every bit of evidence. You swear that oath and I'll believe you. I'll agree to take the case."

"Why?"

"Because Eden and Allie are your family. Just as Jason is mine." He held out his hand, curling his other around the edge of his brother's substantial criminal file. "Do we have a deal?"

Power plays had been her bailiwick for longer than she could remember. She could outlast, outmaneuver anyone. Except maybe one man. This man. But she was out of options and Mara might be out of time. "As long as you understand this is my case. And that means following the law. My rules. My playbook."

"Until it needs to be mine."

It was as close as she was going to get. Desperation overrode common sense. Getting anywhere near

Vince was asking for trouble, but if she was going to find Mara, win her case and solidify her future with the DA's office, she didn't have a choice. "I swear on their lives." She locked her hand around his and braced her heart against what was to come.

"Then we have a deal."

Chapter 4

"Thanks for meeting me, Kyla." Simone slipped into the chair across from her assistant at Monroe's and offered her a small smile. The fifteen-minute drive from Vince's bar to the coffee shop had given her enough time to think. And question. And have second thoughts. Then third...

Vince had been right about one thing: she really wished she'd had Allie and Eden to talk to if for no other reason than to convince her she was wrong about where she and the case were headed. Maybe she was overreacting to something and letting fear get the best of her. Simone might have been able to cling to that belief if Vince hadn't voiced his own similar suspicions. "I hope I didn't interrupt anything."

"Like a date?" Kyla flipped the multicolored scarf behind her narrow shoulders and sent her ebony curls bouncing. "Well, I was deeply involved with this ten-inch-thick textbook on property and tax law. Do you want coffee?"

She'd already had enough to ensure she wouldn't blink for weeks. "No, thanks." Simone shook her head and waved the waitress away. "Were you able to get the information I asked for?"

"I boxed up all your files and left them underneath the desk in your office." Kyla cringed. "Glad you reminded me about the new email monitoring program. Printing the hard copies didn't take me as long as I thought it would and I would have brought it all with me, but there was no way to be sneaky about it."

"Not to worry." Simone added an early morning stop to the office to her mental agenda.

"I also added the background information on Mara and everyone else that's involved, however peripherally, in the case. I'm surprised the copy machine didn't short out."

"What would I do without you?" Simone couldn't wait to start combing through everything from top to bottom. "I appreciate you covering for me today."

"Felt like I was in a spy movie. Nice break from studying for the bar." Kyla folded her hands on the table. "Are you going to tell me what's going on or is this some roundabout method of giving me more 'tests' for homework?"

"I wish that was the case. What did you hear around the office?"

Kyla shrugged, her gaze shifting to the table. "Not much."

"Kyla Bertrand." Simone pursed her lips. "You're a beacon for gossip in that place. Spill."

"Okay, I might have heard that your main witness went missing, and you somehow managed to get a delay from a judge notorious for sticking to his calendar. Your colleagues started a pool on how long you'll have a job."

"What odds are they giving?" Maybe she should place a bet and get a jump start on her unemployment.

"I didn't ask," Kyla said with a hint of defense in her voice. "I never bet against my boss and I plan on you sitting in the big chair this time next year."

"I appreciate your faith," Simone said, even as her own began to fracture. If she blew this case, the career she'd always wanted, had worked so hard for, would be over. And Paul Denton and his coconspirators—whoever they may be—would avoid justice. Something Simone refused to abide. "I wanted to keep you in the loop so you know what not to tell people."

"By people you mean DA Lawson?"

"I mean any people." Simone didn't want to tell Kyla about her growing suspicions of Cal Hobard or her concern others in the DA's office were involved. The farther away she stayed from everyone at her place of work, the better. At least until she got more information herself. "I've hired an outside investigator to hopefully track down Mara. I'm keeping it under wraps. I don't suppose anyone would believe if I called in sick tomorrow?"

Kyla's expression confirmed her thought. "They'll believe you're working on a new angle for the case."

"That works." Keeping people on edge gave her an advantage.

"Come to think of it," Kyla said. "You've never been sick in all the years I've known you. Must be all those plants you eat."

"What is it with people and how I eat?" To be contrary, she reached across the table and snapped off half the chocolate chip cookie Kyla had been nibbling on. "First Vince, now you—"

Kyla slapped her hand on Simone's arm as her mouth dropped open. "Vince, as in the ex-husband you never talk about Vince? Now it's your turn to spill."

"He's a private investigator, and I needed someone outside the office I could trust."

"You can trust your ex-husband?" Kyla's confusion mirrored Simone's. "Is that even possible?"

"When it comes to something like this, yes, it is." Describing Vince to someone who had never met him was a bit like trying to describe the Easter Bunny to a newborn. There wasn't any point. They'd never understand. "I'm going to give him your cell number in case there's more information he needs, information I can't get to. Does that work for you?"

"I'm your assistant." Kyla's defiant brown eyes sparked in that way that had convinced Simone to hire her. "You tell me what you want me to do, I do it. No questions asked."

"Keep that in mind because as we move forward, no matter what, this will all be over Monday morning." Simone picked up her bag and got to her feet. "Keep your head down, okay, Kyla? Let me know if you hear anything else about the case."

"Like what?"

"I'm not sure. But I have this odd feeling my world is about to crack open. I don't want you getting swallowed by it."

"Then maybe it's me who should be telling you to keep your head down. Hey, before you go, answer one thing for me." Kyla waggled her eyebrows. "Any chance in all of this that you'll introduce me to your ex-husband?"

Simone couldn't help it. She smiled. "Something tells me I won't have a choice."

Vince cleaned the last glass, turned off the neon open sign and locked the front door to the bar. The clock had hit 2:00 a.m. or, as he planned to call it from here on out, the hour of regret.

He'd heard of hitting a grand slam before, but how he'd managed to sit through dinner with his ex-wife, agree to work *with* her and dive into what was probably another hopeless missing person's case could easily be added to the record books.

He never should have congratulated himself on knowing what buttons to push to unsettle her. Karma had caught up to him with Simone's offer to reexamine his brother's conviction. When was he ever going to learn?

Vince flicked off the lights, picked up Jason's file and headed down the narrow hallway, passed the bathrooms, to the stairs that led to his apartment. He bypassed the second floor that, until a little over a year ago, had served as the office for Sutton Investigations.

The calm that normally descended when he closed out the rest of the world didn't manifest as he shut his apartment door. Instead, the restlessness he'd brought back from Afghanistan rattled through him, prodding him toward the thin edge of control.

He tossed the file onto the cluttered stainless-steel island. If he cooked, he did so downstairs. If he worked, it was downstairs. His life was...downstairs. The one-bedroom apartment, with its simple king-size bed and matching dresser, the no-frills throwback leather sofa, and a flat-screen TV he used more for background noise than anything, did little than give him a place to sleep.

On the occasions sleep wasn't possible, there was a window to stare out at the Sacramento skyline. Some nights, glancing at the tip-top of the golden Tower Bridge, standing sentry over the city, was all he needed. Other nights?

He grabbed a bottle of water out of the refrigerator, dropped onto the sofa and clicked on the digital music station on the TV. The muted strains of Bach drifted from the speakers and eased the tension that had co-cooned him the instant Simone walked into the bar. His heavy metal music days had disappeared in the desert, replaced by the meditation-inducing melodies of the classical masters. He might not be an educated man, but he was smart enough to recognize genius and artistry.

Vince's gaze landed on the table beside him. He opened the drawer and pulled out the framed wedding photo. Gut-tightening regret coiled as it always did whenever he looked at his and Simone's smiling faces. He didn't recognize that man in the photo, couldn't re-late to the happiness and joy that now seemed as lost as a dream. Was that the last time he'd worn his uniform? He could remember the teasing glint in Simone's eye as she'd walked down that short brick pathway in Napa overlooking a blooming vineyard. Her gorgeous, figure-hugging lace gown that sparkled in the sunshine had nearly undone him. When she'd reached out her hand for his, she'd leaned in and, in barely a whisper, told him the plans she had for him and his uniform in the hours to come. The years to come.

Years that came to a screeching halt months later.

Vince stared into Simone's radiant blue eyes. He could almost smell that perfume of hers that he'd been convinced was part love spell. The ugliness that had followed him most of his life had vanished the day he'd realized he'd fallen in love with her.

And yet he'd left without a fight.

Vince set the frame face down on the table and shook his head to clear the past. Marrying her hadn't been the worst mistake he'd ever made. Leaving her? Yeah, that might be up there with his thirteen-year-old self throwing lighted firecrackers at a patrol car.

And yet, today proved she was still cagey and still knew how to work the angles. There was also her smile, always a weakness of his. He wouldn't kid himself though, her career always came first. It was her trial, her job on the line. She was using his brother as a means to an end and while the idea of that didn't sit well, he certainly understood her reasons for it. That she knew how easy it was to manipulate him should worry him more. Aside from Simone, Jason was the only person he'd ever valued. Thanks to his ex-wife, there was a chance he could get his brother home. So if that meant diving headfirst into his own personal nightmare, so be it.

All he needed to do was stay in control, not like on the Walker case. Somehow he'd have to remain detached, unemotional and see the search out to its end. Whatever that end might be.

Leaving the TV on, he headed into the next room, stripped and dropped naked onto the unmade bed, begging the past to leave him alone long enough for sleep to consume him. His prayers were answered, but only after one last thought shot through his head like a bullet: starting tomorrow, everything was going to change.

Chapter 5

D*ing!*

Simone skidded to a stop halfway down the hall at the DA's office. It wasn't even 7:00 a.m. Who on earth, other than herself, would be in this early? She looked around, pulse racing. So much for a clean getaway. She hefted the file box Kyla had readied for her and darted behind one of the assistant's desks where she dropped the files on the floor.

Determined footsteps headed toward her. She clenched damp palms before readying her smile of welcome, when she turned and gaped, shocked at the elegant woman in the fitted red suit, who strode forward. "Senator Wakeman."

With coiffed silver hair, a steely, locked-down gray-eyed stare and an unbreakable confidence that aided her in her anti-crime and corruption platform, the woman

Simone had looked up to as a pillar of justice stood before her. Simone cleared her throat and approached. "Good morning, ma'am. I'm sure you don't remember me—"

"Simone Armstrong, of course." State Senator Wakeman's handshake was warm and firm. "It's a pleasure to see you again." She motioned her hulking dark-suited guards ahead of her. "I understand you're doing great things here. Congratulations on your conviction rate."

"Thank you, ma'am." Simone resisted the urge to gulp. "Is there something I can help you with?"

"Oh, no, thank you. I'm meeting with District Attorney Lawson to catch up on all the goings-on in your city. I hope you'll feel free to call on me should you need my help with this Denton situation." The faint lines around the woman's wise eyes crinkled slightly. "I was having lunch with the governor yesterday when we heard about the disappearance of your witness. Absolutely dreadful."

"We hope to locate her soon," Simone said. "I wasn't aware Ward was in his office already."

The second the words were out of her mouth, her boss rounded the corner, decked out in his camera-ready suit and killer political smile.

"Simone. Already at it, I see?" The guarded expression on Ward's somewhat pale face spoke volumes given their conversation last night. "I hope I haven't kept you waiting, Senator."

"Not at all. I enjoy speaking with the up-and-comers in the judicial system." The older woman gave Simone a nod of approval. "I'll let you get back to work."

"Thank you, ma'am." Simone watched Ward and

the senator disappear into Ward's office, bodyguards and all. *Whew.*

Simone retrieved her box and hurried to the elevator. Now, given the senator's interest, she knew she was doing the right thing by pursuing the case the way she was. All that remained was to get out of the office—and the parking lot—before anyone else saw her.

Hustling downstairs, she then finished locking the box of files in her trunk and turned around. Cal Hobard stood behind her.

She yelped, pressed a hand against her chest and wondered when, if ever, men were going to stop sneaking up on her in parking garages? "Good morning, Cal." She plastered on her biggest fake smile. "You're in early. Big weekend planned?"

"Did have." Cal's pinched voice echoed in the empty parking lot. "Before one of our attorneys took it on the chin in court yesterday." Cal wasn't a large man, but he loomed taller than most, and his implication was clear. Thin and wiry, any weakness in appearance he might project was offset by the designer suit she knew for a fact he didn't make enough to buy. Nothing about the man rang true to Simone. "Regarding Denton, still not willing to cut a deal, I hear."

"No," Simone said. She rested tapping fingers against her hip. "As I told Ward last night."

"Yes, he filled me in." The shifty eyes and surly attitude made her feel as if she was being questioned by a movie villain. He should join forces with those two bodyguards of the senator's. "I heard he gave you a reprieve until Monday. Maybe by then you'll see this is a complete loser of a case."

Don't do it. Don't rise to the bait. Don't let him get the better...

"Except it isn't," Simone said. "And for the life of me I can't understand why you keep insisting it is. You know Paul Denton's been working this game for years, maybe even decades, and yet you seem perfectly fine letting him skate by on some misdemeanor tax evasion charge. Why?"

"Listen, unlike you, I don't see conspiracies everywhere I look." Cal hefted his briefcase in his hand, glanced away, but not before she saw him flinch. "Not everything is bigger than it is, Simone. The smart move, for you and for the office, would have been to accept a plea and move on. Now look where we are."

"You mean it would be the smart move for your client. Take an easy win, add it to the DA's résumé and make it a talking point of his campaign."

Cal sighed and ducked his chin, his longish blond hair skimming his neck. "Is there anything wrong with that?"

Where did she begin? "Only if you have other reasons for sweeping this case under the rug, which is exactly what you've been trying to do ever since you arrived here. Denton's dirty, Cal." Simone couldn't keep the disbelief out of her voice. "It could be worse than what the evidence so far proves and yet you've fought me at every step. Why don't you want him to go down for these serious crimes? And why, in the span of this whole conversation, haven't you said one word about Mara Orlov?"

"What is there to say? Your witness got cold feet and bolted. If you remember, I warned you that might happen."

"Yes, you did, didn't you?" Simone's mounting unease lessened when she heard another car enter the parking lot. "Be sure to share those opinions of yours with Senator Wakeman when you get upstairs, will you?" She pulled open her door and climbed in but she couldn't close it as Cal stepped in and blocked her.

"Senator Wakeman is here?"

Was that panic in his voice or the same shock she'd felt?

"She's meeting with Ward right now." Simone frowned. "Why? What's going on that I don't know about, Cal?"

"Nothing." The answer came too fast to be anything other than a lie. But the uncertainty that flashed across his features momentarily was gone as quickly. "I don't know how many ways I can say this, Simone, but drop the case. Offer the plea and take whatever Poltanic asks for."

Simone gripped the door handle even tighter and elbowed him back. "If that's what Ward wants, all he has to do is remove me from the case and offer the plea himself. But he won't do that, will he?"

"No." Cal's eyes narrowed. "He won't."

"Because then he'd make this an even bigger story than it is already. He's given me until Monday, Cal. Either get on board or get run over." She didn't bother to check to make sure he was completely clear of her vehicle before she slammed her door. Within seconds she'd screeched out of her space and pulled onto the street. A few blocks later she pulled over. She clenched the wheel and tried to stop her hands from trembling. He knew something. Simone replayed the conversation in her head, wished she'd had the forethought to hit Record on her phone, but that would have been illegal.

She laughed, a small sound that had her covering her mouth. Here she was tiptoeing around a case that could blow up at any time and she was rationalizing legal semantics. Then again, she had learned one thing this morning. Cal Hobard wasn't just any political guidance counselor. He was into this up to his scrawny little neck. The question was, who else was in it with him?

"I hope you still take your coffee black." Simone held out a to-go cup for Vince when he opened her car door about an hour later. Pushing the earlier conversation with Hobard out of her mind, she shielded her eyes against the sun as the hormones she'd given a stern talking to last night resurged.

The rugged bartender she'd spoken with last night had disappeared. In his place stood the man she'd married. Vince had shaved and now presented a more professional appearance than she'd expected. There wasn't a wrinkle in his dark T-shirt, black jeans or the snug jacket that covered those tattooed forearms she'd memorized once upon a time. She glanced down. Even his steel-toe work boots had a shine.

"Appreciate the boost." He drank and gave her a nod she accepted as thanks. "Right on time, as usual. Before we lock this down, I want to be sure you know what you're getting into."

"You mean breaking and entering to gain access to a material witness's apartment?" Simone retrieved her purse and locked up. "I can't say the idea thrills me, but I may as well mark it off my bucket list. I should warn you, I asked Detective Jack McTavish to meet us. He has some information I need and I'm trying to give the office a wide berth today."

"As long as you post bail if he arrests me." He cupped her bare elbow in his free hand and guided her across the street to the Governor's Square apartment complex on 3rd and P. "Your case, your call. Apartment 2F, right?"

When they reached Mara's door, he stooped down, set his coffee on the ground and reached into his back pocket for the small leather case that held his lock picks. She caught a flash of the holstered Glock under his jacket before she looked away, silently reciting the codes he then proceeded to violate. "You still carry?"

"When I'm working." She heard the distinct clack of metal against metal before the deadbolt clicked open. "You ever take those shooting lessons I signed you up for?"

"No." She'd seen the damage that could be done.

He turned the knob and pushed open the door. "After you."

"Thanks."

The muted earth tones, heavy curtains and solid wood furniture welcomed them like an oasis. Simone spotted a stack of folded laundry on the sofa, noted the business and entertainment magazines arranged on the glass coffee table and clung to the optimism she'd attempted to ingest with her own cup of coffee earlier. Unease prickled the back of her neck as she noted the half-completed crossword in last week's paper. Mara did like her puzzles.

"You've been here before." Vince snapped on a pair of latex gloves. "Anything seem off to you?"

"Everything." Mara had joked about needing to get

a maid as she was a hopeless slob, yet the apartment was pristine. "The last time I was here it looked as if a bomb had gone off."

He sniffed the air and winced ever so slightly. "You smell that?"

"It's faint. What is it? Cleaning fluid?"

"Bleach." Vince ducked into the small kitchen and pulled open the fridge.

Dread pooled thick in her throat. Guess she could add bleach to her list of least favorite words ever.

"Simone?"

She spun to find Jack standing in the front doorway. "Oh, hi, Jack. Good morning." She needed to stay calm, not to overreact. Jack would have told her if he'd found something. Mara was fine. Scared but fine. Until Simone knew otherwise, she wouldn't accept anything else.

Jack frowned and closed the door. "How did you get in here? I heard voices."

"Ah…" Simone glanced over her shoulder as Vince popped back into view to examine the fruit bowl on Mara's breakfast counter. "It was open?"

"Vince Sutton, private investigator." Vince joined them, held out his gloved hand. "You must be Detective McTavish."

"Wish I could say the introduction answers all my questions at the moment." Jack's trademark friendliness disappeared beneath a dark look of skepticism directed at her. "Simone? Care to explain?" He was dressed in his usual jeans and white button-down shirt, and the khaki blazer kicked up the casual look enough to be both practical and eye-catching. She couldn't help but compare and contrast the two men. Brooding versus friendly. Pessimist versus optimist. Sexy bad boy versus good-intentioned…what was wrong with her?

"I hired Vince to look into Mara's disappearance." Simone cut to the chase. "He's had a lot of experience with missing persons' cases."

"Sutton. I know that name." Jack's frown deepened.

Simone's cheeks went hot. "Well, he has a good reputation—"

"Had," Vince interrupted. "I've been out of the business for a while. I'm also her ex-husband."

It took a moment for the disbelief to shift out of Jack's gaze. "Right." His slow, rational nod made Simone ache to explain. Not that there was anything to explain. This was a business arrangement between her and Vince. A quid pro quo. He was helping her find Mara and she'd said she'd help his brother. "I didn't realize you two had reconnected," Jack added. "This recent?"

"Very." Simone cringed.

"I'm going to keep looking around so the two of you can discuss this." Vince's tone scraped Simone's nerves as he looked between the two of them, a wall of ice settling in his steely gaze.

"There's nothing to discuss." Simone gave him a strained smile but he still moved off. What? Did he expect her to become celibate once their marriage had ended? Although come to think about it… "Jack, I needed to hire someone without any connections to the DA's office. If this is going to be a problem—"

"It'll only be a problem if he keeps breaking into things. I'm a little surprised at you, Simone. I thought there were some lines you didn't cross."

"There are, Jack." There were. "And no, I'm not

thrilled about it." Simone folded her arms over her chest. "And a crime scene?"

"You don't smell that?" Jack backed up, reaching the hallway that led to the bedroom. "Someone's cleaned up in here. What else have you found?"

"Other than a stocked refrigerator, not much. We were just getting started when you got here," Vince called from Mara's bedroom.

Simone swore. She'd forgotten about his bat-like hearing.

"The smell's stronger in here," Jack said, entering the bedroom with en suite bathroom. As she joined them, she heard the whine of a cabinet being opened. "The sleeping pills used in the deputies' coffee match the brand in her medicine cabinet."

"There's no suitcase," Vince stated, staring into the open closet. "And I haven't found keys. Her purse and cell phone are gone. Car, too?"

"Yes." The more they talked, the less assured Simone became. "What about the notes Russo sent you, Jack?" Simone asked him as he emerged from the bathroom. "Was there anything that seemed strange?"

"He mentioned a few visitors over the past few weeks. She stuck to her schedule faithfully, didn't vary much from her routine. I saw a couple of things that could use a second glance, including some odd license plates on cars that made frequent appearances. I assume you'll want to take a look?" he asked Vince.

"I'd appreciate it."

Simone didn't know whether to be relieved or concerned that the two guys had fallen into a weird professional camaraderie. "We already had all tenants' cars on record," Simone said. "What did you mean about her refrigerator?"

"She's an accountant by trade, correct?" Vince shrugged, hands outstretched. "Where's her office?"

"There's a desk in the dining area." Simone, Jack and Vince returned to the main living space. She pointed at the table and moved aside as both men focused on Mara's belongings.

Jack immediately clicked on Mara's laptop while Vince sorted through mail and receipts. Simone scanned the bookcases, where she noted the collection of mystery novels, books on logic and a DVD collection featuring mostly British detective shows.

"For an accountant, I'm surprised her computer's not more secure," Jack said. "Her passwords are all stored, at least for her emails. Everything that's bookmarked is completely innocuous. Last message she sent was the night before she disappeared. Eleven forty-five, to someone named Gale Alders. They made plans to meet for lunch once the trial's over." He looked at Simone. "Doesn't sound like someone getting ready to vanish."

"She bought all those groceries two days ago," Vince said. "The same day she sent that email. I don't know about you, but if I'm planning on leaving town, I don't replenish the fridge."

Simone worried that the case was about to go very, very bad. She wandered back to the bedroom and stopped short at the foot of the bed. Vacuum marks streaked the coffee-colored carpet; the dresser drawers were closed. She checked the clothes still hanging in the closet. "This place is immaculate," she called out to them.

"Jack's right. Someone definitely cleaned up," Vince said from behind her.

"I need to make a call," Jack said, as she and Vince returned to the living room. Jack headed outside.

"Are you going to tell me what you're thinking?" Simone asked Vince as he pulled the vacuum out of the closet.

"I'm wondering if whoever cleaned up this apartment cleaned up after themselves." He popped the canister off the appliance and, after retrieving a towel from the bathroom, dumped the contents out. She stooped down as Vince brushed his fingers through dust clumps and shards of glass.

"Something must have broken." Simone tucked her hair behind her ear. Bits of glass sparkled.

"Can one of you answer a question for me?" Jack asked as he rejoined them.

"What?" Simone pushed to her feet as Vince stayed crouched.

"How can two deputies be suspended for dereliction of duty regarding a missing person's case that doesn't exist?"

She rounded on Jack. "Ward told me last night he was filing a witness warrant as soon as we were done talking."

Jack winced. "Either he forgot or he changed his mind."

"Ward didn't become DA by forgetting to file warrants," she said. Had Cal Hobard intervened?

"Well, there's nothing on record," Jack said. "So, my question stands."

Vince straightened. "Might this have something

to do with what you didn't want to tell me about last night?" he murmured in her ear.

She lifted her foot and planted her heel on his shoe. She heard him suck in a sharp breath, but he refrained from saying more.

"I just talked to Missing Persons," Jack continued. "They have no report for someone missing, matching Mara Orlov's description." Jack looked down at the dirty towel and pointed to it. "You part archaeologist, too?"

"Someone thought to clean up," Vince said. "There's broken glass here. Crystal, the good stuff."

Simone still remembered the befuddled expression on his face when he'd encountered the crystal jam jar her mother had sent for their wedding present. He'd remarked that they could have used what it had cost for a down payment on a house.

"Trash in the bathroom was empty," Jack said. "I'll check the kitchen."

"You two are like ping-pong balls." Simone left Vince, and struggled for the right words as she approached Jack. "Look, I know this isn't the time, but about Vince and me—"

"You don't owe me any explanation, Simone." Did he have to sound so understanding? "We went out on a few dates, nothing major. I know we're just friends." He opened the counter under the sink and grabbed the garbage can.

They'd had some good times together. Dinner, movies, walks in the park. She liked being around him. He was fun. But as far as attraction went? Well, she'd certainly *wanted* it to be there and maybe if she'd never been involved with Vince, it might have been. Jack was a good guy. He was… Simone sighed. Jack was safe. "Do you?"

"If I didn't before, I do now. Should have listened to Cole. He warned me not to get attached. Leave it be, Simone." He held up a hand. "While I'd be lying if I said I haven't been hoping for more, I can take a hint. No need to hit me over the head with an ex-marine."

Guilt twisted her insides. She hated to disappoint him. "I'm sorry, Jack. I really like you."

"Please don't twist the knife deeper. Not the first time I've fallen for the wrong girl." He angled a smile at her that didn't quite reach his eyes. "It probably won't be the last." He took a cue from Vince and dumped the can's contents onto the floor. "Broken vase it looks like. And what's this?" He hefted a chunk of glass into his hand.

"I remember seeing a crystal clock on her night-stand the last time I was here." The shards Vince had found earlier could also have come from that. "Wait, is that…blood?" She pointed to the bright spot of red in one of the crevices.

"Looks like it to me." Jack grimaced. "Could be hers. Or not."

"You should get a crime scene tech here right away." Vince had joined them.

"Yeah." Jack set the crystal fragment on the counter and stepped away from the debris and can on the floor. "I'll call Tammy in the lab, have her collect all this. In the meantime—hey, where are you going?"

Vince was at the front door. "I saw surveillance cameras at the school across the street. A couple of the neighbors downstairs had them as well."

"I can get a warrant—"

"Someone's going to a lot of trouble to keep this case on the QT," Vince said and gestured at the living room. "A solitary lab tech is one thing, but think about it. You've got a missing witness, two drugged deputies and a cleaned-up crime scene. You also have a DA who, for whatever reason, doesn't appear to be doing his due diligence to locate the crucial witness. This isn't a missing person's case, Detective. This is a lot of planning, both before and after the fact. You request a warrant and whatever else, you'll be letting whoever might be involved know they didn't get away with it."

"The DA already knows I'm looking into Mara's disappearance," Simone said.

"He knows *you're* looking," Vince said. "He doesn't know about me, and he doesn't know about Jack, right?"

"Not as far as I know, no." Simone caught her lip in her teeth. But that could change at any minute. Ward could become aware that Jack and Vince were helping her. This was getting out of control fast.

"Hold on," Jack ordered. "Are you suggesting someone in the police—"

"I'm not, actually," Vince said. "It goes higher up than that, right, Simone?" How she wished he'd stop looking at her like that. "This is your call. You hired me. You're the one who followed her gut and went outside her office. You decide."

How had this happened? Jack was right. She needed this investigation done by the letter of the law if she hoped to salvage the case and her career. The law had been her life for as long as she could remember. The idea of justice, of due process, had settled in her soul before she'd turned ten years old. Without rules, without structure, everything collapsed. People got hurt.

Simone swallowed.

People died. But Vince was right, too. Making Mara's disappearance about anything other than a nervous witness with cold feet could spell disaster for everyone in the long run, especially Mara. Simone had to err on the side of caution, and the safety of the young woman's future.

"Vince, would you give me and Jack a few minutes?" Her ex-husband left them and Simone took a deep breath. "Jack, I'm going to ask you to do as Vince says and keep this as quiet as you can. Not forever. And hopefully, not for long, but at least until Monday." Might as well pile everything into one potentially career-ending weekend and go out with a bang.

She'd never seen someone's faith in her dim right before her eyes and it hurt far more than she'd ever imagined it could.

"You know how much trouble you're in if this goes bad?" Jack asked. "We're not talking sorta bad or kinda bad, Simone. We're talking full-on bad. It'll taint everyone involved."

"I can't worry about that." She felt as if she'd been pushed down a road she'd sworn never to take. Simone Armstrong didn't cut corners; she didn't break the rules and she certainly didn't skirt the law. Something told her, however, that by the time this case was settled, she'd have done all of the above and more. "Please, Jack. Mara's life might depend on it. Tell me you're on board with us."

Jack shook his head and blew out a harsh breath. "Wow. Okay, I'll follow your lead and do my best to keep Tammy silent, but I never thought I'd see the day where you'd trust your ex-husband over everyone you've worked with the past five years."

His anger didn't surprise her; she only wished she could explain everything. But she couldn't. Not to Jack. Maybe not even to herself. "I trusted you enough to include you, Jack. If that doesn't mean much, say the word."

"I'm not leaving you out here on your own, Simone. You need me, you say the word."

"I appreciate that, Jack. And I'm not on my own, remember? I've got Vince."

"Yeah," Jack said. "The guy who walked out on you three years ago. That makes me feel a whole lot better."

Chapter 6

When Vince returned to Mara's apartment complex, flash drive in hand, he found Simone sitting on the stone steps, arms wrapped around her knees peeking out from the ruffle hem of her skirt. He could hear voices coming from the apartment and assumed they belonged to Jack and the lab tech he'd called in.

A chill ran up Vince's arms. The ease with which he'd found himself slipping back into being an investigator unsettled him. It was as if his subconscious was agreeing with Simone's observations from last night.

He'd always prided himself on being meticulous, on trying to see every angle. But that was before the Walker case had become personal, so personal he'd found himself walking a thin line between bringing a perpetrator to justice and doling out revenge.

If Simone wasn't careful, if she didn't somehow separate herself from the victim, from Mara, she was going to find herself falling down that same, slippery, life-changing slope.

It was only a matter of time before the reality of this case—and Mara's fate—would hit her full force. All the more reason to keep things as light as possible while he could, he figured.

"Tell me something." He walked up the stone steps and leaned against the railing. "Do you have some kind of force field that keeps your clothes so clean? They should hire you for a detergent commercial."

She tried to smile, validating Vince's concern. That the strain of whatever had happened to Mara was already taking its toll. "Eden always says I will dirt away with the power of my mind. Any luck at the school?"

"A few well-placed comments about crime statistics in the area got us what we need. I'll take the footage to my place and run through it once I get back from Davis."

"What's in Davis?"

"Gale Alders," Vince replied. "We need a place to start as far as where Mara's mind was in regard to the trial." And he'd rather start with someone local.

Simone looked over her shoulder. "I don't want to leave here until Jack and Tammy are finished."

"Tammy okay with keeping this under the radar for now?"

"It's not the first time Jack's had her do something off the books," Simone said. "And I kicked in a bottle of her favorite tequila to sweeten the deal."

"A tequila girl, huh? You go shot for shot with her yet?" Vince asked. "Does she or Jack know you could drink them both under the table?"

"I don't do that much anymore. Just ask Eden and Allie."

He didn't expect this case to last long enough for him to do that.

"What about the neighbors' cameras?" Simone asked.

"One's been busted for a while, the other is a fake." A good fake, but useless nonetheless. "Simone, if you'd rather go home and work from there—"

"I'm going with you," she said. Maybe his P.I. skills weren't that sharp because he should have expected this from her. "I need something other than files and reports to focus on. I need to *do* something. And please don't ask me how I am. I'm fine, Vince."

Hardly. Simone was a talker when things were going well, but she became loquacious when things turned sour. He'd learned to let her ramble and pace, paying enough attention in case his opinion was requested, but it rarely was. Simone's actions when they used to be together let him know early on that while she may have wanted him in her life, she didn't necessarily need him. Recalling that now kicked his irritation meter into the red. "You trying to convince me or yourself?"

"You never appreciated me psychoanalyzing you, Vince. I'd appreciate the same in return."

Vince tried to reconcile the Simone sitting in front of him with the spitfire he'd married. Three years wasn't so long ago, and yet, right now, it felt like an eternity, but it had obviously been enough to dim her rose-colored glasses. "I warned you this case could get nasty." Although he hadn't anticipated it happening as fast as it had.

"Really? An I-told-you-so?" She stood up, brushed her hands across her butt and pivoted on those needle-thin heels that could pierce a man's heart and dreams. "I'm seeing this through, Vince. With or without you."

"I didn't say I was quitting. We made a deal. I'm sticking with the case until the end."

"Of course you are. You haven't gotten what you want yet."

"Is that how we're going to do this, Simone? You're going to use me as your verbal punching bag whenever you get angry or scared? I'm only asking so I can put on my protective gear if need be."

"As if—"

"Careful." He was in front of her in a flash, trying to keep his memory from spiraling back to the hours spent tangled up in the sheets with her. "Baiting me like that will only make me do something you'll regret."

"Like what?" Hands on hips, she inched up that defiant chin of hers. Lush curls caught the midmorning breeze, ruffling the thin fabric of the white tank she wore. "Well? I'm waiting."

He moved in, cupped the back of her head and whispered, "Yes, you are, aren't you?" With that, he dropped his mouth onto hers. He wasn't certain who was more surprised, but the slight gasp that escaped her lips gave him all the encouragement he needed to draw her in.

There was only one thing more invigorating than kissing an expectant Simone and that was kissing an angry Simone. That was where the passion was, that was the taste that mingled on his tongue as he dueled with hers, and held her so close he wasn't certain whose heart was beating double time.

She nipped at his lip, gently at first, then harder. He grinned as he pulled back, but pressed his forehead to hers. He stared into her defiant gaze. "Any time you want to add sex to the deal, Simone, you let me know."

She stroked his cheek for a long moment before she curled her fingers underneath his jaw and teased his stubble. "I hope you got that out of your system, Vince, because it's not going to happen again."

"Want to bet?" he called after her. She'd already turned and was striding into the apartment complex.

When she didn't respond, he couldn't help it. He grinned like a kid on Christmas morning. He hadn't felt this good, this alive, in ages. But, yeah, he realized she wouldn't be betting him anytime soon.

Not when she knew she'd lose.

"Doesn't look like anyone's home." Simone peered inside the window beside the modest bungalow's front door.

"We'll wait." Vince returned to the car and she followed. By the time she'd closed the door and glanced at him, he seemed comfortable and settled. Not what she had expected.

"So we're just going to sit here? How do you know Gale's even in town?"

"Pet bowls on the porch aren't empty. I heard a dog in the backyard. More excited about visitors than angry at being abandoned. She cares about them. Toddler toys in the yard, picture books on the couch and coffee table. She probably took her kids out for a bit. She'll be back."

He could tell all that by peering into someone's window for five seconds? She sank back in her seat. No wonder he was so good at reading her.

He clicked on the radio and filled the car with the sounds of Strauss, one of her personal favorites. One of those surprising qualities of his, that they shared the same taste in music. She wondered if the powerful melodies were as much a coping mechanism for him as they were for her. She should know that, she realized. She should know a lot of things.

She stared out her window and marveled at the lives people led. The ankle-deep grass was strewn with the toddler toys Vince mentioned. An empty plastic wading pool, no doubt anxiously awaiting the arrival of hot valley temperatures come summer. She couldn't recall the last time she'd thought about the change in season or what followed. Concerts in the park? Barbecues with friends? They seemed almost unheard of for her these days. The only exception, the lazy afternoon spent on Cole's boat, cruising up and down the Sacramento river a few weeks ago, but other than that, every minute she'd had was spent at work. "What is it you're hoping Mara's friend Gale will tell you?" She felt her phone vibrate and dug it out from her purse. Scanning the screen, she then bit her lip to stop smiling.

"Can't say for sure until I hear it," Vince replied. "Everything all right?" He gestured to her cell.

"Eden's losing it. She's sending me and Allie honeymoon pictures." She passed the phone to him with the most recent photo of Eden's hand shoving a flailing Cole into a lake. "She doesn't do well doing nothing for long."

"If they're doing nothing, they're not honeymooning properly." Vince sent her a tempting glance and instantly, her cheeks went hot. This happened whenever she thought of their own honeymoon in Cabo. They didn't leave their room for three days.

"Given what I've heard from Eden, I have no doubt

they're honeymooning just fine." Nonetheless, Simone was anxious for her friends to return to the city. Working with Vince was fine, up to a point, but there was a shorthand, a language she shared with Allie and Eden that made her feel more productive and…grounded. "How much are we going to tell Mara's friend?"

"As much as we need to," Vince said. "Less than we have to. Mara's apartment was washed down, Simone. Professionally. I know you trust McTavish, but can you honestly tell me you haven't considered the possibility that someone he works with could be involved with this disappearance?"

"At this point, I wouldn't rule anyone out." Simone hated to admit it, but he could be right. "I know where your thinking leans, Vince, but this isn't exactly easy for me. I've put everything I am into the system." Without the law as her compass, what did she have?

"Tell me something I don't know."

"Just because you think I'm stuck up—"

"I've never once thought that, Simone." Vince shook his head. "I might have said it once or twice, but I've never really believed it."

"I wouldn't have guessed that you still do this."

"Do what?"

"That thing you do when no one else is around. And don't act like you don't know what I'm talking about. You're a nice guy, Vince. Charming even." He'd have had to be to get past the emotional defenses she'd built up. "It's too bad no one else sees it."

"Maybe you've always brought out something different in me." He reached toward her and leaned in.

She jerked back, grimacing. "You can't be serious. I told you no se—"

He paused, arched a brow and then clicked something open resting on the floor of the backseat. "Relax." He handed her a chilled bottle of water then grabbed one for himself. "I already made my move. The next one's yours. I always keep a cooler in the car on a stakeout. And don't get overexcited. I'm too old to do anything of significance in a car these days."

Considering he was more fit than she remembered, she found that difficult to believe. "Sorry." She twisted off the cap and drank. "You make me nervous."

"Good. And back at ya."

She tried to cross her legs, found it impossible and slouched in the seat. "This can't be all that the job is? Sitting around, waiting for people to show up?"

"More often than you'd think. Disappointed?"

"Surprised, I guess. Not that we ever really talked about your job very much."

"We didn't do much talking about anything if memory serves." He drank down half his water, keeping his gaze straight ahead. "We based a marriage on sex. Not the best idea for any relationship, let alone for two people each used to being in charge. Being together wasn't our mistake, Simone. Getting married was."

Simone scraped at the label on her bottle until it started to peel. She wasn't going to apologize for being a control freak, but she'd never considered their marriage a mistake. Exactly.

"There was more between us than that," she said. She'd loved him. At least she'd thought she did. She'd definitely wanted him, but once she had him, she hadn't known what to do with him. "Or maybe I wanted there to be." He'd been a challenge she hadn't been able to resist. Not when her feelings for Vince had been so…

powerful. "I told you when you proposed I wasn't cut out for marriage."

"Why? Because your parents stink at it? That's a bit hypocritical considering your lecture last night about rising above your circumstances."

The backdoor reference to his brother wasn't lost on her. As if he needed to remind her about the deal they'd struck. She'd already gone through his brother's file. There wasn't anything new to be found. But the second she told him that, he'd be gone and she couldn't risk it. Not when she still needed him.

"There's a difference. I know how not to break the law. It's not as if I had a shining example of marital bliss." She dismissed his accusation. "My father's on his, wait, third, no, fourth wife and Mother's probably stalking number six as we speak."

"What happened between us had nothing to do with your parents' inability to commit to each other. Nor did it have anything to do with mine hurting each other whenever the mood struck. The truth is neither one of us was willing to step back from the life we already had to make room for the other and build something new."

Condensation dripped from the water bottle onto her skirt, seeped into the material and left a splotch that in ordinary circumstances would have had her diving for a napkin. "Is that what happened?"

"You really want to get into this now?"

She looked around, then back at him, finding that, yet again, an irritated Vince got her insides revving almost as strong as one of his kisses. "You have somewhere else to be?"

"I don't see what use rehashing our history is going to do other than tick both of us off. We gave it a shot, it didn't work. It's disappointing, Simone, but it's not a tragedy."

"You're right." She shifted into the corner of the seat, dismissing what she thought sounded like doubt in his voice. "We both know what happens when we argue."

"We'd probably turn this car into a convertible with all that repressed steam you've got building up."

Repressed... She faced him, cheeks flaming. "If that's you asking who I've been sleeping with..."

"No one." Vince shrugged and finished his water. "Not recently at least. And you can tamp down on that righteous indignation, your highness. It's none of my business who you've been hitting the sheets with."

"Jack and I have been going out."

"Going out, not staying in." Vince shook his head and laughed. "Let me guess. You like him as a friend, just not *that* way. Please don't tell me he got that 'it's not you, it's me' speech."

Simone glared at him.

Vince laughed. "Man, I so owe that guy a drink."

"You'll probably owe him half your bar by the time this case is over. He's got our back, Vince. He doesn't deserve your disrespect."

"I never said I didn't respect him. He likes you, Simone. He might even be in love with you. If we'd been living in the Stone Age, he'd have pummeled me with a club."

"That's ridiculous." At least she hoped it was. "I mean, I know he has feelings for me. But he understood."

"That you only want to be friends? Yeah, I'm sure he was thrilled to hear that."

"Where's all this coming from? You're the one who

walked out on me, remember? You're the one who decided he didn't want to be married anymore. You decided not to fight for us."

"Hindsight's always twenty-twenty." He didn't sound angry. In fact, he sounded amused. "You think back on that day, Simone, really think back without adding your spin on things and tell me what you truly remember. Then we'll talk about why I left. And speaking of leaving, I bet that's Gale coming down the street." He pointed to the rearview mirror.

Simone twisted around. The woman pushing an overstuffed stroller looked like a typical harried mom, with a toddler leaning out of his seat to try to grab at fallen leaves and a younger child in a baby carrier strapped to her chest.

"Matches her DMV photo," Vince said. "Right down to the spiky hair. You coming?"

"Of course I am." She hauled herself out of the car, leaving her purse inside as she stood beside him on the sidewalk, the sound of baby talk bursting against her ears.

Vince reached into his pocket well before Gale reached them, suspicion clouding her dazed eyes. "Are you two lost? Can I help you?"

"Gale Alders?" Vince asked in what was his sweetest tone, she knew. He held out his ID then dug out a card to hand to her. "I'm Vince Sutton, a private investigator from Sacramento. This is Simone Armstrong. Do you mind if we ask you some questions?"

"Oh." Gale's eyes went wide. "Is this about Mara? She mentioned your name a few times," she told Simone, as her toddler made a break for it and stuck one leg out of his stroller.

"Mar!" the boy cried as his stuffed elephant took a nosedive onto the concrete. "Mar! Baba."

"Whoa, big guy. Hold up." Vince bent down and settled the little boy in his seat before retrieving his toy. "Your mom needs to get you inside before you speed off."

Eyes the same shade as his mother's widened in silent shock as the boy looked at Vince. Simone's breath caught in her chest. She knew the feeling.

"That's the quietest he's been in days." The relief in Gale's voice had Simone smiling in sympathy. She'd never been around many kids. And babies? The very idea of them petrified her. She knew how easy it was to mess up someone's life from day one. She'd never subject an innocent kid to that, not with her messed up mind-set. "Please. Come on inside," Gale said. "Let me get them down for their naps and we can talk. I'm so glad to meet you." She touched Simone's arm as she passed her. "Mara's gone on and on about how great you've been with this trial."

Simone managed to keep her smile in place as she followed Gale into her small, though comfortable, home. She jumped back before the door closed as a white streak of fur bolted out the front.

"That's Niko," Gale said. "He came with my husband, Dave. And the cat's fine outside. I'll be just a few minutes."

"Nice place," Vince commented as Simone sat on the edge of the sofa. "Cozy."

"Homey," Simone agreed. Everywhere she looked she saw photographs or kids' drawings or mementos from marriage and family. A familiar face caught her attention. She stood up, crossed the room and reached for the framed picture of Gale and Mara. "They're close."

"Seems that way."

"That went faster than I anticipated." Gale emerged looking bedraggled, but relieved, if not happy. "He probably wore himself out on the slide at the park. Thank goodness for that elephant Mara gave him last week. Puts him right out. Can I get either of you something to drink? I'm sorry this place is such a mess—"

"It's fine." Simone returned the frame to its spot on the cabinet shelf. "Please don't worry yourself. We won't stay long."

"Okay." Gale sat in the chair beside the sofa. "Do you need character references for Mara? Is that what this is about?"

"Actually," Vince said and covered Simone's hand with his when she was about to speak. "We're hoping you can help us. Mara didn't appear in court yesterday and we're trying to locate her."

"What do you mean she didn't appear?" Gale's gaze sharpened. "When I talked to her a few days ago she was anxious to get this over with."

"That was my impression as well." Simone tugged her hand free. "But I'm afraid we've been unable to find her. You said you spoke with her earlier this week?"

"Um, yes." Gale pressed her fingers to her temple. "We have Sophie's christening next month. Mara's our daughter's godmother. You're saying she's missing?"

"Did she say anything else to you that might indicate where she would have gone?" Vince asked. "Or why she would have left town?"

"No, nothing," Gale said. "She's one of those people you can set your clocks by." She looked to Simone. "But

I'm sure you know that already. She's always been reliable. I'm sorry, but I need to call her."

"Of course," Vince said.

Simone forced herself to remain passive. She couldn't let her mounting concern show, not until they had answers to give her friend. It wouldn't do anyone any good to panic and, as Simone knew from personal experience, sometimes having no answers was the best way to cope with a situation. Sometimes the truth hurt too much.

Gale pushed to her feet and retrieved her phone from the diaper bag on the back of the stroller. A heavy pressure built up in Simone's chest as she watched comprehension slide over Gale's face. "Mara, it's Gale." She turned her back on Vince and Simone but not before Simone caught the tears welling in the woman's eyes. "Please call me as soon as you get this message. No one's upset with you, I promise. We're just…worried." She clicked off. "Something's wrong. She's never more than a few inches away from her cell phone."

Simone was silent. Part of her had been hoping Mara would answer.

"She doesn't go off without telling anyone," Gale added. "Have you tried her parents? Or her brother? He's living in…um…" She squeezed her eyes shut and pressed the phone against her forehead. "Los Angeles, I think? Maybe she drove down to see him? I'm sorry. My brain's gone all fuzzy. What if something's happened to her?"

"We're not jumping to any conclusions yet." Vince urged her back to her chair. "Can you tell us if she has any special jewelry she wears? Anything she wouldn't have left behind?"

"There's a cross." Gale tapped the hollow of her throat. "A small one her mother gave her years ago. Other than exchanging the chain, she's never taken it off."

"How long have you known her?" Simone asked.

"A year maybe? We met at a coffeehouse right after I found out I was pregnant with Sophie. She'd just started her new job and we got to talking. We hit it off, you know?"

Simone nodded. She knew all too well.

Gale gestured toward the hallway. "My husband travels a lot so Mara's been my backup. This case she was testifying in, she told me it wasn't any big deal, that she'd be finished in no time. That wasn't true, was it?"

"Not really, no," Simone said. "She was my main witness in the Paul Denton case."

"Denton." Gale frowned. "I'm sorry. I don't pay much attention to the news these days. Everything's animated or education-related."

"It's a case that could have far-reaching implications." She didn't want to worry Gale any more than they already had. Not when she knew what it was like to be concerned for a friend's well-being. "Would you do us a favor and let us know when you hear from her?"

"Yes, of course. And you'll do the same?"

Vince got to his feet and stood next to Simone. "Absolutely. We appreciate your time, Mrs. Alders."

Simone was shivering before they'd returned to the car. She wasn't giving up, not yet. Not until she knew for certain. "Now what?"

"What do you think we should do?" Vince reached over, about to flip on the AC, looked at her, then shrugged out of his jacket and draped it over her. "You always get cold when you're scared."

"I'm not scared." She was petrified, but she couldn't surrender.

"And if I said the sky was blue?"

"I'd say it's pink. I'm at a loss here, Vince. My brain says call out the National Guard, but we can't do that."

"Not without exposing this to the media, no. I'm going to drive you back to your car and you're going to go home."

"What? No, there's nothing I can do—"

"There's something you have to do and you know it. You need to rebuild your case against Denton if we don't find Mara in time. Find a way to get her evidence admitted without your star witness."

"Right. You're right." Simone nodded, hating that he was able to detach from reality, do what was necessary. "I need to concentrate. Regroup. You'll keep me up to date on everything you're doing?"

Vince nodded as he started the car. "I'll report in as soon as I have something. I promise. Focus on your work, Simone. It's what you do best and right now, it's the only thing you can do for Mara."

"You didn't have to walk me to my car," Simone told him once they were back in Sacramento and heading down P Street.

"Humor me. Besides, I want another look at Mara's apartment." A quieter look. A solitary look. Given everything Vince had learned about the young woman, no, she wasn't one to disappear on a whim. Nor was she someone who wouldn't have made contingency plans should something have gone wrong.

And something obviously had.

"You can't break in again." Simone's eyes narrowed.

"I don't have to." He pulled out the key he'd stashed in his pocket this morning. "Found this in a box on her desk. It's a spare."

"You always did have an interesting relationship with semantics."

At least he'd made her smile. All the bad stuff between them, the years, the resentment, the anger, he'd gladly let all that go if it meant protecting her from what he feared was coming.

"My car's right there. You can go on—hang on. What's this?" She pulled a large manila envelope from under her wiper.

"Secret admirer?" Vince teased. "Maybe Jack left you a memento of your time together."

She flipped the envelope open. "You know if I put you two in a cage match he'd kick your butt."

He'd never been so tempted to snort in his life. Then again, he knew better than to challenge a man in love. He stepped off the curb but turned when he heard her sharp intake of breath. "What's wrong?" The color had drained from her face. Her hands trembled around the envelope's contents. "Simone, what is it?"

She shoved whatever it was back inside and shook her head, her lips pressed so tightly together they disappeared. "Nothing. It's another case. Another…it's nothing." She waved him off and pressed her key fob to unlock her door. "I'll wait to hear from you if you find anything in Mara's apartment, okay?"

He stayed where he was as she threw her bag and envelope into the car, started the engine and pulled out sharply enough to leave skid marks. Who was she kidding, another case? She'd made it perfectly clear since she'd shown up at his bar that the Denton case had her complete attention. She was lying to him. The question was about what? And why?

Chapter 7

Vince stood outside the glass door that led into the major crimes division. His blood pounded so hard through his veins he was afraid he might burst a vessel. The last eighteen months threatened to drive him back to his car. He'd always prided himself on being true to his word, especially when it came to promises he'd made to himself. Clearly, not stepping foot in a police department was going to be one he couldn't keep. Then again, cracks had formed in a lot of promises the second Simone had strolled back into his life.

He should have known his snowball of good intentions would only pick up speed and threaten to wipe out his senses.

At least this time wouldn't end with him in jail for assault while two parents were forced to identify the body of their dead teenager. An image of Mara Orlov's smiling face and green eyes came to mind and momentarily, at least, erased the memory of Sabrina Walker.

"Sutton?" Jack McTavish sidled up beside him, a large take-out bag in one hand.

Vince caught the wariness in the detective's face, but the shell-shocked expression had vanished. Maybe he'd been wrong about the cop's feelings for his ex-wife. Maybe he'd just been projecting his own. Vince needed to remind himself why he was really here, instead of dwelling on Simone's social life, which, after all, had nothing to do with him.

"What brings you here?" Jack asked. "And where's your partner in crime? If it's about any lab results—"

Vince held up a hand. "I know how long lab results take. I went back to Mara's apartment. Took another look around."

Jack's face went like stone. "You've got to be kidding me. So, what? You're here to turn yourself in? Please, make my day and let me arrest you for something."

"I'm here with a peace offering." He glanced around at the throng of uniformed deputies milling about, heading to the elevator, the staircase or banging on the uncooperative soda machine at the end of the hall. "Is there somewhere we can talk?"

After a brief hesitation, Jack sighed. "Yeah, sure. Come on back. You eat yet?"

"No." He'd planned to fix something when he got back to the bar to check on his manager and staff. Yet again he found himself following the detective, this time around desks and chairs into a room filled with uneven tables, an oversize refrigerator and an abundance of coffeemakers. Coffee, even cop coffee, would really hit the spot about now. "You mind?"

"Help yourself," Jack said. "There's an extra burger in the bag if you want. I keep forgetting my partner's still on vacation."

"Honeymoon, right?" Vince sorted through the stacks of mugs for the biggest one then filled it to the brim. "I'm having a bit of trouble wrapping my mind around Eden getting married." In all his life he'd never met a more independent, opinionated, yet devoted friend in his life. The connection Simone had with Eden and Allie had done a lot to redeem his faith in human beings.

"Not as much as I'm having accepting the fact she's going to be working with us."

Vince swallowed fast, the scalding coffee burning his throat. He coughed and covered his mouth, eyes watering. "What?"

Jack grinned as he sat down and emptied his bag. "Simone didn't tell you about that?"

"Must have slipped her mind." He set his mug down and joined the detective. "Eden working with cops? Yeah, that'll take some processing. And here. Before I change my mind." He pulled a flash drive out of his pocket and set it on the table. "I found this in one of the origami lotus flowers in her keepsake cabinet." One of the cleverer hiding places he'd come across. The more he looked into Mara, the more that didn't add up.

Jack unwrapped his burger, exposing the trademark cheese collar oozing out of the bun. He cast a wary eye to the device. "I assume you know what's on it?"

"Among other things? Her personal journal," Vince told him. "I skimmed through most of it. Plug it in and it takes you to a password-secured server. All those innocuous sites you found on her laptop? I'm guessing that was camouflage. This girl isn't some computer novice."

"Let me guess. You were a hacker in a past life."

"I know enough to get by." Employing a few technologically gifted individuals at the bar kept him in the game. Travis had been thrilled to show off his skills, skills Vince had been able to utilize. "Mara's password is Sophie2086. Her best friend's daughter and their address." The way his stomach growled reminded him he'd skipped breakfast so he began to eat. "Simone and I spoke with Gale Alders a few hours ago."

"Did she have any idea where her friend might have disappeared to?"

"No. In fact, she confirmed what Simone already suspected. Mara's not one to take off. And you and I have been around long enough to know this isn't going to end well, Jack." It felt like a relief being able to say out loud what he'd only hinted at with Simone.

Jack flinched. "Chances are it's going to destroy whatever case the DA has against Denton. How convenient for Ward."

"Is it?" Vince wasn't so sure. "Given what I've read, Denton doesn't strike me as the type to pull off something as daring as this. He's a numbers guy. Behind the scenes and if anything, he's probably being downgraded as a liability to whomever he's working for. Simone's shared her theory with you, I take it?"

"That she suspects he's a small cog in a bigger machine?" Jack nodded, wiped his mouth and went to get his own coffee. "Yeah, she's convinced Denton's the tipping point of some massive criminal enterprise. One of the reasons we're keeping him on his own in custody."

"You ever know Simone to be wrong about something like that?"

"No."

"I'm guessing the idea that she's using Denton as some kind of bait to go after the big fish sits as well with you as it does with me."

Jack hesitated. "I haven't known her as long as you have—"

"I haven't known her at all for the last couple of years," Vince reminded him. "She's still the same Simone in a lot of ways. But in others?" He couldn't explain it. He'd been knocked for a loop when he'd first met Simone; there had been that tilting-the-world-off-its-axis attraction that made everyone who came before fade into the shadows. The Simone who'd walked into his bar last night? That Simone was deeper, edgier. Definitely more intriguing.

The tight smile Jack offered was clear to Vince. He didn't need a translator to understand that the guy was telling him to tread carefully. Jack spoke softly, "All I'll say is, Vince, if you hurt her again, we're going to have a problem. Not that that makes any difference with respect to the case."

As if what Vince wanted when it came to Simone had ever made a difference. "She's asked for my help, Jack. There's nothing more than a business agreement between us."

"And, I might have accepted that if I hadn't gotten the 'you're a good friend' talk this morning. So this flash drive is really a peace offering?" He veered back on topic with the talent of a seasoned cop.

"Add it to whatever other information you'll be getting down the road. That said—" Vince finished his burger, wadded up the paper and leaned his arms on the table "—I do have a question for you."

"Figured as much." Jack waved his fingers. "Let's have it."

"What other case is Simone working on?"

"Other case?" Jack suddenly focused on anything other than Vince. He seemed particularly interested in a napkin under his coffee mug. "Nothing that I know of. Why?"

"When I dropped her at her car, someone had left a large envelope on her windshield. I didn't see what was inside, but whatever it was freaked her out. Scared her." He didn't even have to ask his next question to know he'd hit on something. Jack's eyes had gone pinprick-intense. "What?"

"I ran a background check on you when I got to the office," Jack said. "I wanted to know who she was working with. Besides you being her ex."

"I would have done the same," Vince assured him. "You could have asked me and saved yourself the time. I don't have anything to hide."

"Also talked to a few cops you worked with. And the two who arrested you."

The burger churned in his stomach. "I'm sure they gave you an earful."

"They told me you went crazy on a kidnapping and murder suspect from the Bay Area. Broke his jaw, six ribs, ruptured his eye socket."

Vince flexed his hand as the ghostly pain of slamming his fist into the monster's face vibrated up his arm. He could still feel the blood slipping through his fingers, could still see the mutilated body of sixteen-year-old Sabrina Walker lying in the corner of an abandoned warehouse. "Don't forget the bruised kidney and concussion."

"Must have been tough when the case went sideways."

Anger simmered in his gut, swirling around the lunch he regretted eating. "Your point?"

"I need to know you've got the right frame of mind for this. I need to know you aren't going to lose control when it all comes to a head."

"I wouldn't have taken the case if I thought otherwise," Vince lied. The last thing he needed was to admit Jack McTavish was right to be concerned. That anger, that rage, it wasn't buried as deeply as Vince wanted. It never would be. But if it meant helping to get his brother out of prison, he'd take the risk. "What isn't she telling me?"

Jack swore, leaned over and looked out the open door of the break room. Vince glanced back and saw a dark-haired, compact man standing by a glass-walled office, whom he recognized as the department's lieutenant. Santos?

"You know about Chloe Evans, right?" Jack asked.

"The girls' friend who was murdered when they were nine? Yeah, some." He hadn't heard a lot of it from Simone as it wasn't a topic of conversation she delved into very often, but he'd done his own digging. "The four of them were camping in Simone's backyard. Chloe got up in the middle of the night to go to the bathroom and never came back." No matter how long he worked this job, or how many horrific things he'd seen during his military service, he was always affected by how the murder of a child never ceased to haunt those connected to the victim. "They found her body in a field a few days later. Strangled, I think. The killer was never caught." The latter fact was explanation enough as to why Simone lived her life—did her job—the way she did.

"He's resurfaced. Chloe's killer," Jack added as if he needed to explain. "It happened during the Iceman case, when Eden got caught up in all that. It started with notes, flowers and mementos of that weekend. Eden, Allie, Simone, they've all received something. He was likely behind a federal agent getting shot as well."

"Could be a coincidence," Vince argued, but that same prickly feeling he got when he'd read up on Mara's case resurfaced. "Unsolved cases bring out the conspiracy theorists and obsessives."

"That's what we thought until a package was sent to the former detective on the case. Since he died last year, his wife turned it over to us."

Vince waited, feeling as if an anvil was about to drop on his head.

"It contained Chloe's missing tennis shoe. One of those details about the case that was withheld from the press," Jack said. "He's back."

"Back? Back how?" The abject fear Vince had seen on Simone's face earlier made sense. "Why wouldn't she have told me?"

"Simone? Are you kidding? She barely talked to me about the case. She won't talk to anyone, really, not even Eden or Allie."

"And I let her go off on her own. You're saying they're being stalked? All of them?"

"I'm not saying anything officially," Jack said. "Because I can't. I also can't tell you that the Chloe Evans murder investigation has been reopened and we're trying to keep that out of the media for as long as possible. It's been weeks since we'd heard anything new from him. But if what you're saying pans out and Simone did receive—"

"I'll find out what it was." He should have known Simone wouldn't be willing to confide in him about something as personal as Chloe's murder, but he wouldn't have expected she'd put herself in danger. Which was exactly what she'd done by leaving him out of the loop. She knew how he felt about being blindsided. "Tell me she's not the most stubborn person you've ever met," Vince muttered.

"Until recently I'd have put her in second place behind Eden, but given the last few weeks, she's inching into gold medal status. The only ones who've ever really been able to get through to her are—"

"Eden and Allie. I figured." Vince scrubbed his fingers across the bridge of his nose. "We'll keep them in reserve for now, but it'll get easier on us once they're back in town. In the meantime, is your lieutenant in on this? Has there been any discussion about getting them protection?"

"I believe there was a cursory conversation with Simone that ended with an anatomically painful suggestion as to where we could stash that idea."

"Well, isn't that too bad?" Simone would be surprised what he was anatomically capable of. "Can I get a few minutes with you and your boss?"

"Can I tell him what this is about specifically?"

"Sure." Vince got to his feet and finished the last of his coffee. This agreement with Simone was turning into quicksand. The more he struggled to break free, the deeper he sank. "You can tell him Deputy District Attorney Simone Armstrong just earned herself a bodyguard."

Chapter 8

Defiance overrode reason as Simone unlatched the lock on her patio door and stepped outside. Bypassing the cushioned chair, she carried her wine to the railing. It was twilight, and she attempted to lose herself in the view of Capital Park nestled in the distance below. No one was going to scare her into not living her life.

They might, however, give her an epic headache and turn her into one of those foolish teenagers in a horror movie who goes to check on that weird noise in the attic. Idiots deserved what they got. Yet here she stood. In the open air.

The afternoon had both dragged and sped by. No matter how hard she tried, she couldn't get those photos—and the thought of whoever was behind them—out of her head. She'd stared down murderers, gang members and drug dealers, ignored their threats, and pushed to see justice done. No way was she going to let a handful of photographs scare her into giving up whatever Chloe's killer wanted of her and her friends.

What did he want? He'd gotten away with one of the most heinous crimes someone could commit. Why come back now and make them relive the nightmare of Chloe's death? Unless he hadn't been able to before now for some reason. And the reason was what she'd spent the better part of the afternoon looking into. Searching for recently released violent felons who had served at least twenty years. She'd gotten halfway through the depressing list before taking a break and had used the Denton case as a palate cleanser.

She'd considered texting Eden and Allie. They needed to be warned what might be waiting for them when they got back into town. But she knew her friends well enough to know that they'd cut short whatever plans they had. Life couldn't stop because some maniac had put them in his crosshairs. Besides, whatever had been done so far had been done within the city limits. Odds were her friends were safer where they were.

She drank and, despite the chill running up her spine, remained where she was and scanned the street and surrounding buildings. For once the neighborhood didn't bring her the peace she longed for. Not the markets and art gallery, not the yoga studio or bookstore.

When she spotted the familiar black sports car pulling into one of the remaining parking spots across the street, her breath caught. She couldn't tear her eyes away from the sight of Vince climbing out of his car before he grabbed a couple of bags out of the backseat and started toward her building.

Her lips curved, halting in midsmile when he stopped

in the middle of the street and looked up. Was it possible, even from this distance, he was scowling at her? Again, she stayed where she was as he disappeared below, no doubt checking himself in with the doorman by flashing his pseudo badge and ID. Little did he know one of the reasons she'd chosen the upscale loft apartment building was its security: card-only-access elevators, former law enforcement security, doormen who knew how to handle just about any situation.

Her knuckles whitened around the stem of her glass. Chloe's killer wasn't going to win. She wasn't going to let him. He'd taken enough from them already; he wasn't going to rob them of the fragile peace they'd found. A peace that would only be solidified when he was caught, put behind bars. Or put in the ground.

Simone drank deeply. She was beginning to sound like the avenging angel she'd been accused of being.

The doorbell rang.

She dropped her chin against her chest, squeezed her eyes shut. "Yeah, I'm going to need more wine." Barefoot, she headed inside, leaving the door open to allow the Delta breeze to play against the lightweight curtains.

She flipped the deadbolt and pulled open her door. She did her best to stop the little dance her insides did at the sight of him, but within seconds it had turned into a full-blown jig. Was she ever going to get him out of her system?

"Just once I'd love to see you in some kind—any kind—of color." His gaze skimmed the white silk pajama set she'd climbed into minutes after she'd gotten home. He stopped briefly on her breasts that tightened beneath his heated stare. Any impulse to cross her arms slipped right out of her mind as she planted her free hand on her hip. Hiding from him in any sense was useless. Besides, it wasn't anything he hadn't seen before.

"How much did you bribe my doorman to let you up?"

"Not a penny. I got through on pure charm. Relax." That grin he used whenever he was up to something beamed brightly. "Jack called ahead and vouched for me. I'm on the list and everything."

"You talked to Jack without me?" Was that a good idea?

"Do you mind?" He hefted one of the bags. "These are getting heavy."

"Wimp." Forget that she'd seen him bench-press twice her weight. Simone bit the inside of her cheek and stepped back, unnerved at how he maneuvered her apartment like he knew it. She locked the door, then followed to the kitchen, hiking herself onto one of the two barstools as he unpacked enough groceries for a week. "I take it you have something to report about Mara?"

"I do. I also have some questions for you about the Denton case." He gestured to the second bag that he'd set on the floor. "Thought maybe we could bounce ideas off one another. After you take a nap."

"Why would I take a nap?" She leaned her chin in her hand and scowled at him.

"Because you have a headache. Right there." He reached across the counter and poked a finger between her eyes before he removed his jacket and started searching her cabinets. "I picked up that teriyaki tofu salad you like from the health food store."

Was there anything he forgot? "I'm not hungry." But she was itching for a fight. How nice of him to accommodate her.

"Tell that to your headache." He stepped in front of her when she got up and headed to the fridge. "Take ten, fifteen minutes, Simone. Turn your brain off and give your eyes a break. We can continue the verbal joust when you're feeling better."

"You know you lost your right to boss me around when you served me with divorce papers." As much as she hated to admit it, the idea of a power nap held massive appeal.

"We all make mistakes."

She froze in the doorway of her bedroom, uncertain if he meant for her to hear him or not. Their divorce a mistake? Sure, she'd considered that more often than she cared to admit. She didn't like failing. That Vince might somehow feel the same way? She shook her head, dismissing his muttering. Not going to do it. Not rising to the bait...or whatever it was he was dangling before her tonight.

Dinner, more wine, and then she'd send him back to his bar, after looking at whatever he thought needed her attention. She sank onto the gold duvet–covered mattress, embraced its cushiony depths and closed her eyes. A minute, she told herself. She rolled onto her side, drew her knees up, feeling more secure than she had all day. Five seconds later she was out.

It wasn't often that Vince's plan for Simone went off without a hitch. That he didn't hear a peep out of her bedroom had him checking on her, a wave of protectiveness washing over him as he stood in the doorway.

Strong and independent to a fault. So hurt she refused to let anyone—even someone who loved her—in. It might take an entire flash of nitro to blast through those defenses of hers, if he was so inclined. He had to admit, the more he thought about it, the more he was.

He retrieved the folded blanket from the nearby chair, draped it over her. He stepped back and watched her sleep. Yeah. He was so inclined. He'd never in his life met anyone more pristine than Simone. Everything about her—from her clothes to her countenance to her apartment décor—screamed elegance, the absolute opposite of everything he'd ever known in his life.

He'd missed this. The polish, the beauty.

He'd missed her.

Vince clicked on the soft bedside table lamp, turned off the overhead and drew the door almost completely shut.

Once he got over his initial anger he realized he shouldn't have been surprised that Simone hadn't confided in him about Chloe's killer. Why would she when they had virtually nothing to do with one another any longer. That said, he wasn't about to let his ex-wife put herself in jeopardy because she was too stubborn to admit there was a maniac stalking her and her friends. It was all he could do not to read her the riot act for loitering in full view on her balcony. In yet another of her white ensembles. She may as well have been a beacon daring whoever was watching her to take a shot.

Come to think of it…he looked toward her bedroom. He'd bet that was exactly what she'd been doing.

So foolish.

That Simone hadn't shared whatever was in that envelope with either himself or Jack hadn't sat well with either of them, which meant there was only one solution to make sure they all stayed a step ahead of whoever this maniac was.

Whether Simone liked it or not, she was stuck with him.

He knew living spaces often reflected their owners. Simone's was no different. The open-air loft didn't allow for clutter. A small dining room table sat in front of the patio door that led out to a spacious balcony extending the length of the unit. He spotted a high-tech treadmill in the far corner, one of the few he'd ever seen not being used as a clothes rack. The entire wall in front of him was windows, the bottom half of which were draped with—what else—white fabric. Not a lot of privacy, but enough that he didn't feel she was particularly exposed. At least she kept the curtains drawn. On Monday he'd set up an appointment with the head of building security. He planned to be blunt about what was going on and what he needed the guards to be on the lookout for. He also wanted to see the full system up close and personal. While Simone hadn't asked—and she'd be ticked off to no end when she found out—he wasn't taking any chances with her safety. Not when they were dealing with someone who had murdered a child.

Once a person crossed that threshold of evil, there wasn't a lot they wouldn't do.

As Simone napped, he put himself on a mental timer and took the staircase up to the loft where he found her office. *Well, well, well.* He stuck his hands on his hips and looked around. "Not quite the tidy one here, are we?" Or maybe the clutter was representative of how she was feeling. Off-kilter, uncertain. Scared. He'd seen the fear behind the headache, pounding just as fiercely. He could only hope that would ease as well while she slept.

The solid wood desk was piled high with files and notepads, scattered pens and piles of sticky notes thick enough to wallpaper a small home. The bookcases that lined the wall behind her were stocked with law texts and assorted novels. There was a small bathroom off to the side, a flat-screen TV in the corner, and there, sticking out from under a hardback law text on the table behind the desk, was what he wanted.

The envelope had been wrinkled, no doubt from her nervous fists clenching it closed. The pictures he found inside, however, reignited the frustration at her keeping this to herself. She could have at least talked to Jack about it. After all, he was up to speed on the Chloe Evans case. It crossed his mind, yet again, that a number of his problems with Simone could be solved by her friends' return. He'd said as much to Lieutenant Santos and Jack, and while they hadn't verbally agreed, he'd caught a flash of understanding between them.

The photos curled his stomach. The image of Simone walking out of this building; another of her heading into her office, talking on her phone; and yet one more of her coming out, presumably on the same day as she was wearing the same clothes. This time she was in the company of a beautiful young woman with tight black curls and a smile wider than the Grand Canyon. Another picture, another day, another…he stopped. This one was different. This one…he set it down and leaned his hands on the desk to examine it. It appeared to be a photocopy of what looked like an old newspaper clipping showing the outskirts of a crime scene, tape stretched in front of three young girls, a crowd behind them.

The grief on Simone's, Allie's and Eden's childhood faces as they clung to one another transported him to what must have been the day Chloe had been found. For an instant, all Vince saw was nine-year-old Simone, in the center of her friends, her arms wrapped around them as if she could protect them from the world, golden hair spilling over the shoulders of her white summer dress. Tears streaked her cheeks, glistened in her defiant eyes.

He'd seen plenty of death in his life. While he hadn't held much grief at the loss of his parents, he'd seen friends die in battle and some, much later, by their own hand. He'd sat by his one-time boss from the security agency as he lost his battle with cancer. His relationship with death was a tedious one, but just then, he knew Simone had lived through something he could never understand.

What he could comprehend finally, now that he saw the pictures, was her reluctance to talk about it. She and her friends had been through this together, were going through it together now. Convincing her they couldn't do this alone any longer, that would be the trick. And that would happen once Eden and Allie were back in her orbit.

He made quick work of taking pictures of the pictures, then emailed them to Jack, cc'd Jack's lieutenant. He slipped the photos back in place, under the book, then picked up her phone and emailed her contact information to his own phone before he made a call. Then he went downstairs to wait.

"What on earth are you doing?" Simone hugged the warm blanket around her shoulders as she wandered out of her bedroom, blinking.

"Replacing the locks on your doors." Vince depressed a new lever on her sliding glass door. The extra security looked like something the military would have developed. "Headache gone?"

"Mmm." Never one to admit he was right, Simone looked behind her to the front door. He hadn't touched that one. Yet. "How long was I asleep that you were able to turn this place into Fort Knox?" Better yet, why was he doing this? Did he think whatever had happened to Mara made her a target?

"A couple of hours." He slipped a handful of tools into a duffel bag and zipped it closed. "I also installed a security camera outside your front door." He pointed to the small monitor on the kitchen counter that displayed the empty third floor hallway. "It'll feed into the system downstairs once I activate the wireless feature."

"What? No alarm that barks or an air raid siren?" She rubbed a hand down her face. "Vince, I'm sure you're doing what's best—"

He smirked and continued to pack up, the muscles in his arms tightening, straining the tattoos marking his skin. Were there more than she remembered? There was a wing, here, on his forearm she didn't recall.

"Of course you're doing what's best." She fell into the old dance with practiced ease. It was kind of nice, him taking care of her, but she didn't want him worrying about her. She could take care of herself. She always had. Never mind the fact she'd thought about changing the locks herself, especially when those "mementos" began appearing. She didn't need him. She didn't need anyone. Wanting him? She shifted on her feet. That was something entirely different. "Do I want to know what caused this sudden attention to my safety?"

"You already know. You ready to eat?"

Her stomach growled in response. She clutched the

blanket corners tighter. "What do you mean I already know?"

"You're working a high-profile case and your main witness has disappeared, remember? Wouldn't want the same thing to happen to you."

Just as she suspected. Except for the first time since they'd reunited, she didn't believe a word he said. Challenging him would only open up doors she preferred stayed firmly shut. She didn't want to talk about Chloe, or how she felt about the reappearance of Chloe's killer. Not with him. Maybe not with anyone.

"You said you had something you wanted me to look at with Mara's case?" She climbed up onto a kitchen stool and he pulled a paper container from the fridge. When he poured her another glass of wine, her heart— and attitude—softened. Or maybe she was still too sleepy to fight him. She'd forgotten how nice this could be, a quiet evening in, conversation, a meal. Even with the Denton case and Mara's disappearance looming.

She stabbed her fork into the spinach salad dotted with sesame seeds, fried tofu and assorted vegetables. The spicy dressing exploded on her tongue and woke the rest of her up.

"I went through the camera footage from the school across the street from Mara's apartment." He hefted his bag onto the chair beside her and pulled out a stack of papers and photographs. "When I talked to Jack this afternoon—"

Caution flags waved in her mind. "That's right. Exactly when did you—"

"After I was done at Mara's. I wanted to give him some of what I found."

"What did you find?"

"If you don't stop interrupting me I'm going to kiss you again."

Silence pounded against her ears. She clamped her lips shut and refocused on her dinner, wishing that didn't sound so appealing.

"Thank you," Vince said. "I located a flash drive she had hidden in her desk. I was able to access her private server and download the documents she'd stored before I passed it over to Jack."

"Something tells me you neglected to tell him about the copying part." Skirting the edge of the law, just as Jack had warned.

"He followed through and gave me copies of Deputy Russo's notes and reports. Which in turn gave me something to look for as I went through the school security tapes." He sorted through a stack of photos and pulled a few out. "Russo's observations were spot-on. Mara was as predictable as the sunrise, but there were some people that caught my attention. I printed out some stills. Do you recognize him?"

Simone set her fork down long enough to examine the picture. It was dark, had to have been taken in the dead of night, but in the halo of the street lamps, she recognized the blond-haired man and long beige trench instantly. "Cal Hobard." Well, that sealed it, didn't it? "He works for my boss."

Vince blinked as if that was the last thing he expected her to say. "This guy works for the DA?"

"Campaign consultant. Puppet master, take your pick." Appetite gone, she shoved her plate away and stared at the photo. "When was this taken?"

"That one? About a week before she went missing."

Recognition dawned. "He's in more than one?"

"Oh, yeah." He slipped another free and placed it on top. "A few over the last couple of weeks. This one though was taken around 4:00 a.m. the morning she disappeared."

Her mind raced. She'd thought there was something off with Hobard, but what possible reason would he have to communicate with Simone's witness outside the office? Wasn't he the one who kept reminding her what was at stake should the case against Denton fall apart? The entire reason for him wanting her to cut a deal? It was ridiculous to think he had anything to do with Mara's disappearance. Yet there he was. Caught on film. The morning she disappeared. "What about Mara? Any sign of her during that time?"

"No. But the apartment building's parking lot is being paved, remember? She'd have had to park on the street and her car hasn't been seen in the area for as long as she's been missing. The neighbor with the fake security camera saw her go downstairs with a thermos, come back, then leave again about a half hour later. Insomniac neighbors," he added. "A detective's best friend."

"So she did leave on her own." The relief she'd been hoping to feel at the revelation didn't descend. Not with the heat of his gaze radiating through her. He knew she wasn't telling him everything, but how could she when she wasn't sure what everything was?

"Did the neighbor say whether she had a suitcase or not?"

"No. Purse, car keys. Had her cell in her hand. But she was definitely alone. Whoever cleaned up probably took it to make it look like she left town."

Arguing with Vince's gut was more difficult than arguing with the man himself. Still, she shook her head. "She knew how important court was. I can't imagine—"

"Then let's come at this a different way. She wasn't a social butterfly, right? She didn't date a lot?"

"No." Simone shook her head. "She'd been set up a few times, but said she wasn't interested in dating right now."

"Is it possible she was looking for more evidence in the case? Something to cement what you had against Denton? Could she be trying to help you?"

Simone had considered that. "She agreed that there was more to Denton's case than we'd charged him with. But I told her this would be enough."

"Because you were hoping to get him to talk."

"I didn't tell her that." Guilt rose up and had her swallowing hard. "I always keep the details of my cases as quiet as possible. I need her to verify where the books came from. I see it as the tipping point. Once I get that on the record—"

"Mara doesn't agree?"

"She's angry with him. Not only about the fraud he'd committed and made her a part of, but because he was sloppy and cost innocent people their jobs. A lot of those businesses were only there for show and when he closed them, people got hurt. She thought they deserved more than having to stand in the unemployment line."

"One of the entries I saw talked about a new offshore account she connected to one of Denton's shell companies, an LW, Inc."

"What account?" Simone frowned. "She didn't say anything about that." And she didn't recall the forensic accountant she'd hired for his expert testimony mentioning it in his report, either.

"The entry in the flash drive was dated last week. When was the last time you talked to her about her testimony?"

"Before that. I had Kyla cover all my calls unless it was an emergency. But Mara wouldn't have done anything that would have jeopardized the case."

"What do you mean?"

"I needed Mara's reputation intact. I didn't want to give the defense anything to use against her when she was cross-examined. If they thought she'd gone rogue and tried to dig up dirt on her boss—"

"And as she's just lost her job. Okay, I get it. They'd think she had some kind of grudge against him."

Obviously Mara was even more determined than Simone had given her credit for. "We need to know what she was looking for. What she found. Something important enough that she'd drug two cops and take off in the middle of the night."

"I'm more interested in why this Hobard guy was lurking around her apartment," Vince said. "Maybe we can kill two birds."

She flinched at the image. "Mara's still got stars in her eyes, Vince. She still believes anyone can make a difference by doing the right thing. She doesn't know how evil people can be."

"Let's hope she hasn't found out the hard way."

Chapter 9

"Bad news?" Vince asked as Simone paced the living room, muttering to herself, cell phone in hand. He'd spent the better part of the last day and a half planted either on her sofa or at her dining room table as they sorted through Mara's files and notes, combining them with the information Simone had on the Denton case. There wasn't any doubt in Vince's mind Mara had gone off on her own to delve deeper into Denton's criminal connections. "Simone?"

"What?" She faced him in the dim light of the loft. "Oh, it's fine. Allie's taking a couple extra days in LA."

"That's good. She meet someone?"

Surprise erased the exhaustion on Simone's face. They were closing in on midnight Saturday, more than twenty-four hours since they'd dug in. They were still waiting on the warrant to access Mara's GPS on her hybrid. The cell phone company was dragging its heels when it came to her records, enough so that Vince had a contingency plan in place if it went on beyond tomorrow morning. He knew Simone wanted everything done aboveboard in case she needed to use it in court, but Mara was running out of time. Bureaucratic red tape had gotten in his way once before; he wasn't going to let it happen again.

"The only people Allie meets aren't exactly in a position to date. What she did get was an offer to tour some new psychiatric facility in a prison. I'm betting this time tomorrow she'll be shoulder-deep in serial killers and repeat sex offenders." She shuddered.

Yeah, Vince thought, because she and Allie were so different. "It's always the quiet ones who surprise you." He got to his feet, stretched and gathered up the empty water bottles he'd been collecting. "It's time we called it a night."

"What?" Simone swung on him, tugging on the hem of her white tank as she shook her head. "No, there's still more we can—"

"No, actually, there's not." Vince tossed the take-out containers and paper plates into the trash, wiped down the counters. He motioned to the scattered papers that had been taped to walls with enough vehemence he felt pretty certain she wouldn't be seeing her security deposit anytime soon. "We've gone over all her notes, all your notes. All my notes. We've scoured the websites, and now it's a waiting game. Unless you want to start driving around while we wait for those GPS records—"

"Jack said he'd have them by morning."

"Then other than wearing a path in your hardwood

floors, there's nothing more you can do tonight. Tomorrow we'll hit the ground running."

"Kyla said she'd be here first thing to do your bidding." She surprised him by following his lead and cleaning up. "If you're back here by nine—"

"I'm staying."

"What? No. Why?"

"Because I don't feel like driving," he lied. "And because I'm just going to turn around and come back tomorrow. I brought clothes. You've got a spare shower upstairs. I'm housebroken, remember?" Besides, he wasn't leaving her alone as long as that creep was out there taking pictures of her. "Lock your bedroom door if it makes you feel safer."

"That's not what—" She sighed. "Why do you always do that? Make it seem as if you're less than you are? More dangerous than you are?"

"I've always been dangerous." Dangerous was what kept him alive. "You chose to ignore it."

"I chose to see through it." She dumped the plastic bag of trash on a chair and stood across from him, hands planted on the counter. "You are, hands down, one of the most honorable people I've ever met, Vince. Why else would I have married you?"

"Because you like a challenge."

She grinned. "I married you because you were a good man. You still are. Whether you believe that or not."

"A good man you couldn't be bothered to come home to." When she opened her mouth to argue, he held up a hand, shook his head. "We don't need to do this. Not tonight, and not when I have the brain power of a gnat who's hit a windshield."

"Maybe I want to talk about it."

"Talking won't change what happened. Besides, neither one of us is who we were back then. We're older." And in his case, far more cynical. He'd been a powder keg most of his life, one that had finally gone off last year. They'd survived each other once. He wasn't sure they would again. "I'm not angry, Simone," he said. "I'm aware I didn't make our time together easy."

"See? Honorable." He'd have to be blind not to see her struggling against wanting to say more. Nor could he look away as she walked around the counter, stood in front of him and planted both palms flat against his chest. There was nothing he could do to stop his heart from thudding against her touch; there never had been. He'd been hers from the moment they'd met. As if she didn't know it.

He caught her hands, wanting nothing more than to slip his fingers through hers and lead her into that sanctuary of a bedroom. "Get some sleep, Simone." He pressed his forehead against hers, silently willing her to understand. He needed her to go before he brought her into the darkness he fought against every day. "I'll see you in the morning."

"Okay." She nodded, slipped free of his hold. "But I won't be locking my door." The smile she gave him as she disappeared around the corner vibrated through every cell in his body.

"Great." Vince sighed and stared at the ceiling. "A cold shower it is."

Darkness was not a control freak's friend. The ceiling fan whipped its soft, repetitive noise through the room, and Simone, in a futile attempt to soothe herself, dropped an arm over her eyes and willed the mental carousel of thoughts to stop spinning. It didn't help. If anything, the whirling only picked up speed.

Mara's disappearance, her job stability, her ex-husband asleep on her couch…

Maybe what she needed was a good stiff…drink. She groaned and kicked free of the suddenly heavy bedcover.

How long had she been lying to herself? Attempting to convince herself Vince was out of her system? She'd realized it the second she'd seen him standing behind the bar, looking sexy as ever surrounded by bottles and glass, that stolid, determined expression blanketing his face. One look from him, one quirky smile had been enough to short-circuit the control she'd instituted years before when she'd convinced herself she didn't need him in her life. And that kiss the other day? She blew out a breath. What on earth was she supposed to do with that?

She knew what part of her wanted to answer that.

How he'd put the brakes on her carnal offer confused and enticed her. They were adults. Given their history, no-strings-attached sex made sense. Then again, what didn't make sense at two in the morning? Hadn't they done enough damage to each other? What could she possibly be thinking to consider opening herself up like that again? Except the more time she spent with him, the more she remembered why she'd fallen so hard for him in the first place, pushed the lessons she'd sworn never to forget to the side.

Simone kicked her feet on the bed, reminding herself of a two-year-old in the throes of a temper tantrum. Why was she even thinking about this? About him? She'd made her move, however subtly, just as he'd bet her she would and still he'd turned her down. That should have been enough to turn her off. Instead he'd only revved her up more.

"He's *too* honorable if you ask me." She flipped onto her side, pounded her fist into the pillow.

She stared at the clock. At this rate, come morning she'd be lucky if she didn't rival one of those zombies who survived the apocalypse. Something was barreling toward her full steam, and no matter what strategy she considered, she knew she was about to get run over. She needed to grab hold of something: logic, rationality. Normalcy. If she even knew what normal was.

Chloe. Tears burned behind closed lids as she drew in a shuddering breath. The terror of their friend disappearing lodged anew in her chest; fear, uncertainty and guilt wrapped around her soul.

Most kids grew into adulthood. It was gradual.

Simone and her friends hadn't had that luxury. They'd become acquainted with the harsh world before any of them could reach double digits. She could pinpoint the day, the hour, even the minute her childhood had ended.

She jumped out of bed, tugging her tank down over her stomach and short shorts before she pulled open the door. Silence welcomed her, not surprisingly since she'd never known Vince to snore. She tiptoed into the kitchen, and cast a quick glimpse toward the sofa that was bathed in the glow from the streetlamps outside. She crouched down, opened the cabinet beneath the island. The hinges squeaked.

"What are you doing up?"

Simone yelped and shot upright. She locked her hand around the bottle of Scotch and pressed the other against her racing heart. "What are you, some kind of ninja?" If she got through this week without having a coronary it would be a miracle. "Honestly, normal people make noise when they move."

"Normal people don't skulk around the house at this hour." He stood there, wearing only his jeans, hands on his hips, looking like some kind of warrior god who had invaded her home. All that was missing was a sword and those leather strappy things crisscrossing those distracting abs of his.

*Don't look. Don't look. Don't...*she dragged her gaze across his chest, to the six- or was that an eight-pack trailing down to his waistband. She shook her head, trying to erase the image, but it only managed to lock it in place.

"I couldn't sleep." She set the bottle down, clicked on the light under the stove and grabbed the closest glass. "This." She tapped a hand against her head. "It won't stop."

"Want to talk about it?"

"We've been talking all day." She poured herself a good couple of fingers, downed it in one shot and waited for the buzz to take hold as her throat burned. "The only thing that's going to stop it is to put an end to it." To all of it. Her eyes watered as she poured another glass. And Vince was very much a part of all of it. "I'm beginning to think I shouldn't have taken this case."

He reached over and tugged the bottle out of her grasp. "This only brings up all the doubts and insecurities, leaves you questioning every decision you've ever made. Does wonders with guilt, let me tell you. Like fire in the brain."

"Feel free to join me." She retrieved another glass,

but he shook his head when she handed it over. "What? Wrong brand? I might have some whiskey around here—" She didn't remember him being so picky before.

"I don't drink." He capped the bottle, set it aside.

"This late? Well, make an exception because there's a lot to drink about if you ask me."

"At all, Simone. I don't drink at all anymore. I stopped."

"Yeah, right." He'd been known to put a six-pack away without nary a blip of intoxication. "Why? Wait, back up. You're serious."

He didn't respond.

"But you own a bar. How exactly does that work?"

"One day at a time," he said as if they were discussing nothing more than the latest sports scores. "I had a rough couple of years," he said. "Things got bad for me after the Walker case. Really bad. In here." He tapped his temple in the same way she had moments before. "I couldn't pull out of the thoughts, the doubts. Plus, I didn't exactly hit the genetic jackpot when it comes to alcohol addiction. Caught sight of myself in the mirror one night and saw my father." He shrugged. "Not a pretty picture. As far as bottoms go, though, I've heard of worse."

"I'm so sorry." The aftertaste of the Scotch turned bitter. She was well aware of the violent household he'd grown up in and that alcohol was at the center of it. The military had offered him an escape, a purpose, but not before seventeen-year-old Vince had finally had it and swung back hard enough to land his father in the ER. "I didn't know—"

"We could fill a library with what we don't know

about each other, Simone. And don't apologize. It's my problem, not yours. I'm not your responsibility. I never was."

He might not have meant it as an accusation, but it struck her like one. "Are you in recovery? Do you go to support groups?"

"I've gone to meetings. This is something I've come to terms with. It's who I am. It's probably who I've been for longer than I care to admit. And, come to think of it, I should have told you before now, if for no other reason than you thought you were hiring someone else."

"What?" It took her a second to understand what he meant. In an instant, the haze that descended evaporated. "Wow. You know what? That's insulting."

"It is?" He rubbed his chin.

"That you'd think I'd be so callous about you admitting you have a problem." It was all she could do not to take a swig out of the bottle but he was right. Drinking herself into oblivion wasn't going to do any good other than leave her with a hangover in the morning.

His eyebrow arched in that way that made her tummy itch. "I don't recall saying that. But I'm not the guy you married, Simone."

"You're telling me—" Words failed her, but she didn't stop moving around the counter to stand in front of him. Staring at him, feeling the heat of him radiating against her, she realized he'd never been more correct. He wasn't the man she'd married. He was more. So much more. "I'm not judging you, Vince. How can I when I have plenty of weaknesses myself? Wait."

She pressed a hand against his chest, felt his heart pounding. "Is this why you didn't want to work for me? Were you afraid this case would threaten your sobriety?" She frowned and his eyes lit up. "Then yes, you should have told me. I would have understood. I don't want to be the reason you start drinking again."

"My drinking isn't the reason I wanted to say no." He looked down at her hand, hesitated, then lifted his gaze back to hers. "It isn't the *only* reason. I didn't want to take the job because being around you is…difficult."

"Oh, come on. I'm not that bad, am I?" Her attempt to laugh ended when she saw the pained expression on his face.

"You said we're being honest with each other, Simone. So let's be honest. There's still something here. Nothing's fizzled out between us. That spark we had, it didn't go away. It only got hotter. Judging by that look, I'm guessing you agree."

She smoothed her hand down his chest, skimmed her fingers along the front of his jeans. "Maybe."

"I'm also betting it scares you as much as it does me." He dipped his head toward hers. An inch, maybe two, but enough to capture her attention and her imagination.

She couldn't argue with him. She couldn't breathe. The last time they'd slept together had been so intense, so powerful she hadn't had time to think, or to contemplate what would happen when reality crashed through their honeymoon hangover. Only then had they begun to see—and admit—that neither of them had any clue how to be married. It had been easier to give up and part ways. "Vince—"

"Everything I've ever done, ever seen, you're what really scares me. And I have no idea what we're going to do about it." He lowered his voice, stroked his finger down the side of her face. "But before this case is over, it's safe to assume we both know where we're going to end up."

She moved in, that rational part of her mind clicking off as she brushed against him. His eyes darkened as his hand skimmed down her neck, over her shoulder, trailing teasing fingertips along her arm to that sensitive bend in her elbow. "Is it really going to take us that long?"

"It *should* take us that long." He caught her wrist and drew it up to his mouth, pressed his lips against the skittering pulse beneath her suddenly too-hot skin. "You have enough running through your head, keeping you up at night, without adding us to the mix."

"There's one thing wrong with your theory." Simone locked her arms around his neck and pressed herself into him in every way she could manage. How his firm body melded into hers stoked every bit of desire she felt. "You were part of the reason I couldn't sleep."

She kissed him, deep and slow, reveling in his surprise, and finally his acceptance. There was no frenzy, no urgency, only her need to be close to him, to have him touching her, kissing her, reminding her that she was, when all was said and done, still alive.

He let her take what she needed, matching her moment for moment as he brought her in tight against him. He wanted her, still wanted her, and that knowledge set her to wanting more.

"Simone." His whisper against her lips did little to break through the fog. "Simone, stop. I meant what I said." He drew his hands up her sides, grasped her shoulders and set her on her feet. "Tonight isn't the night."

She hooked her heel behind his calf and tugged his hips against hers. "You sure about that?"

He squeezed his eyes shut and set her back. He stepped away, as if he needed the extra space to breathe. "Man, I'm going to need another shower."

He was serious. "You mean it?" Her cheeks flooded with warmth. "You don't want to keep this going?"

"Oh, I want to. But there's this horrific honorable tag you've labeled me with that keeps getting in the way. The last thing I want you to wake up with in the morning is regret. When the time comes, Simone, I don't want anything, including the past, coming between us."

He headed up the stairs and she waited until she heard the shower running before she withdrew into her bedroom, back into her bed. The blankets did little to warm her against the chill of loneliness that she was only now beginning to understand had become a part of her.

Simone tried to relax but was unable to stop herself from counting the passing seconds, her body taut, her mind braced for the weight of responsibility that was bound to return.

The mattress dipped behind her. She gasped as his arm slipped under her and scooped her against him. She curled into him as she'd always done, her head on his shoulder, her leg braced between his. She slipped her hand down his chest, lower, her fingers resting above his waistband. He pressed a soft kiss against her forehead, brought their linked hands up close to his heart as a solitary tear trickled out of the corner of her eye.

He always knew.

"Go to sleep, Simone."

She closed her eyes. The carousel slowed. The thoughts faded. And she slept.

Chapter 10

"I come bearing coffee! Come and get it while it's hot!"

Simone shot up. Her front door had just slammed and someone was calling to her. She shifted her legs against something, or rather someone else, solid. "What time—" She leaned over Vince to grab her phone and resisted the urge to shiver as his hand slipped beneath her shirt. His fingers brushed the base of her spine.

"I've missed this." His voice was soft and sweet, his breath warm against her neck.

"It's after nine. How can it be after nine?" She shoved her hair out of her face and stared at him. "I was a teenager the last time I slept this late."

"If there's a compliment in there, I missed it." His sleep-tinged voice made her insides tingle.

"Get up!" She scrambled over him and rolled out of bed, barely dodging his searching hands.

"If that's your mother, she does know you're a grown woman, right?"

"As if my mother ever cared about what I do with—" She looked over her shoulder as he sat up. Her heart skipped a beat.

"With what?" He scooted back against the headboard as she searched her dresser for something to throw on. "People like me?"

"People like you?" Had she heard him right? She hugged the oversize white T-shirt and matching pants against her chest. "You mean men?"

"Men. Red-blooded, hardworking males." He grinned.

"I often have," she tossed back, verbally dancing on that thin line to the conversation they'd started last night. Now was not the time to take her up on her offer to…reconnect. "Now would you please—?"

"If you're expecting me to hide in the closet, think again." He crossed his arms over his chest.

"I wasn't going to ask you to do that." She turned her back on him so she could strip, drag on her underwear and then her clothes. "I was going to suggest the bathroom."

"I sit corrected."

"Vince! Would you please—"

There was a quick knock and then…"Hey, boss lady, your coffee's getting cold."

Simone squeaked and leaped back as her bedroom door swung open. "Morning, Kyla." She readjusted her waistband and reached for the cup as her assistant turned gleaming eyes to the bed. "Ah, I overslept."

"Yeah, I can see why."

"You know when you smile that wide I can see the

fillings in your molars." Simone tried not to be blinded by the tropical pattern of orange, red and turquoise mingling on the young woman's maxi-dress.

"Uh-huh. You must be Vince." Kyla pushed Simone out of the way and strode over to Vince. "It's nice to finally meet you. I've heard so little about you."

Vince shook her hand before he threw the covers back.

"Oh, wow!" Kyla's hands shot up to cover her eyes. "That's more of an introduction than I expected."

"Relax." Simone laughed. "He's wearing pants. He wore pants all night."

"He did?" Kyla's flushed embarrassment shifted to disappointment. "Well, that sounds positively uncomfortable. Exactly how does that—"

"It's nice to meet you, Kyla." Simone could swear he was actually enjoying himself. "I appreciate you coming over here on your day off. I assume you have some information for me?"

"I do, indeed, Vince." She nodded and her curls bobbed accordingly.

"Wait, *you* called *her*?" Simone couldn't quite come to terms with the surreal situation in her bedroom. "When?"

"Yesterday afternoon. He had an assignment for me." Kyla blinked at her. "You told him he could use me. I can't thank you enough."

"Oh, for the love of—" Simone grabbed Kyla's shoulder and steered her out of the room, then leaned in to glare at Vince. "You. Out of bed. Now."

"I wish you'd make up your mind. Get in my bed. Get out of my bed…"

Simone slammed the door.

"I like him." Kyla's bright eyes looked like over-blown Christmas lights as she unloaded chocolate croissants and popped an additional coffee cup out of the travel container. "Not anything like I expected."

"Who did you expect exactly?"

"Well, he's really got that action-movie-star thing going on, doesn't he? Can he do an English accent? 'Cause, he is—"

Simone growled in the back of her throat.

"Okay, all joking aside," Kyla laughed. "You're going to be glad he called me. I spent yesterday afternoon poking around a little, trying to find out what I could about Cal Hobard."

Simone, who was sipping coffee out of one of the cups Kyla had brought, stopped midslurp. "Vince had you looking into Cal Hobard?"

"He just wanted some basic background information. Education, family, employment history and such. I've got a report ready to—"

"Tell me you did this at home and away from your office computer."

Kyla frowned. "Most of it."

Most of it? Simone pinched the bridge of her nose. "Did Vince happen to mention we think Hobard might have something to do with Mara's disappearance?"

"He might have mentioned there were some concerning pictures. It's not any big deal, Simone. I needed to grab some passwords and file names from the system."

"You hacked into the private server of the DA's office. Kyla—"

"It's not the first time I've done it. All the assistants do."

"You're not supposed to. Kyla, we're already dealing

with one missing person because she was poking her nose into something she shouldn't. I can't worry about you, too!" Was she going to have to get handcuffs for these reckless independent young women who kept entering her life?

"I'm also not supposed to be left in the dark when it comes to my boss getting the rug pulled out from under her at work. You think I wasn't already poking around after our clandestine meeting at the coffee shop the other night?" Kyla shoved a croissant across the counter. "Eat something before your bad mood wears off on me. And then maybe I'll tell you and your bed buddy what I found out."

If there was one thing Vince excelled at it was picking up on tension.

"You sicced her on Hobard?" Simone demanded when he headed to his duffel to pull on a clean shirt.

"I asked her to run a background check. Basic info." He tugged on socks, then his shoes. "Nothing that would bring any attention to her." Given how Simone had asked the question, he could only guess her assistant hadn't exactly followed instructions. He looked at Kyla, who had her arms crossed tightly over her chest. "What else did you do?"

"She wormed her way into the server at the DA's office and downloaded his passwords and account information."

"I downloaded everyone's," Kyla corrected. "And I told you, all the assistants do it. It saves time when we have to request certain information."

"And what if someone had caught you?" Simone demanded.

"I'd be out of a job, which I could be anyway if you don't save this case."

"I'll agree with Simone that it wasn't the best idea in the world," Vince told her and avoided Simone's laser-hot gaze. "And I'm assuming since Simone looks as if she's about to blast off into orbit that you did it from your work computer."

"If I'd accessed the information from home *that* would have sent up red flares," Kyla told them. "I download all personnel information at least once a month. I hadn't done it this month yet, so there's nothing to worry about."

"Nothing to worry about until the psycho working in our office finds out about it."

"We don't know Hobard's a psycho and stop getting ahead of yourself," Vince said. "Here. Have some sugar." He broke off a chunk of pastry and popped it into her open mouth. "You get cranky when you haven't had any in a while."

"I don't appreciate you putting her at risk," she mumbled and covered her mouth.

"At some point you're going to have to accept you can't protect everyone from everything, Simone. The sooner you stop trying, the happier you'll be. So, Kyla." He picked up the envelope and pulled out the papers. "Why don't you give us a rundown on what you found."

"I'm going to have to ask Eden to borrow her white-boards." Simone sank onto the sofa and curled her feet under her, nibbling on her second croissant in as many hours. If she wasn't careful, by the time this case was over, she'd gain ten pounds. She pointed a finger to the list of businesses Cal Hobard had been affiliated with over the years, and drew a mental line to some of those same names Mara had linked Paul Denton to. "If I was looking at this objectively, I'd say it's purely circumstantial," she said and earned a frown of disappointment from her assistant. "It could be as simple as they shared the same banking representative or investment counselor. The law, government, can be incestuous. Everyone into something with everyone."

"Not everything has to be proven in a court of law." Vince circled another name, drew a line to another one on the paper attached to it. "Right now we're looking for the smoking gun Mara found."

"Assuming she found one." Kyla hitched her sandaled feet in the rungs of the barstool. "Did you also suggest someone might have provided her with information to lure her out?"

"That's our worst-case scenario. Speaking of—" Simone checked her phone "—I haven't gotten a call from the car manufacturer about the GPS warrant. Have you?"

"Jack said he'd let us know when it arrived," Vince said. "Want me to give him a call?"

Simone shrugged. Vince went out on the balcony and left Kyla and Simone staring silently at the fruit of Kyla's Saturday afternoon labor.

"I'm sorry I got upset with you," Simone said. "I know you were only trying to help."

"I don't care that much about my job, Simone. Not if it means losing this case."

"You might not care, but I do. I also care about your future and getting fired from the DA's office right before you take the bar exam can tank your career plans."

"Then I adjust my career plans." Kyla turned admiring eyes on her. "You've never let anything or anyone get between you and what you want. Nothing interferes, not even him."

"That's not—" Simone began, but had to stop when she realized Kyla had struck a nerve. "Moving on, please."

"Mara's journal and notes—"

"Vince sent you copies of those, didn't he?" Simone may as well surrender. It wouldn't be the first time. She'd spent her life pushing everything aside to get to where she wanted to be career-wise. She'd accelerated her education, taken every opportunity offered, and, when push came to shove, she'd turned her back on her marriage and the man she thought she loved because it was easier than trying to find a balance. She pressed a hand against her sternum, forced herself to breathe. This must be what regret felt like. "Why doesn't he tell me these things?"

"Because he has freedoms you don't and he doesn't want you getting caught in the legal backlash. You ask me, you should turn the case over to him and stay out of it. That way you can claim ignorance and distance yourself if it goes really bad."

Simone smiled. "You're too young to be this savvy."

"I learn from the best." Kyla hopped off the stool and retrieved her laptop from her bag. "I found this awesome new computer program—"

The patio door slid open.

Vince's expression was stoic, his jaw tense. "We've got the warrant. They have a last location for Mara's car."

"Where?" Simone untangled her legs and gripped the edge of the sofa. "Vince?"

"Off Highway 160 near the Antioch Bridge."

"The Delta," she whispered. As she stood up, her knees wobbled. "Okay, so maybe her car broke down and she had to go find help. Do they know—?"

"We need to go, Simone." Vince took her by the shoulders and stared into her eyes. "We need to go now."

Chapter 11

The pressure built inside of Simone the longer they drove Highway 160, and deeper into the Sacramento Delta region they went. Neither she nor Vince had said a word since leaving her apartment. Part of her didn't want to know where they were going. Or why. She didn't want to speculate, didn't want to hope...

A helicopter circled overhead, the buzzing and constant hum thundering in her ears.

Inside, she willed Vince to drive faster. The strong sun sat above the horizon. Red and white with a dash of yellow for added impact. As they neared the scene, he pulled onto the gravel-strewn shoulder. He parked. Turned off the engine. Waited.

"It's such a beautiful place," Simone said. "I've always loved this part of the valley, the river. Peaceful. Do you know how many different bird species migrate through here?" Maybe if she kept talking, maybe if she didn't get out of the car…maybe. *Maybe…*

"I do not." He sat back, rested his arms on the steering wheel and followed her gaze over the bank of the sun-kissed river.

Shrubs and brush and thick, wet grass mingled and meandered for endless miles, hypnotizing even the most troubled of minds. The eleven-hundred-mile stretch of oak woodlands was a welcome and more scenic means to connect the central valley to Stockton and surrounding cities.

"I remember learning about it in school. I feel like I should know. One of those factoids that should have stuck in my head." Why couldn't she remember?

"I can go talk to Jack if you want," he offered. "You can stay here."

"No." She shifted her attention to the trio of deputies who had joined the detective. At least one EMT vehicle had wedged itself into the narrow space between the road and the river, light spinning against all the solitude. Another patrol car pulled up, stopped briefly before moving on down the road. In the distance, she saw the telltale silhouette of a tow truck approaching the scene. Mara was her responsibility. Always had been. Always would be. No matter what they found in the river. "This is my job, my case. I need to do it." She opened the door, braced one foot on the ground, then stopped. "Thank you. For being here. For doing this. I know it wasn't easy for you."

"Simone—"

She got out of the car and slammed the door, heading across the street before she could stop herself. When she felt his hand brush against the small of her back, she didn't want it to matter, but it did. That he was here mattered very much.

Engines rumbled, an odd cacophony against the quiet air. The acrid stench of gas and diesel permeated her nose, poisoned her thoughts. She stopped and stared at a pair of black skid marks arcing from the highway and followed their path to the deep trenches in the mud and grass. Trenches that didn't stop until the river's edge.

"Jack?" Vince guided her away from the investigators who were cordoning off the area with neon yellow tape, a slash against the lush, shaded beauty of billowing oaks and the occasional, drooping willow.

The detective acknowledged them, saying, "Heck of a way to start a Sunday."

"Heck of a way to start any day," Vince replied.

"True enough." Jack nodded. "Look, Simone, I told Vince on the phone there wasn't any need for you two to come down. We've got hours of work—"

"Is she in there?" Her question sounded clipped, irritated, even to her own ears, but she couldn't apologize for something she couldn't control. Jack looked to Vince, and Simone's temper rose. "He works for me, remember? Talk to *me*, Jack. Is Mara in there?"

Jack grimaced. "Can't say for sure until we get divers in."

"When will that be? Where are they?" She scanned the area, didn't see a sign of any water rescue team. "How long has it been? Shouldn't they already be in the water?"

"We're doing what we can, Simone. We've got two missing rafters down at the American River. The teams are stretched pretty thin, so they could only spare one diver. Rescue has to take priority over recovery."

"She must be so cold." Simone hugged her bare arms around herself and shivered. "I can't stand thinking of her—" She turned away, unable to decide what emotion to surrender to. Or if she should just turn off.

"I keep a suit in my car," Vince said. "If your guy has extra equipment, I can dive."

She spun, hand clutching her throat as she stared at him. "You'd do that?"

"Unless there's some regulation against a civilian aiding the police in a case like this? Jack? You told me you read my file," Vince said. "If that's true, you know I was a combatant diver in the Corps."

"Yeah." Jack nodded and pulled out his phone. "This is good, but give me a second to call it in." He disappeared around the other side of the EMT vehicle.

"You're really willing to go down there?" Simone asked.

"You hired me to do a job." Vince headed to his car, opened his trunk and rummaged around in the back. "I don't get to choose where that takes me." He dragged out a black dive suit, shook it out, draped it over the car and shrugged out of his jacket, which he handed to her. "Put this on before you rattle the teeth out of your head."

She tugged the jacket on and buried her nose in the soft lining. Vince's soothing scent of citrus and spice was everywhere. And Vince. "How long has it been since you've been diving?"

He shot her one of those "don't ask" looks as he ditched his shoes and socks, stripped off his shirt. When he unsnapped his jeans, she turned away, the flush on her cheeks filtering through to the rest of her. "Nothing you haven't seen before, honey."

She didn't want to smile. Hadn't she thought the

same the other night when she'd found him at her door? Her knuckles whitened as she gripped the edges of his jacket tighter.

"Nothing you didn't want to see last night."

"You're trying to distract me again." If only she could articulate how much she appreciated it.

"Maybe. Now we just have to hope this thing still fits."

She shouldn't have been as entertained as she was by the sound of him struggling into the wet suit. Jack reappeared, a young, redheaded woman in her own curve-hugging suit trailing close behind as they came toward Vince's car.

"Simone, Darcy. Darcy, Assistant DA Simone Armstrong," Jack introduced them. "And that back there is Vince Sutton."

"Nice to meet you, sir, ma'am." Darcy offered a firm hand and a friendly but tempered smile. "I'm sorry we're meeting under these circumstances."

"Me, too." Simone figured the young woman was about Kyla's age. Bright-eyed, energetic, but there was a caution about her that told Simone she wasn't someone who jumped into things without thinking them through.

"Darcy has over three years with the local volunteer rescue group," Jack said. "She'll give you a quick run-through before you head under."

"Sounds good," Vince called. "And while I'm sure Simone doesn't mind being ma'am'ed, please drop the sir. It's Vince." He moved from behind the car and joined them, torso still bare as he held out his hand.

"Follow me, Vince. Sooner we get in, sooner we get out."

"Lead the way." Before Vince followed, he took hold

of Simone's hand and pressed a soft kiss on her lips. "Whatever we find down there, this isn't over. If anything, it's just begun."

He moved off, leaving Simone to wonder if he meant the Denton case or whatever hadn't happened between the two of them last night.

"I really don't want to like that guy," Jack said, his back to Simone. "But he doesn't make it easy."

"Tell me about it." Heart in her throat, Simone watched Vince strap on his tanks, nod to his diving partner and head toward the water.

"How long have they been down there?" Simone sipped toxic coffee from a paper cup that had been pushed into her hands by an eager rookie.

"Not long." Jack glanced across the water. "I know it feels like forever."

"No." She slipped her sunglasses on. "Forever is what it must have felt like to Mara." The crime scene unit was getting a jump start on the tread marks, while patrol officers controlled the traffic issues that cropped up with a closed section of the highway. She'd never seen Jack in action. Watching him interact with his fellow officers, observing how he commanded a situation without being controlling or combative, she was impressed. No wonder he and Cole made such a good team. They had the same temperament, the same attention to detail. Most important, they shared the same dedication to finding out the truth.

"Hard to believe it was only a few weeks ago Cole brought us down this river in his boat." Jack's wistful disbelief aligned with her own. "Really could have done without this image in my head."

"It seems every place I've considered beautiful has been marred in some way." Simone's throat thickened with emotion. "Never thought I'd be adding the Delta to my list."

The tow truck's engine continued to idle as it hugged the side of the road, hovering like some giant metal grim reaper.

"If this turns into a murder investigation…" Simone found herself stumbling over the words. "*When* this turns into one, I'd appreciate you giving Vince as much access as you can."

"I thought you'd hired him to find her." Jack tapped away on his cell phone, glanced up every few seconds to keep track of all the goings-on.

"He won't let this go." Simone refused to tread lightly any longer. "And I don't want him to." One of the things they had in common.

"It would make it easier on me if you made him official through the DA's office. You know how tricky things got with Eden and the Batsakis twins. Consultants are one thing. Independent contractors are another."

Considering she had no idea what she'd be walking into when she went into the office tomorrow, she couldn't promise anything. "I'll do what I can," she said. "Fair warning, though. Vince isn't an easy man to say no to." She looked at him. "And he loathes red tape."

"Noted." Jack's expression had her wishing her feelings for him were different. He was a great guy, but he wasn't Vince.

She wandered away, looking for something, anything to distract her as the seconds ticked by. An outcropping of rocks decorated by bright wildflowers called to her. As she approached, something on the ground glinted against the sun. A flash. Bright. Blinding. She stooped down and stared at the knotted gold chain with a tiny cross.

The tears she'd been holding in check dropped onto her cheeks. She dipped her fingers into the gravelly dirt, started to lift the necklace free, but stopped herself. She'd be breaking procedure, contaminating evidence. She could see part of the chain had been coated red, no doubt with blood. She didn't want it to matter, but it did. It took every ounce of control she had to look over her shoulder and gesture to one of the evidence techs. "This is Mara's," she whispered and pointed to the cross lying on the ground as if it were a gravestone.

"Detective!" A shout from the bank's edge had her jumping to her feet and scurrying over to Jack. The river rippled. A few seconds later Darcy and Vince broke the surface.

Darcy held up her thumb. Then turned it down.

"They found her." Simone's whisper barely broke through the noise as deputies, technicians and EMTs scrambled to organize. The tow truck rumbled to life, moving out to adjust position and back down to the edge of the river.

Simone couldn't tell if her heart was beating so fast she couldn't feel it or if it had stopped altogether. Darcy and Vince swam toward shore, gear still in place as they grabbed hold of the tow rope and dived back in. Time stopped. Or did it speed up? One minute the bank was filled with people issuing orders and making space and the next, a small blue hybrid vehicle emerged from the water's depths.

Simone set her coffee on the ground, took determined steps to where they stopped the car. She could see Vince and Darcy walk out, snapping off masks and unlocking their tank straps.

Every promise she'd ever made to Mara echoed in her ears. Every conversation they'd had, every joke they'd shared. Crime scene investigators snapped pictures, nodding and motioning their okay to open the door. There was a brief discussion where it was noted the window had to be broken to gain access as this particular model of car didn't allow for slim jim access.

Simone jumped when the driver's window exploded. The door was unlocked and opened.

Mara Orlov's body spilled out onto the muddied bank.

A sob caught in Simone's throat. Tears blurred her eyes as she moved in.

"Simone—" Jack moved toward her, but out of the corner of her eye, she saw Vince catch hold of Jack's shoulder and pull him back.

New orders were shouted. The clang of metal doors and squishing shoes scraped against her senses. She could smell putrid water and as she looked down at the young woman's body; scraggly brown hair; vacant, translucent eyes, rage took refuge in her heart.

Simone stood over Mara, remembering the wonder-filled eyes, the dazzling smile, but all she saw now was the pale face and a thin red welt around her throat.

"Simone." Vince came up behind her, his hands falling on her shoulders in a gentle embrace. "They need to do their work. Come on. They'll take care of her. Come with me."

She let him lead her away, only because she didn't know what else to do. He brought her back to his car, left her leaning against the hood as he changed out of his wet suit and into his clothes.

She looked up into the sky, rocking back and forth. Where had the morning gone? Heat had descended but was tempered by the cool Delta breeze. The sigh she released left her sapped of air, as if she hadn't breathed in hours. It hurt. Every inhale, every exhale, made her feel like she was going to shatter into a million pieces.

She looked down when he joined her, noticed the layers of mud caked on her shoes and white slacks. Her feet felt heavy, like anchors pulling her into her worst nightmare. Again.

"I was wearing white the day they found Chloe." She surprised herself by speaking. "A white sundress with lace edging. Hand-done. One of those imported fabrics my mother was obsessed with. Funny what sticks in your mind. I can remember the colors so vividly. That thick green grass, the deep purple of the wild violets in the field. Chloe's red hair." And with those words, she was over the mental mountain she'd imagined. "Every color you can think of was somewhere right in front of me. It hurt. Sensory overload, you know?"

"You were nine years old," he said. "I imagine more than your senses were overloaded."

"I knew," she continued as if he hadn't spoken. "I knew she was dead before they told us. There were these expressions on the cops' faces, the lead detective. I saw that same determined anger on Jack's face before they opened that car door." She shivered. "It was so quiet that day. It seemed so strange, all those people, everyone waiting for news, you could hear the wind brushing through the trees. Rustling the leaves. Like now." She closed her eyes and focused on that one soul-saving sound. "Do you hear it? Even with the engines and the voices, you can hear the silence. Like the entire Delta is pressing in on us."

"Like it's trying to protect itself from the outside world."

"Or protecting itself from us." She drew his jacket around her and rested her head against his arm. "I wear white so I don't forget. Every day I get dressed, everything I wear, it's so I remember that there's always someone, something to fight for. It's the promise of everything that died that day. Not only Chloe, but for us, too. I've never been able to explain it, not until I heard Eden talking to Cole a few weeks ago. Whoever we were meant to be died in that field with her. Every time I step into a courtroom, every time I face down a crook and do everything I can to make them pay for their actions, I'm doing it for Chloe. Because maybe if I make enough of them pay, she can finally rest in peace." Before now, she had never been able to put it into words. It was as if Mara's death had unlocked something inside her. Broke something inside her.

She loathed the gratitude she felt as he slipped his arm around her and drew her in, needing it more than she could say. "She is at peace, Simone." He didn't sound condescending or apologetic. He sounded like the Vince she knew, the Vince she'd loved: strong, dedicated and solid. "How could she not be with the way the three of you have lived your lives?"

"We promised each other we'd live not only for ourselves but for her." A solitary tear escaped her control, but instead of wiping it away, she let it fall.

"For the record, I don't think she'd mind if you added a bit of color to your world."

She appreciated his teasing. "I should have paid closer attention to Mara. I should have talked to her more, made certain that she understood what she'd given me was enough. Instead I let her get caught up in my excitement at the prospect of bringing down some criminal overlord who might not even exist. God." She pressed her fingers into her eyes. "What if I've been wrong all this time, Vince? What if Denton is just some schmuck who was defrauding clients and the IRS?"

"The fact that we've pulled Mara's body out of the river should be all the proof you need you were right." He pressed his lips against the top of her head. "Blaming yourself isn't going to get any of us anywhere. From everything you've told me about her, there's nothing you could have said to stop her from pursuing some mysterious connection she found. Everything I saw in her apartment told me she loved puzzles and figuring things out. You can't take on everyone's mistakes and decisions. Do you have tunnel vision? Absolutely. I've seen evidence of that myself."

"Geez, Vince, not Jason again." She planted a hand on his chest and tried to push away, but he kept holding on to her. "Not now."

"It was only an example and stop using my brother as a convenient barrier between us." As he was never one to coddle, she welcomed his terse comment as a sign of normalcy. "That situation is what it is. You're not wrong, Simone. Not about Denton and not about your boss and Hobard. The question is what are you going to do about it?"

"Do about it?" This time she had enough strength to break his hold. She sat up, brushed the dampness from her cheeks and handed him back his jacket. "What do you think I'm going to do about it?" She stalked around to the passenger side of the car. "I'm the Avenging Angel, Vince. I'm going to make whoever did this wish they'd never been born."

Chapter 12

"I told you I wanted to go to my office," Simone said as Vince bypassed the turnoff. He'd been hoping by the time they got back to Sacramento her temper would have cooled. No such luck. If she'd been raging before, now she was in full-blown fury mode.

"I know what you told me." Patience, he counseled himself. She's in pain. "I'm not letting you anywhere near your office—or the DA—until you get your head on straight. We need a plan. Your main witness is dead. I don't have to be a legal expert to know Lawson is either going to want to offer a deal or cut Denton loose altogether. He won't have a choice unless you find another way to present your case." He hit the gas and took the next turnoff, which led toward her loft. "You're due in your boss's office tomorrow morning, right? Let's go over everything we have and see what else we might have missed. Maybe have some fresh eyes take a look at Mara's journal entries."

"Fresh eyes?" She looked at him as if he'd lost his mind. "I'm not bringing anyone else into this mess."

"You think I'm enough? I'm touched."

"That's not what I meant."

"I know what you meant. You don't want to put anyone else at risk."

"I don't have to worry about you," she said. "You can take care of yourself."

"Now I really am touched." He reached over and took her hand, forcing his fingers between her iron-tight fist. "You are not alone in this, Simone. But until we have all the information about what happened to Mara, going in half-cocked is only going to get you fired and negate everything you and Mara were trying to accomplish."

"She was twenty-three." Simone's whisper cracked the wall around his heart. "She'd barely started her life, a life that she wanted to have meaning. You and I both know it wasn't an accident her car went into the river."

"What we know and what we can prove are two totally different things. Jack said they'd have lab results by tomorrow, right? Let's hope it's early enough to make a difference in your meeting with Lawson."

"And Hobard." She gripped his hand so tight he lost circulation. "I want to know what he was doing near her apartment all those times. I swear if he had anything to do with this—"

"All the more reason to go in prepared for anything."

"Did you have a plan in place when you beat the crap out of your murder suspect?" She snatched her hand free.

He took a slow count of ten before he answered and

only after he turned into her driveway, inserted the garage keycard the doorman had given him Friday night and drove inside. "I did have a plan, actually."

"And how did that work out for you?" The anger in her eyes blazed hot in the dimness of the parking lot.

"It didn't. He's still alive." There were days he wished he'd succeeded, to know that the monster responsible for the brutal murder of Sabrina Walker was erased from existence. Then there were days he realized he'd crossed a line. A line he was going to make sure Simone never even got close to. "Why do you think I'm telling you to take some time? You don't want to live with what I do, Simone. Trust me. No one does."

Her brow furrowed enough that he knew she heard him. Whether she understood what he was saying was something else.

"Tell you what." He parked and killed the engine, palmed the keys. "You go upstairs, toss those clothes and shoes in the trash and take a long hot shower. If, when you're done, you still have the desire to destroy your career, ruin your reputation and make enemies of just about everyone in law enforcement, I'll take you someplace where you can work out your aggressions in a more productive manner than unmanning your boss and his underling." He had a punching bag with her name on it.

"You hate my career," she countered. "Why do you care what happens to it?"

"You're a brilliant lawyer, Simone. I've always thought that." That she'd confided in him about why she only wore white no doubt required a reciprocal admission. Not much harm it could do now, anyway. "What I didn't like was how I disappeared around it. Do you realize we've talked more about the law, procedure and my work as a P.I. in the last three days than we ever did in the months we were together?"

"It never occurred to me that you were interested. You always distrusted the police and the judicial system."

"I seem to recall asking you to convince me I was wrong." Not that she'd ever heard him. "And I don't distrust all police. I know there are good ones. Like Jack and Cole. And the two detectives who were working the Walker case."

"You can say that given what happened?" Her eyes glinted.

There was the law-abiding prosecutor he loved. "They could have testified against me. They'd seen enough of what I'd done, but they put the attention back on Sabrina Walker, on the fact that she wouldn't have been found without me. Not entirely true by the way."

"I've read the report," Simone said. "You're underestimating yourself again."

"I nearly beat a man to death with my bare hands, Simone." He could still feel the bruises, still feel the blood on his hands. And he would do anything to feel more remorse than he did. "As much as you want to believe I'm still the man you married three years ago, something like that changes you. You know it does. It just happened to you a lot sooner."

"Is this the equivalent of you talking me off the ledge?"

He took her hand again, raised it between them and pressed his lips against her fingers. "You jump, I jump. Nothing else to it, Simone. You've got me for as long as you want me." He started to get out of the car, but she tugged him back.

"What if I do? Want you?" Her other hand came up and touched his face. She leaned forward and kissed him. Gentle, questioning, tempting. And it was all he could do not to take what she offered.

"Simone," he murmured against her lips. "You're not in the right frame of mind—"

She sat back, stared at him, disbelief shining in her eyes. "You're saying no to me again? Seriously?"

"Yeah, I'm starting to doubt my own intelligence. But don't worry." He shifted toward her, her mouth only a breath from his. He brushed a kiss on either side of her lips, stroked that sensitive spot under her ear and waited for her to shiver. "Consider this a rain check, not a refusal. Now let's get upstairs before I change my mind."

She flattened her hand against his chest, moved it lower, until her fingers brushed against the front of his jeans.

He tried hard not to exhale fire. "Come on, Simone." This time when she pulled back, he broke free. He waited for her to get out of the car and gather her purse. There was no denying he wanted her. He would always want her. But not when her head was filled with images of a dead friend and her heart overflowed with guilt.

The familiar silence descended as they walked to the elevator. Stretched to the ride up and followed them to her front door. "Last chance, bud. You sure you won't change your mind?" She slipped her key into the lock, arched a brow at him. "Shower's nice and large. Remember?"

He stared at her, jaw locked, letting her read his mind.

"Fine. See if I ever offer again." She pushed open

the door and disappeared down the hall. Vince waited, waited...she yelped. "What on earth are you doing here?" He heard her ask her friends and pocketed his keys. He waited, listened, not wanting to intrude. "Allie, you said you weren't coming back until... Eden? You two still have days left—"

"Vince called," Eden outed him despite their agreement to make their arrival seem spur-of-the-moment. "He told us about Mara. He said you needed us."

"I—he did? But he didn't tell me—Vince?" Simone's voice broke as he reached for the doorknob and drew the door closed.

"Sutton."

Finding Cole Delaney leaning against the trunk of his car seemed like the fitting end to his day. He did a quick inventory of his most recent actions. Nope. Nothing to warrant an official police visit. He supposed he could chalk this up to the cop's wife upstairs in Simone's apartment.

"Detective." He'd met Delaney only on a few occasions, the most recent being his and Simone's wedding. Cole hadn't changed much. He still had that boy-next-door look about him with dark blond hair and a special twinkle in his eye despite the "don't mess with me" attitude. Vince supposed he could attribute all but the attitude to honeymoon jet lag. And the gold wedding band on his finger. "Problem?"

"Appreciate you letting us know what's been going on." Cole uncrossed his ankles and held out his hand. "Simone's either going to kiss or kill you. Hope you're prepared."

"For both, actually." He'd known he was taking a

chance by notifying Simone's friends, but as soon as he'd talked to Jack this morning about what they expected to find in the river, he hadn't thought twice. Calling in reinforcements was the only thing to do. The only thing he knew he could do that might actually make a difference where Simone was concerned.

"Have you talked to Jack?"

"I'm on my way in to the station now to get filled in. Why don't you come with me? Catch me up on your side of things so I'm not flying blind."

Vince hesitated, gripped his keys and then slipped them back into his jacket. "You still want me involved?"

"You're involved whether I want you to be or not." Cole's lips quirked. "For the record, I'm fine with it. One thing I've learned is not to turn down help from smart people. Even P.I.s with anger issues. Besides, I'm betting Simone would never speak to me again if I tried to lock you out of this now."

Despite the rotten day, Vince's mood lightened. That they understood each other would make getting this case to a satisfactory conclusion a lot less painful for all involved.

"Car's over here." Cole inclined his head toward a blue SUV. "So, Vince, don't hold back. Fill me in on what you've been up to the last three years."

"There, I bet you feel better." Eden skidded to a halt, passed a filled wineglass to Simone and stared at her, her green eyes going wide. "What are you wearing?"

Simone looked down at the jeans and purple T-shirt. "What's wrong?" She tugged at the hem as she asked. She knew this was a bad idea, but her suddenly blinding closet didn't look right. Nothing looked right. Nothing

felt right. The white had brought her so much com-
fort all these years, but now? What she'd finally found
in the bottom drawer of her dresser felt as confining
as a straitjacket while at the same time she couldn't
remember feeling so exposed. "Vince said something
about adding…you know what. This isn't working. I'm
changing."

"Allie!" Eden set the wine down and dived forward,
grabbed her wrists and hauled her into the kitchen. "We
won't need an angelic intervention after all. Look!" She
did something with her hands that reminded Simone of
a model on one of those spinning car displays. "Color!
You're so shiny. I'm going to call this the Vince effect."

Allie had pulled her head out of the refrigerator and
was looking at them, her jet-black hair a sharp contrast against the soft lavender of her capris and matching tank. She blinked. A slow smile spread across her
lips. "This is what we in my profession would call a
breakthrough."

"And bare feet." Eden clapped like a five-year-old
greeting Santa. "Oh, this is a happy, happy day."

Simone laughed, then slapped a hand over her mouth.
She shouldn't be laughing. Not with everything that had
happened. Not with Mara…tears burned.

"Eden!" Allie pointed a finger at her then the wine.

"On it." Eden dashed away but returned quickly with
their glasses. She wrapped Simone's hand around the
stem. "Drink. Allie, you know what to do."

"I already called. Two supersized supremes with
extra cheese are being prepared this minute."

"Did you tell them no mushrooms?" Eden asked as
she pushed Simone onto the sofa before she curled up
next to her.

"Of course I didn't." Allie sounded as if she were placating an irritable child. "What would pizza with my best friends be without you picking off the fungus?"

Gratitude drove away the sadness. Vince might have done well in the distraction department the last few days, but no one distracted her better than these two. Eden with her sharp edges and acerbic views, Allie, all rounded and optimistic. They balanced each other. They balanced her. When Allie dropped down on the other side of her, a bit of Simone's world righted itself again. Not quite as sturdy as before, but as close as she was going to get until this case was over.

"We're sorry about Mara," Eden said. "Kyla filled us in while we were waiting for you."

"Kyla." Simone tried to break free of their hold, but they wouldn't let go. What was it with people and not letting her move when she wanted? "I should call her and let her know—"

"She knows," Allie said. "And what she doesn't, she will be told. Cole said he'd have Vince call her."

"Where is Cole? You didn't ditch him already, did you?" Simone's own attempt at teasing didn't come close to striking home. She felt trapped between emotions she couldn't get a handle on.

"Please," Eden snorted. "He's stuck with me for the rest of his life, poor guy. He said something about taking Vince to the station."

"Why to the station?" Vince hadn't done anything wrong as far as she knew. Had he?

"Relax. The fact Vince called us earned him serious credit."

"With all of us," Allie added. "Maybe even enough to make us forgive him for breaking your heart."

Given what she'd learned in the last few days, it seemed she'd done most of the breaking. "We both gave up. There's no one to blame."

"Spoken like someone in the midst of a rekindling," Eden said. "So we'll hold off on the girlfriend bonfire and give him a pass. For now. At least until things settle down."

Simone hadn't realized how much she'd needed to hear those words. "I'd appreciate that."

"Looking at this place," Allie said, "I'm thinking this compulsion you two share of taping notes all over the place is a cry for help. I've seen serial killers' homes less obsessive than this."

"Do you pack that silver lining of yours wherever you go?" Eden rolled her eyes. "Just because you have more brain capacity than the rest of us—"

"I needed to see all of it." Simone could barely see the sanctuary of her home beneath the facts, records and figures of what, in the last few hours, had turned into a murder case. She grasped Chloe's pendant and slid it across the chain. "I didn't understand that before, Eden. How it helps put the pieces together."

"No two cases are ever the same." Eden frowned. "You've got a lot going on but no real connective threads. It's there," she added when Simone's confidence took a nosedive. "We just have to dig it out. You want to talk about what happened today?"

"Other than watching them pull the body of a twenty-three-year-old kid out of the river?" Simone shrugged, as if she could push aside the images circling in her mind. "What's there to talk about?"

"How about the fact you're blaming yourself." Allie kicked off her shoes and tucked her feet under her. "That you believe her death is your fault. That you should have seen it coming because Simone Armstrong is an all-knowing omnipotent being."

"That's not fair." Simone bristled.

"We all do it," Eden said. "We have control issues and we all know why. Something goes wrong, someone innocent gets hurt or worse, someone dies and we blame ourselves because at the moment there's no one else."

"The only person responsible for Mara's death is the person who killed her," Allie added.

"I know," Simone sighed. "You're right, but…" She wasn't sure she ever wanted to feel anything ever again.

"I realize you're hurting," Allie said. "We hurt for you. You're angry and you're confused and you're feeling guilty, all of which are understandable. But we know you, Simone. Once you've taken some time and let things sit, you're going to come out swinging. And you'll have us right by your side."

"She was one of us," Eden said as Simone stared at the wine in her glass, the liquid rippling as she spun the stem. "Which makes her ours now. Whoever is responsible, we're going to get them. We're going to set this right."

"Speaking of setting things right." Simone took a deep breath, glanced upstairs and sighed again. "There's something I need to show you. Something Vince wouldn't have mentioned on the phone. Give me a second."

She retrieved the envelope from under her law text and went back to her friends in the living room. She didn't think anything could lessen the impact of the photos but seeing Mara's body, replaying the image over and over in slow motion, did the trick. "These photos were left on my windshield Friday when Vince and I got back from visiting Mara's friend in Davis." Because she knew the pushy journalist in Eden would rip them out of Allie's hand, she gave them to her first. "I haven't had a chance to examine them yet and with everything else that's been going on—"

"Let me guess." Allie's eyes sharpened into that therapist gaze she wore so well. She rested her elbow on the back of the sofa and pressed her fingers against her temple. "Our dry spell on gifts has come to an end."

"Sicko is upping his game." Eden flipped through the pictures.

Simone stood still, toes curling, bracing herself for the reaction she expected. Eden's eyes went hard, her face unreadable as she handed photo after photo to Allie.

"You should have told us immediately," Eden said.

"So you could what?" Simone fell into the defense she'd crafted days before. "Cut your honeymoon short because some maniac's taking pictures of me? Nothing's changed, Eden. There's nothing new. There wasn't anything either of you can do."

"I don't know about you, Eden, but I can't wait to get home." Allie's statement, accompanied by a knowing look aimed in Simone's direction, made her realize her mistake. "Maybe he's left something for us as well."

"I should have thought of that." She should have asked Jack to check their homes and offices right away.

"What did Vince say when you showed him?" Eden asked.

"I'm surprised he didn't try to lock you in a safe room so he could go after this monster himself," Allie said with a strained smile.

"He doesn't know," Simone said. "And before you two get any ideas, I don't plan on telling him. He's already turned this place into a fortress because of the Denton case and Ma—" She cleared her throat. "He's already acting protective and that's with him not knowing." Not that the idea of Vince as a bodyguard didn't have its appeal.

"Correct me if I'm wrong," Eden said after a moment. "And granted I didn't get to know Vince all that well during your first go-around, but I seem to remember him being a stickler for the truth. You really think lying to him is the way to go on this?"

"How can you not tell him?" Allie frowned. "Aren't you two sharing that *magic moment* again?"

"Man, we really need to find you a boyfriend," Eden muttered. "But I agree. How can you be doing whatever you're doing with Vince and not tell him what's going on with Chloe's case?"

"It's none of his business," Simone said. "I—" She looked from one to the other, but when she found both her best friends looking at her with disbelief and disapproval, she caved. "I hired him to find Mara. That's all this was supposed to be. I needed him to help save the case."

"Bet that surprised him," Allie said from behind her wineglass.

"What's that supposed to mean?" Simone snapped.

"It means the two of you never had a particularly loquacious relationship," Eden explained. "You two lived very separate lives even while you were married."

"You don't get to give me marital advice until you've at least had your first real disagreement," Simone countered.

"Then my advice stands." Eden grinned. "And you were right about the makeup sex."

"Getting back on point," Allie said, waving her hand in the air. "Tomorrow you're taking these pictures to Jack. What you decide to tell or not tell Vince is on you, but he's going to find out." The buzzer sounded and Allie leaped to her feet and grabbed her wallet. "I'll go down and get the pizza. And keep pacing all you want, you know we're right. Lying to Vince isn't going to get you anything but trouble and if you ask me, you already have plenty of that."

"Nothing like a suspicious death to kick a company into complying with a court order." Lieutenant Santos entered the conference room of the major crimes division and closed the door behind him. Slight in stature, he commanded a presence that reminded Vince of his time in the military. Santos didn't miss a trick and prided himself on being directly involved with every investigation. Cops might have his grudging respect, but Lieutenant Santos earned Vince's with his handling of this case, especially on a Sunday when Vince was certain he'd rather be home with his wife and kids. "Now that we have a victim, the company who manufactured the GPS system in Mara's car should get us her complete history within the hour."

Jack polished off his latest cup of coffee. "Better late than never."

"No guarantee it'll yield anything." Cole glanced at Vince who had taken the look-and-listen approach.

Organized chaos seemed to be the best way to describe the department since Vince and Cole had arrived. It was as if the cops were taking Mara's case as personally as Simone.

"Has anyone been able to get in touch with her family yet?" Vince asked.

"We've left voice mails on her parents' phone and brother's," Jack said. "Both the coroner and the lab have moved her case to the top of the list and we've shifted the evidence Tammy collected in Mara's apartment to authorized. We hope to have some preliminary results by morning."

"What about Gale Alders?" Vince hadn't been able to stop thinking about Mara's friend and the fact she probably hadn't slept since his and Simone's visit. "She shouldn't hear about this on the news."

"She's on the list," Jack confirmed.

"I should be the one to tell her," Vince said. "I promised we'd keep her up to date." When was he going to learn not to make promises he was loath to keep?

"You sure?" Cole sat back in his chair and pinned him with a skeptical look. "It's not the best part of the job."

"I've handled worse." Vince meant what he said. "Are we done here? I'd like to get back to Simone's."

"Would you now?" Cole arched his neck to look at Jack before focusing on Vince. "Any particular reason?"

Aside from wanting to see her? "You didn't tell him?" Vince looked to the lieutenant then to Jack.

"Tell me what?" Cole asked.

"Someone left these on Simone's windshield the other day." Jack dug through the stack of papers on the table and pulled out a file, slid it toward Cole.

Cole flipped through the photographs Jack had

printed. The quiet rage that settled on the cop's face mirrored the anger simmering inside Vince.

Cole muttered, "I'd ask why Simone didn't say anything, but I already know the answer."

"She didn't say anything to any of us," Jack said. "We only found out about it because Vince was with her at the time."

"She didn't share with me, either. She still hasn't," Vince added. "But I knew something was wrong. Takes a lot to freak her out."

"I don't suppose anyone thought to check—" Cole began.

"I stopped by your boat that night along with Eden's old place and Allie's house, and again yesterday," Jack said. "Didn't see anything out of the norm. Looks like he's got Simone in his sights for the moment."

"And we thought he'd got his kicks by making sure I found Eden hanging in that meat locker. Now he's moving down the line."

"It's a theory," Lieutenant Santos said. "Meantime, Vince is sticking close to Simone. He knows what to look for."

"And what's that?" Cole asked.

"I'll know it when I see it." He'd dealt with his share of criminal minds over the years. "I don't want her to get hurt any more than the rest of you. And she won't as long as I have something to say about it."

"Does Simone have anything to say about it?" Cole asked.

"Not really, no." Vince wasn't tempted to apologize in the slightest. "She doesn't want to let me in on this part of her life, so be it. Not the first time we've been down this road. However, I've updated all her locks, added a few extra security precautions and will be meeting with the building manager tomorrow so everyone's brought up to speed. Might not hurt to add more patrols around her building."

"Already done," Lieutenant Santos said. "Allie, too. Cole, whatever you want, you say the word."

"If it were me, I'd say let him come. But I don't want that creep anywhere near my wife. You want to put some extra cars on the marina, do it. I'm not going to let pride get in the way of her safety."

"Just don't tell Eden about it, right?" Jack chuckled, but when Vince looked at the other detective, he didn't find a hint of humor in the man's eyes. "Be nice if we could get some kind of handle on what the guy's plans are."

"Let's hope we don't find out too late. I'm going to get going. Oh." Vince stood, then reconsidered. "Since it looks like we're all open and aboveboard here, you should know Simone has a meeting with the DA first thing in the morning. She should have some backup about how the case is progressing. Lieutenant?"

"You thinking they'll take her off the case?"

"I'm thinking watching them try is going to make for some fabulous entertainment. Whether they do or don't won't matter. She wasn't going to give up before. She certainly isn't now that Mara's dead."

Chapter 13

"I don't need a babysitter, Vince." Simone exited the elevator and headed toward her office. Late night and two bottles of wine aside, she'd been up since the crack of dawn, pounded out a good forty-five minutes on the treadmill and drank enough water to fill a canal. By the time she'd gotten showered and dressed, she found Vince in the kitchen brewing coffee.

While he hadn't said anything about the white-and-blue flowered shirt she'd found in the back of her closet, the approval in his eyes when he'd looked at her boosted her confidence. "I need time to get my head together before meeting with Ward." She needed to get her head around a lot of things.

"Is my presence that distracting?"

"We both know it is." Few people had arrived yet as it wasn't even eight, but she found Kyla, bright-eyed and eager, sitting behind her desk, typing hard on her keyboard as if exorcising a demon.

"Good morning." She stood and walked around the desk to take Simone's jacket. "I've got a new pot of coffee brewing. All your notes on the Denton case are arranged on your desk. I've also got Judge Buford's and Mr. Poltanic's phone numbers for you in case you need to contact them."

"Thanks, Kyla."

"Poltanic is Denton's defense attorney, right?" Vince asked.

"Slime bucket." Kyla looked a bit sheepish. "I've heard. Sorry."

"Apt description." Simone nodded. "I can't recall any client he represents who shouldn't be on the FBI's most wanted. Did you bring something to keep you occupied?" she asked Vince.

"You mean my coloring books? Absolutely. I even sharpened my crayons."

"A simple yes would have sufficed." Simone flipped through the stack of phone messages from last week as she wandered into her office. She heard Vince ask Kyla a question and caught the flash of color as her assistant headed to the break room. When the door clicked shut, she spun around. "Vince, I don't have time—"

"Make time." He moved toward her like lightning. His arms were around her in no time; she could feel every inch of him pressing against her. She didn't have time to catch her breath before he kissed her.

It took a lot to surprise Simone, and that Vince could still manage to thrill her to the point of breathlessness said a lot about him. Every kiss felt like the first one.

The way his lips devoured hers had her abandoning all thought other than how much she wanted him.

Her hands went slack. The papers she was holding fell to the floor. She reached up, locked her arms around his neck and opened herself to him.

She heard him sigh in approval as he sank into her, his mouth on hers. Simone urged him back, guiding him until he was against the door and rattling the glass wall beside them.

"This distracting thing is becoming a habit." Simone used a finger to trace and tease his lips before she dived in and took more.

She loved the feel of his mouth, his strength, his confidence. How he knew to hold her, to send her pulse rocketing into the stratosphere made her heart soar. So much so that he must have known it and felt it. He held on to her hips and switched their places, now her back was to the wall.

He abandoned the kiss, pressing his mouth against the side of her neck as his fingers trailed to the hem of her skirt. She was breathing hard and murmuring his name as the fabric went higher, exposing her bare skin to his searching fingers. "Vince." She bit her lip, arched her neck.

"Silk." He was panting as he rested his forehead against hers. She pressed her lips together. She couldn't stop herself from wanting, needing to feel more of him. "I've been wondering about that ever since you walked into my bar."

"I—" She gasped as his fingers slipped beneath the edge of her panties. "Oh." She dropped her head back, barely registering anything else as she felt him touch her, caress her, stroke her. She moaned and drew him as close as she could as he whispered in her ear to let go. But she couldn't. Not here. Not now. Not with people outside… "I can't…" His touch lightened, but the pressure didn't ease. If anything it only built her up faster, higher than she thought she could go.

Her entire body quaked as the orgasm ripped through her. She rode it out, pulsing against him, not wanting to let him go.

She went lax, still holding on as he tugged her skirt in place and took a step back. It was only a step but it felt like a mile.

She stayed there, against the wall as they caught their breath. "That can't have been enough for you," she said. She reached for him. "Let me—"

He shook his head, held up his hands. "It's fine." He flinched, backing up toward her desk to sit on the edge. "Trust me, there's nothing I love more than watching you fly. Almost nothing," he offered a weak smile. "Feel better?"

Her face flushed. She shoved her hair in place, shaking herself back to reality. "That was so completely unprofessional I can't even say." She stooped to collect the confetti of notes and messages.

He grinned. "I'd love to hear you describe it for me. In excruciating detail."

"Was that supposed to help me prepare for my meeting?"

"It was supposed to remind you you're a powerful woman who knows what she wants. You want to find out who's responsible for Mara's death, find a way to keep this case going. You needed to get rid of all the clutter you've been collecting the last few days."

"If that's decluttering, consider me a fan." She

smoothed her shirt, wiggled to readjust her underwear
and ignored the knowing smile clinging to his lips. She
walked to her desk. She stopped, brushed her hand over
his shoulder and leaned in. She kissed him. Stroked
his face. Stared into the eyes that had equal parts chal-
lenged and loved her all those years ago. "Once this is
over, I'm thinking we should go on a date. A real date.
Dinner, conversation. Dessert."

"Sounds like a plan to me. Just remember." He caught
her hand in his and squeezed. "It doesn't matter where
we start. We both know where it's going to end."

"Denton's lawyer has officially filed a petition with
the court to dismiss the charges against his client."
Simone had barely entered the conference room and
already she was under fire from Ward Lawson.

She lowered herself into one of the padded chairs,
folded her hands on top of the thick files she'd brought
with her and focused her attention on the DA. As much
as she hated to admit it, Vince's idea of stress release
had managed to reboot her. The nerves, the uncertainty,
the self-doubt? They'd all vanished under his touch.
"Yes. I'm due in court at one to respond. I plan to ask
for a continuance so we can reevaluate our case."

Bookended by his assistant on one side and Cal Hobard on the other, Ward looked more prepared for a
stump speech than for reading her the riot act. There
was charisma to be sure. How else would he have gotten elected? And the man wore a blue power suit better than anyone else. His conviction record was stellar.
Ward Lawson was a talented lawyer. Talented enough
that his political future could be whatever he wanted

it to be. Depending on who he chose to surround himself with.

Which brought her to Hobard, who continued to radiate some semblance of control despite the strained lines on his face and the ghostly exhaustion in his eyes.

"Is that what you think this situation calls for?" Hobard asked, smoothing his hand down his tie. "A reevaluation?"

Simone resisted the urge to clear her throat or reach for the glass of water a few inches away. "I'm aware this isn't the outcome we hoped for."

"Your main witness in the case is dead, Simone," Ward said. "That's as far from hope as we get."

Heat radiated up her spine. So much for civility. "I'll be sure to pass your condolences to her family and friends, sir. In the meantime—"

She was cut off by the arrival of a half a dozen of her coworkers entering the room, their assistants right behind. Bringing up the rear were Jack McTavish and his boss, Lieutenant Santos.

"I apologize that we're late." Lieutenant Santos slid into the chair beside Simone while Jack stood behind her. "We were waiting on the ME's report as well as the forensic results."

"I wasn't aware you'd be joining us, Lieutenant," Lawson said. "I assume Ms. Armstrong requested your attendance?"

"No, we came here all on our own," Jack said in a determined tone. He lifted his arms up and down. "No strings, see?"

Simone bit the inside of her cheek as Santos ducked his head to hide his own smile.

"I assume the audience is here to witness whatever

you plan to dole out, so let's not keep them waiting."
Simone dragged her gaze slowly around the room, meeting each coworker's eyes. A few looked away. Others glared in open hostility. "Yes, Mara was our main witness—"

"Your only witness," Hobard said.

"Her testimony would have authenticated the accounting records we've used to build our case, yes." Simone took a steadying breath. "But that doesn't mean we don't have other avenues of prosecuting Mr. Denton. The accounting records are only part of the effort." Granted the most important part, but still.

"Judge Buford's a stickler for details, Simone." Ted Jones, who had considered Simone his main competition in the office ever since she'd been hired, spoke up. "If you don't have any other evidence to support the charges against Denton, you're out of luck."

"I am more than aware, but thank you for the reminder, Ted." She returned her attention to her boss. "Which is why I'm currently exploring other avenues of investigation. It's always been my belief the current charges were a starting point with Denton. Given the events over the weekend, there's no doubt someone is worried where this case is concerned." She shifted her gaze to Hobard. "Otherwise a twenty-three-year-old accountant wouldn't have been murdered."

"There's no evidence to suggest Mara Orlov's death was anything but an accident," Ward said. "Is there, Lieutenant?"

"As a matter of fact." Lieutenant Santos cleared his throat. "The preliminary examination on Mara's vehicle indicates she was hit from behind, then again on the passenger side, probably in the hopes of sending her into a skid. They found trace evidence of black paint on her car. The tire marks found at the scene support that claim. Broken glass from a headlight and taillight were found fifty yards or so from the site. Also, the car went into the river in neutral." As Santos spoke, the scene played in Simone's head like a horror movie. Mara must have been so scared. So alone. Had she cried? Screamed? Fought back? Simone swallowed and tried to focus on the lieutenant.

"We also found physical evidence of an altercation near the scene. Blood found on an outcropping of rocks matches the victim's, and lacerations around her neck indicate something had been ripped from around her throat. A necklace was found nearby, blood evidence still intact. When we have a suspect, we'll have something to compare to."

Simone kept her eyes pinned to Hobard and her boss, watching for any flutter of recognition.

"Is there an estimated cause and time of death?" Hobard asked.

"Blunt force trauma. Her skull was caved in. Probably on that rock," Jack answered. "The coroner is placing time of death between 2:00 and 8:00 a.m. Friday morning. That's as close as we're going to get considering the damage water does to a body."

"Her GPS signal was lost at eight minutes after three Friday morning," Santos added.

"All factors taken into account, Mara Orlov's death is being ruled a homicide."

"A homicide that occurred in the early morning hours of the day she was scheduled to testify. You told me to come in here this morning with information," Simone said. "That's what I've brought you."

"I believe you told me you'd find your witness."

"We did find her." The deep voice from the doorway had her clenching her fists as everyone around the table, male and female, shifted to attention. "I couldn't help but overhear," Vince said. "I thought a clarification was in order. You wanted her found, we found her. Not in the way anyone wanted, of course. If you dismiss the case against Denton, you're never going to get another shot at him. Trust me, he'll either be gone or he'll be dead. Whoever killed Mara is going to see to that."

"And who are you exactly?" Hobard asked in a frosty tone.

Simone pursed her lips. She could just imagine the image Vince projected to the room full of law enforcement people and attorneys. While there had been a time she'd have been mortified, given the stricken expression on the DA's face, her ex-husband could not have timed his arrival better.

"Vince Sutton. I'm a private investigator hired by Ms. Armstrong."

Ward looked at Simone. "I don't recall authorizing funds—"

"I didn't ask for authorization," Simone said. "I'm paying him myself."

"I bet you are," Ted muttered under his breath.

"To be completely aboveboard," Simone said as Jack and Vince both inched forward into her peripheral vision, "Mr. Sutton happens to be my ex-husband. He's also a former marine." She turned a too-bright smile on Ted as he lost two shades of color in his face. "In case you'd like to continue this conversation with either of us after the meeting? His expertise has been invaluable to the case, which we're continuing to build." She shifted back to the DA. "I understand this is a difficult situation for you, sir, and I will completely understand if you believe terminating me from my position is the best way to save face for this office."

"I'd be lying if I said we hadn't been discussing that option," Ward said.

Hobard didn't look convinced. He did, however, seem more curious than he had only moments before. "Honestly, Simone, can you build an entirely new case against Paul Denton?"

"We owe it to Mara to try," Simone said. "I get it. You're all here at the gallows hoping I'll be swinging in the wind in the next few minutes. You want my job that badly? Stick around. It might be yours." She pulled out an envelope from her stack of papers and set it in the center of the table.

"Simone, what are you doing?" She felt certain Vince's hand on her shoulder was meant to dissuade her, but instead, his support only emboldened her.

"I'm going into that court this afternoon and I'm going to get that continuance." She stood and gathered her files. "If I don't, then you have my resignation."

Vince pushed his way past her and reached for the envelope.

"Leave it." She touched his arm, lowered her voice. "It's what has to be done."

"You're going to let these jerks push you into quitting?"

"Vince is right, Simone." Jack joined in, followed by Santos. "This isn't your fault. There's no reason to fall on your sword to protect this office."

"This isn't about me. It's about Mara. And it's about convicting Paul Denton." And anyone else he might be involved with. Their support meant more than she could say, but this was the only play she had. She looked at Hobard, who was staring at her in a way that made her squirm. "On the case or off, I'm going to find out who killed Mara and why. Now if you'll excuse me, I have an appearance to prepare for."

Before Vince or anyone else could stop her, she walked out of the conference room, head held high. It wasn't until she was safely back in her office, seated at her desk, her gold fountain pen gripped tight in her hand, that she gave in to the fear.

How on earth was she going to pull this off?

"I don't suppose either of you knew she was going to do that?" Vince followed Santos and a shell-shocked Jack out of the building. Never in a million years would he have expected Simone to threaten to resign her position. This job was everything to her. It was a part of her. Without it, she'd lose herself. As much as he'd resented her job in the past, he couldn't let her do this.

"You mean did we know she was going to offer herself up on a silver platter? No freaking clue." Jack scrubbed his hands down his face. "Any ideas what to do next?"

"No way is she going to win that continuance." Santos motioned them to a more private area away from surveillance cameras. "Judge Buford's good, but he's also a realist. We all know rebuilding a case like this is next to impossible, especially if we can't use evidence we've already gathered."

"Then we need to find another way for her to win," Vince said.

"You have an idea?" Jack's eyes lit up.

"Kyla said this Buford judge is a stickler for professionalism. Would you agree?" Vince asked. His mind raced ahead of him. Oh, boy. It was a doozy of a plan, but if it worked…

"Definitely." Santos eyed him warily. "His is the one courtroom my guys don't play around with. It's all business with Buford. What are you thinking?"

"That you'll need plausible deniability." Vince nodded. "I can work with this. Just gotta call one person and I can make it work. I'll see you two in the courtroom at one."

"If Cole finds out about this, I'll be divorced even quicker than you were." Eden tucked an errant strawberry blond curl under the black wig and checked her appearance in the visor mirror of his car.

Vince surprised himself by chuckling. "If it works, no one will be the wiser." That said, if Simone found out he was about to manipulate her court case, she'd cut off his… "Five minutes should do it, ten if you can manage. Don't push it. We want him late for court, not suspicious."

"He's a defense lawyer." Eden checked her teeth and scrubbed off a smear of bloodred lipstick. "Suspicious is his middle name." She pulled out a dark pencil and added a beauty mark above her lip. "What do you think?" She batted mascara-thick lashes at him.

Vince looked for the Eden he knew beneath the hair and makeup, not to mention the come-hither tank and push-up bra. "Can you even breathe in those jeans?"

"Men." Eden's lips curled. "Don't you know we willingly sacrifice oxygen for the perfect look? Are you sure this is where he comes before court?"

"Kyla heard it straight from his paralegal's lips," Vince said. "Coffee run fifteen minutes before court. Double shot, double sweet espresso with an almond biscotti."

"And a diabetes chaser no doubt. I keep telling Simone I'm going to steal that assistant of hers," Eden mumbled as she readjusted herself. "But no, the girl has to have her heart set on being a lawyer."

"Nobody's perfect. You good to go?"

"If I don't break my ankles in these shoes."

Vince looked down at the floorboard. Her wedge sandals looked tame compared to the stilts Simone often wore, shoes that played a supporting role in the erotic fantasies that had been playing in his head since this morning. He spotted a black luxury sedan pull into the lot beside the shop. "There he is."

"You sure?" Eden squinted from their spot across the street. "He even looks like a stooge."

Truer words were never spoken. "Hop to."

"Yes, sir!" She saluted and got out of the car. Once she got five steps away, she stopped, circled back and leaned in through the open window. "One thing. I don't know what you and Simone have got going on, but you hurt her again, I'm coming after you. And you know what I do to people who hurt my friends."

"I do indeed." He'd read the papers. "And under-stood."

"Good." She patted the car and headed across the street. She'd added some kind of testosterone-boosting wiggle that had him blushing. Forget Cole divorcing Eden. If the detective found out about Vince employing his wife as a decoy, he'd be in big trouble.

Vince set his phone on the dash. Twelve forty-five.

Twelve fifty. Twelve fifty-five. "Okay, Eden. That should do it." Vince tapped his fingers on the console. "Don't press our luck."

The door swung open and out flitted Eden, coffee cups in both hands, a bright smile on her painted lips, and a rotund, flustered-looking Silvio Poltanic trailing behind.

Eden laughed, threw her whole body into it and bent forward. As expected, she drew Poltanic's gaze south. When she popped back up, she jerked her hands. The lids flew off the cups. Coffee spewed and landed all over Poltanic's tailored suit and tie.

Vince smiled. He admired Eden's purposeful ineptitude. She tried to help the lawyer, even attempted to use her shirt to wipe off his, but he hoisted his own bag and coffee out of the way and raced over to his car. Horns blared as he left skid marks out of the parking lot.

Eden scurried across the street, ducked into the car and ripped the wig off. "How are we on time?"

"Five after one. You are a genius."

"Now *that* you can tell Cole. Just don't fill in the details." She kicked off her shoes, shook out her hair, but thankfully left the clothes in place. "You can drop me off at the station. No, wait." She dug around in her bag and let out a sigh of relief. "Sweatshirt. Okay. Yeah. Station, please. Then get your butt to court. I bet you don't want to miss this."

"All rise."

Simone stood, butterflies the size of pigeons fluttering in her stomach. Paul Denton did the same from his place at the defense table. She didn't see his family in court, but that wasn't surprising considering the last-minute scheduling. Where was Denton's attorney? His poor client looked apoplectic.

"Where's Vince?" she asked Jack and Lieutenant Santos, who were seated directly behind her. After his defense of her in the office, she'd expected him to be here.

"No idea," Jack said.

When the doors opened, her hopes soared, but instead of Vince, DA Ward Lawson and Cal Hobard strode in. They didn't sit, but stood at the back wall, unreadable expressions on their faces.

"They may as well be holding a scythe," she mumbled.

"Keep the faith," Jack said.

Judge Buford banged his gavel on the bench. "Miss Armstrong. You've had a difficult weekend."

"Yes, Your Honor."

"I appreciate you making the time to be here this afternoon given the circumstances." He motioned to the court reporter to stop. "Would you please convey my sympathies to Miss Orlov's family. It's a tragedy to lose someone so young, not to mention conscientious."

"Of course, Your Honor." The beautiful sentiment wasn't lost on her. He couldn't say more and keep his objectivity where the case was concerned, which only made the statement more powerful. "I'm certain they'll appreciate it."

He motioned to the reporter again. "Mr. Denton? May I ask where your attorney is? This hearing is being held at his request after all."

"I have no idea." Paul Denton stood, his hands shaking. "I only know he told me my case would be dismissed this afternoon."

Judge Buford tilted his glasses down. "Did he now?"

"Your Honor, I'm happy to give the defense additional time to make an appearance," Simone offered.

"You might be, Miss Armstrong, but the court is not. I assume you have a motion of your own?"

"Yes, Your Honor." Whatever was going on with Poltanic, she didn't care. "While the state fully admits the loss of Miss Orlov and her testimony damages our case against the defendant, we respectfully request a continuance so we can reevaluate our strategy."

"It's the court's understanding that the evidence you planned to use was to be authenticated by Miss Orlov. Are you saying you have additional evidence you can present in its place?"

"I'm working on it, Your Honor."

"By yourself?"

"Lieutenant Santos and Detectives Jack McTavish and Cole Delaney are working with me. I've also hired a private investigator at my own expense. I realize this is asking a lot of the court, but the charges against the defendant are significant enough to warrant careful examination."

"He's also entitled to a fair and speedy trial."

"Agreed, Your Honor."

"Mr. District Attorney, I see you lurking there." Judge Buford waved his fingers. "Approach, please."

"Sir." Ward did as was asked and pushed away from the wall to stand beside Simone. "I'd like to add that Ms. Armstrong has the full support of my office behind her. Whatever she needs, we'll make sure she has at her disposal."

"You will?" Jack coughed to cover his comment.

"Hmmm." Judge Buford eyed the courtroom. Simone's

pulse hammered. She wouldn't follow his line of sight, wouldn't remind herself that pesky Benedict Russell was hunkered in the back row, scribbling furiously for the next morning's edition of the *Journal*. "While I did grant you an extension last Thursday, I'm afraid given the circumstances that would be an undue hardship on the defendant."

Simone's spirits dipped. "Of course, Your Honor. We understand."

"I'm inclined to deny the request—"

"Wait!" The doors to the courtroom burst open and Silvio Poltanic dived in. He tripped over his own feet racing to the defense table. "I'm here! I apologize, Your Honor. There was this woman, with these—" He cupped his hands over his chest, his face going red. "She had these legs." His hands went to his ears. "And coffee, coffee everywhere as you can see." Poltanic wiped his hands down his coffee-stained pants and shirt.

Simone stared, astounded that anyone, especially an attorney who had spent as much time in Judge Buford's courtroom as Poltanic had, would arrive in such a manner.

"Mr. Poltanic, get a hold of yourself," the judge ordered.

"Yes, sir." Poltanic gasped, bent double and took deep breaths.

"I think he might stroke out," Santos said as sounds of Poltanic's wheezes echoed in the courtroom.

Simone heard the door swing open. Vince stepped inside, taking barely any notice of the scene before him and circled around to sit beside Jack. "What did I miss?" he whispered a bit too loudly. He looked at Simone, his expression blank. "What?"

She narrowed her eyes.

"I respectfully request all charges against my client be dropped," Poltanic managed finally. He gripped the edge of the table for support. "With the death of the state's main witness it's clear they no longer have a case. A trial of any kind at this point would be vastly prejudicial—"

"Enough." Judge Buford's nose wrinkled, no doubt due to the odor of coffee and panic-fueled sweat permeating the room. "I find it completely disrespectful to the court that an attorney would request a hearing of this magnitude and then arrive late to the proceedings. Your client's rights are paramount at this point, Mr. Poltanic, and for that reason alone I'm not going to hold you in contempt—"

"Contempt for what?" Poltanic screeched.

Simone cringed as recognition dawned on the defense attorney's face.

"Forgive me, Your Honor," he said.

"Miss Armstrong. I'm giving you seventy-two hours. Either return to this court with a new strategy, or the charges against Mr. Denton will be dismissed."

Simone's ears roared. "Thank you, Your Honor."

The judge banged his gavel loud enough to drown out Poltanic's stuttering protests.

Simone dropped into her chair.

"Congratulations, Simone." Ward patted her awkwardly on the shoulder. "You pulled it off after all."

"Thanks." She pressed a hand against her brow. Beads of sweat sank into her fingers. "That shouldn't have worked."

"What was that?" Ward asked as he moved off.

"Nothing. Just, I'm ready to get back to work," Simone said.

"Seventy-two hours. Don't waste them." He moved off, only to be accosted by Benedict Russell as he strode out of the court.

Jack grinned. "Congratulations, Counselor. You did it."

She turned and looked at Vince, completely unconvinced by his innocent act. "Did I?"

"It wasn't me standing up there talking to the judge," he said. "Now how about we get back to business?"

Chapter 14

"You all have been busy." Simone dumped her brief-case and purse onto her kitchen counter.

Clearly Eden, Allie and Kyla had all spent the better part of their day reorganizing all of Simone's notes on the Denton case and attaching highlighted portions of Mara's digital journal. Her walls and half of her windows were wallpapered to the point of blocking out part of the sun, but it was the oversize map of the Central Valley that caught her attention. "What's this?"

"That's what we're working on now." Kyla stuck a small red ballpoint pin into a location, then made a tick mark on the chart beside the map. "We're going through everything in Mara's GPS records and tracking her movements."

"Looking for patterns," Eden mumbled around the pen in her mouth. "If it can work for chasing serial killers, surely, we can find something on an accountant."

"It's interesting," Allie said from her spot in the corner of the couch. Reading glasses perched on her nose, another set stuck on top of her head, she waved a finger in the air for attention. "Mara's remarks in her journal are quite detailed. Much more than I'd expect from a young professional just starting out."

"She was a brainiac." Simone couldn't let herself think of Mara as anything other than a lost witness at the moment. Once they closed the case, then she could grieve, but until then, it would have to be business as usual. "You've read her school transcripts. I've never seen such a brilliant record. She's like the gold standard for every employer out there."

"Yes, I noticed that, too," Allie said.

Simone glanced at Eden, who looked up. Her brow furrowed. Even Kyla seemed to pick up on the odd tone in Allie's voice.

"I can hear the wheels turning." Eden sat back and rested her bare feet on the edge of her chair at the dining room table. "But I can't quite understand the words. What do you have, Allie?"

"I'm not sure. It's just…odd." She drew her laptop closer. "Give me some time here. Go on with whatever you were doing."

"Mara was in Stockton a lot." Kyla stood back to examine the map. "Does she have family there?"

"As far as I know her parents are back east and her brother's down south." Simone focused on the map again. "How many times did she go there?"

"I'm up to six so far, but that's only in the first two weeks of the time period we're working off," Kyla answered.

"We figured since the case began six months ago, that was a good starting point," Eden explained.

"She always took Highway 160. Why? I-5 would have gotten her there and back faster." Simone trailed her finger along the path. "This route would have cut at least a half hour from her trip. I don't remember her ever saying anything about Stockton."

"Did she go to school there?" Kyla asked.

"Not according to her records," Allie said. "Ivy League all the way, private scholarships and grants. No student debt."

"Must be nice," Kyla said. "I'm going to be paying my student loans after I start collecting Social Security. This address keeps popping up near the airport. Eden, can you do an online search and see what it is?"

"On it." Eden tapped away on her laptop. "Have you seen Vince this afternoon?"

"What?" Simone kicked off her heels and got a bottle of water out of the fridge. "Oh, yeah. He showed up in court just as I was granted the continuance."

"Wait, you got it? You won?" Kyla whipped around so fast she knocked the container of pins to the ground. "Sorry, but wow!" The hem of her peacock-blue dress skimmed the floor as she scooped up pins. "That means the DA can tear up your resignation letter now, right?"

"Your what?"

Simone concentrated on her water as her friends shouted protests. When they finally calmed down she managed to explain. "They had to believe I was all in on this case. And they did." She didn't, however, have any illusions that her stay of execution would be permanent. She was on borrowed time and everyone knew it. "If this case goes south they're going to need a scapegoat."

"But if you win, you'll be the highest-profile lawyer in the office," Eden said.

"Yeah, I'm sure Ward will love to share that spotlight." She waved them off topic. "I can't think about that right now." She couldn't think about a lot of things. "You guys hungry? Vince said he could bring something from his bar if you wanted."

"I'd love one of those double-stacked burgers they do," Eden said and gestured Kyla over to look at the screen. "And maybe some fries and onion rings."

"One heart attack, check." Simone shook her head. Eden's eating habits, when she remembered to eat, were absolutely atrocious.

"I wouldn't mind the baked salmon," Allie said. "Where is Vince, by the way? I'm surprised he's not attached to your hip."

"He dropped me off. He's driving out to see Gale Alders to tell her about Mara." She'd offered to go along, but he'd wanted her to get to work. No doubt he thought he was sparing her the emotional upheaval of having to break devastating news to a victim's loved one. She'd never understood how police officers did all the notifying they did. She wouldn't wish that on anyone let alone Vince. "I'll text him and let him know what to bring... back." Simone set her phone down and looked first at Eden then Allie. "Would you two care to tell me how you know what's on the menu at his place?"

Eden's eyes darted. "Every bar serves burgers."

"Not everyone serves salmon. Allie? Your turn since Eden's playing dumb."

"I'm an adult. I can play whatever I want," Eden protested.

Allie's eyebrows pinched as if she was carefully

choosing her next words. "We might have gone there a time or two since he opened. You know, just to check things out. See how he was."

"A time or two?"

"Okay, half a dozen," Eden said. "He makes a really good burger. And before you ask, I doubt he ever knew we were there. He was either behind the bar or in the kitchen, and Allie and I made sure to sit as far from both as possible."

"One time we even went in disguise." Allie grinned. "I was a blonde."

"You've been stalking my ex-husband?"

"Are you really going to keep calling him that after what happened this morning in your office?" Kyla asked.

Simone's face went lava-hot. She gulped down more water.

"Hey, it doesn't take long to get a cup of coffee." Kyla shrugged and dumped the last of the pins onto the table. "I was back at my desk before you guys were, um, finished."

"Ha!" Eden's eyes hadn't been this filled with wonder since she'd gotten a look at the giant cotton candy booth at the State Fair when they were kids. "You two had sex in your office?"

"No, we did not," Simone snapped, then, at Kyla's knowing look, backtracked. "Well, kind of. It wasn't exactly reciprocal. He, well, he was helping me to—"

"Yeah, I'll just bet he was." Eden's laughter tugged a smile out of her.

"You want to say something, too?" Simone asked Allie.

"Vince is a smart man," was all her friend said in her

perfect, annoyingly analytical tone. "Clearly he knows when the woman he loves needs…"

Eden leaned her chin on her hand. "You know, the more I get to know him, the more I like him. I might even be able to forgive him for walking out on you."

Yeah, Simone was thinking the same thing. Wait. Whatever color embarrassment had flooded into her cheeks drained at Allie's observation. Did Vince still love her? Was it possible…?

"Earth to Simone!" Eden snapped her fingers in the air. "Where did you go? Oh, wait. Never mind. Carry on."

"You could have taken a longer break," Simone whispered to Kyla as she resumed her text to Vince.

"I did." Kyla grinned. "I hid out in the break room until the windows stopped rattling."

"Window rattler." Eden cackled. "That is so going on my blackmail list for later use." She elbowed Simone out of the way as she attacked the kitchen cabinets. "And since you're putting in an order, would you please ask lover boy to stock up on some actual food? You know, cookies, ice cream, chips?"

"And have him throw in protein, too?" Allie called. "Some peanut butter would be nice."

"I'll have him bring dinner, but I'm not having him do a grocery run."

"Fine, I'll go once I'm done here," Kyla said. "If this first part of the list is any indication, we're going to be at this for a very long time."

"Answers take time," Eden said before she let out a pitiful whine. "Honest to Pete, Simone? Is this rice cheese?"

"It makes a good grilled cheese."

"Even I know that's wrong," Allie said. "Guys, come here." She waved them all over and pointed to the screen. "I've been going through Mara's school files. Look at this yearbook picture from her high school. Does anything look off to you?"

"Not really," Simone said, wishing she didn't have to look at the smiling face of the young woman she'd promised to take care of. "She looks exactly the same."

"That's my point." Allie held up Mara's photograph next to the screen. "The hair's different, but not by much. And look here, there's a small scar above her clavicle. See?"

"Barely." Eden leaned in and squinted, then grabbed the glasses off Allie's head and put them on. "So what?"

"According to Mara's medical records, she got that scar two years ago in a bicycle accident. So what's it doing in her yearbook picture from over seven years ago?"

Simone stood up straight. "That doesn't make any sense."

"Neither does the fact that almost all her trips to Stockton took place between midnight and 6:00 a.m.," Kyla said.

"What is going on?" Simone demanded. "It's like her life is falling apart right before our eyes."

"If it was her life," Allie said. "I want to do some more checking, but it's looking more and more like Mara wasn't who she said she was."

"Then who was she?" Simone asked, but none of her friends had an answer.

"I appreciate you coming to tell me in person." Gale Alders sat in the same chair she did the other day, but the fragments of hope he'd seen in her eyes before had vanished. She looked drawn, exhausted, but the house, surprisingly enough, was immaculate. "Dave came back early and took the kids out. I needed some time." Tears welled. "Sorry. I still can't believe she's gone."

Somehow Vince had managed to slip his mask of detachment in place before he'd knocked on the door. "I know how difficult this must be and I'm sorry to have to ask you some more questions."

"No, no, ask away. Anything if it will help find whoever did this to Mara."

"The police have been having a difficult time getting in touch with her family."

"I'm not surprised. Mara said her folks traveled quite a bit and she and her brother weren't close."

Vince considered that. "I don't recall seeing any family photos in her apartment. I don't suppose you have any?"

"No, I'm afraid not. She was friendly enough, but didn't seem too keen on talking about her past, you know?" She reached behind her and pulled out the stuffed elephant he remembered from her son's stroller. She squeezed it in her hands. "She loved my kids. Absolutely doted on them. Especially Christopher. He's going to be upset to have forgotten this."

Funny. The one photo he did remember seeing was of Mara and the boy. And the elephant. He knew one thing from having searched Mara's apartment. She was smart. Beyond smart. She was clever. Whatever she'd been doing out on that highway, she'd have had a reason. He'd bet she also had a backup plan should anything go wrong.

"Would you mind if I looked at that for a moment?"

He gestured to the elephant. The gray animal's cartoon-like face stared back at him as he squeezed and prodded. "Your son called him Baba."

"Short for his favorite bedtime story. Mara was the first one to read it to him. She always told him an elephant never forgets."

He felt a hard corner deep inside the elephant's belly. "No," he said. "They really don't." Flipping the elephant over, he examined the seam, looking for easy access. There, in the crease between the neck and body, his finger slipped into a small hole. Two hidden snaps on the inside broke apart.

"What are you doing?" Gale sat forward as he pried open the animal, dug his fingers in and pulled out a small metal box. He slid the lid forward. "What is that?"

"It's a key." He pulled it free and held it up.

"To what? Why would she have put it in Baba?"

"Excellent questions," Vince said. "I'm going to need to take this with me."

"You want me here in the morning, or at the office?" Kyla hefted her bag over her shoulder and headed to the front door.

"I could use you," Eden said. At Simone's irritated glare she feigned innocence. "What? I could."

"You're not stealing my assistant."

"You want to steal me?" Kyla's posture straightened. "Am I in demand?"

"I'll loan you out," Simone told her. "But only for as long as this case goes. Back here by eight?"

"You got it. Night, guys."

"Drive safely." Simone yanked open the door. She found Vince and Cole juggling numerous bags on the other side. "Well, hello. I was beginning to wonder where you'd gotten to."

"Hey, Vince. Cole." Kyla batted her lashes at Vince before she grinned at Simone, who grinned back. "I'm out. But I'll be working from home later, so if you need anything you can reach me on my cell."

"Oh, wait. Before you go." Vince looked at the bags he carried, then at Cole. "The one in your right hand. Yeah. BBQ pork sliders, as ordered."

"Officially the best bosses ever!" Kyla plucked the bag from Cole's hand and darted around them. "See you tomorrow."

"He's not your boss, either!" Simone yelled after her. "Stop poaching my people," she ordered and waved them inside. "You'd better feed these two before they start gnawing on each other's arms."

"Unloading!" Cole called as he disappeared into the kitchen.

Vince remained in the hall, arms full, as she closed the door.

"What?" she asked.

"Just enjoying the view. I missed you."

How did he make her blood pressure spike with so few words? "I missed you, too."

"When was the last time we said that to each other?"

Unfamiliar nerves jangled to life inside her. Something had shifted since she'd last seen him. Blossomed. Rejuvenated maybe. "How did the meeting go with Gale?"

"More productive than expected, actually. We'll talk about it while we eat."

"Speaking of eating." Eden ducked around the corner, eyed them and then the food, and grabbed some of

Vince's bags. "This is going to go cold while you two act googly-eyed, so I'll take them. Feel free to continue behind closed doors. No window rattling!"

Vince looked a bit like a deer caught in headlights. "What was that about?"

"Let's just say what happens in my office doesn't necessarily stay in my office. Kyla outed us."

"Awesome." He should have sounded more pained than he did, but what surprised her more was how he wrapped his free arm around her and drew her to him so easily. She wasn't sure if he thought she needed the quiet moment, or if he did, but she didn't pull away. Instead, she slipped her arm around his waist, rested her ear against his chest and listened to his heartbeat. "I realize this isn't the time, but just so you know, I made an appointment for us to visit Jason."

"What for?" The instant she said it, she recognized her mistake. "Oh, no, Vince, that's not what I meant." But his body had gone tense, as if another word from her was going to cause him to snap. "Of course I know what for."

"Because of the promise you made to talk to him? To look into my brother's case again to see if you could get him out of prison?"

"Yes. That. You know what we've been dealing with. I can't just shift focus—"

"I'm not asking you to shift focus. I'm asking you to respect our deal."

"And I will," she snapped. "Just…let me save this case and my career before I jeopardize it again, all right?"

"Yeah. We all know how important your career is."

"Hey, you two." Allie poked her head around the corner. "Not to interrupt this stellar reality show you've got going on, but might I recommend calling a truce to eat dinner? We've got a long night ahead of us."

"Vince." Simone reached out, but he moved too fast and was already gone.

Probably in more ways than one.

Chapter 15

"Looks like you're taking a road trip to Stockton in the morning." Cole set his empty take-out container on the coffee table beside the key Vince had discovered.

"Be still, my heart," Simone mumbled.

"Ignore her." Eden waved a dismissive onion ring in her direction before she bit into it. "It's all those seeds and soybeans she eats. Causes a serious erosion of any sense of humor."

Vince almost smiled. There was something oddly soothing about being surrounded by Simone and her friends. He'd never felt left out exactly when he and Simone had first gotten together, but he'd never felt as if he'd exactly fit, either. This time was different.

Or was it?

Simone's forgetfulness when it came to Jason's case shouldn't have come as a surprise. If it was forgetfulness.

He knew where her attention was, where it always was, and it was never on him. Maybe that grand sacrificial gesture yesterday in front of her coworkers and boss had been just that: a gesture.

She'd known what buttons to push when it came to getting what she wanted and she'd wanted him on this case. Whether she'd actually follow through? That was the question.

"According to the online search engine, that address Mara went to so many times is a motel right near the Stockton Airport," Allie said. "We couldn't pull up a street view, but it seems odd to me. It's not the best area, and in fact most of the surrounding buildings have been abandoned or are scheduled for demolition."

"Maybe that key opens one of the rooms," Cole said.

Simone picked up the key, hefted it in her hand. "Why would someone hide a key fob in a toy? Fobs are usually for cars, right?"

"We considered it might be to her glove box," Cole told her. "We stopped at the evidence lab to check. No joy."

"So frustrating." Simone gripped the key in her hand. Frowned.

"What?" Vince abandoned his roast beef sandwich as she pried up the edge of the plastic. "Simone?"

"Hang on." She slipped her long fingernail between the metal and plastic then twisted the key. It popped free. She had to squint to read out the brand name. "Does that mean anything to anyone?"

"It's a line of lockboxes," Vince said. "We used to recommend them when I was working security until they had a massive recall for not being as fireproof or waterproof as advertised."

"They didn't find any lockboxes in her apartment, did they?" Simone asked Cole.

"Not that I saw on the evidence sheet. We can check the crime scene photos to make sure, but we would have remembered that."

"I don't know about you guys," Allie said, "but I'm betting now you have an idea about what to look for when you get to that motel."

"You going to tell me what's going on with you and Vince or do I have to guess?" Eden carried the last of the empty containers and glasses into the kitchen.

"Nothing new," Simone replied.

"Oh, this is new. Otherwise you wouldn't be in here stewing. Come on." Eden hopped up on the counter. "What's up?"

"Just because you're awash in marital bliss doesn't mean the rest of us are destined for the same fate."

"Getting annoyed with me isn't going to solve whatever your problem is. Look, even I can tell this is different than the first time you two got together. What's getting in the way now?"

Simone sighed and planted her hands on her hips. "He thinks I've gone back on my word."

"About?" Eden asked.

"When I asked him to take Mara's case, I had the feeling he wouldn't, you know? Too much history. Too much baggage. Plus, he'd gotten out of the business after what happened with his last case."

"Yeah, Cole was telling me about Vince's walk on the dark side. Who can blame him?"

"Not me, and I don't." She should be, though. "I

might have sweetened the pot a little to make sure he came on board."

"I'm not a dentist, Simone. I don't like to pull teeth." Eden circled her hand in the air. "Get on with it. What did you do?"

"I told him I'd look into his brother's case again. See if maybe there was something that would qualify Jason for a reverse in sentence or an early release."

"Wow." Eden whistled. "You were desperate. You spent weeks mulling over that case after Vince walked out."

"Which is why I know there's nothing there."

The light dawned and Eden nodded. "But you led him to believe otherwise. Classy move. Surprisingly deceptive, and the sort of thing I might have done. I'm kind of impressed."

"I didn't have a choice," Simone whispered. "Vince is good at what he does and I couldn't trust anyone else to help me."

"But you asked him to trust you with his brother's life. Again." Eden jumped down, but not before Simone caught the look of disapproval on her friend's face. "That's cold, even for you."

"Thanks for the support." The criticism stung.

"Given what that guy's done for you in the last few days, you owe him, Simone."

"I realize that." She'd be lying if she said she wasn't hoping that maybe she and Vince could actually make a go of things again. Maybe not marriage, maybe not even permanent, but she couldn't deny being around him, being with him, made her realize what a mistake she'd made three years ago. She'd let him walk out of her life without a fight. "What am I supposed to do exactly? If word gets out that we're together just as I go poking my nose back into the case—"

"How about you pass off Jason's file to an objective third party and see what they might find?"

"That's—" Simone blinked. "That's actually a good idea."

"Gee, thanks. I'm all warm and gushy inside." Eden's mouth twisted. "Now go get me Jason's file and I'll see what I can come up with."

"Wait, you? You want to do this?"

"I'd like to take a run at it, maybe work on it with Cole. See if he has any ideas. Problem?"

"No. I'll just go—" Simone backed out of the room.

"Yeah, you do that. Cole! Let's hit the road!"

A few minutes later, Eden tucked Jason's file into her bag and headed out with Cole.

"Guess I'm off, too." Allie stretched her arms over her head and let out a yawn. "There's a bubble bath with my name on it."

"Have a good evening, Allie." Vince pulled out his phone, sent a quick text, then set it on the coffee table. "I'm going to take a quick shower myself." He walked upstairs with barely a glance in Simone's direction.

"Whew. Cold front moving in. I don't know what you did, but please fix it." Allie brushed a kiss on her cheek. "I like having him around. He keeps you on your toes."

"I can stay on my toes just fine," Simone called, but the only response she received was the door slamming. She finished cleaning up, keeping an ear on the running water upstairs. When he didn't seem to be in any rush to return, she sat on the bottom step and waited.

When the door did open, she could feel the residual

waft of steam against her back. "Do we need to talk?" she asked when he walked by clad only in his jeans.

"Not tonight, Simone."

"Look, I'm sorry I forgot about your brother's case." She couldn't remember ever feeling so tired before. "I promise, as soon as we get through this week—"

"Please don't promise me anything more." He set his bag on the coffee table, rummaged around a bit before he checked his phone and stretched out on the sofa. "And I said not tonight."

"Since when do you sulk?"

He threw an arm over his eyes as if to block her out. "This isn't sulking. This is me wanting to get some sleep. We'll head out first thing and see what we can find in Stockton. Unless you'd rather hang out here and work with Eden and Allie."

"I said I'd come with you. I'm coming."

"Then get some sleep. Something tells me it's going to be another long day." And with that, he went silent.

Irritation mingled with anger. They were back to square one, not talking, letting things fester, except this time she knew it was her fault. There was only one thing he hoped to get out of this arrangement and for all intents and purposes, he believed she was trying to get out of it. It wasn't something she could deny. Which meant he was right. There wasn't anything to talk about. Yet.

"Good night," she said softly as she got to her feet, turned out the lights and disappeared into her room. Her last thought before climbing into bed was the hope that somehow tomorrow would end differently.

"Headache?" Vince glanced at Simone as she continued to rub her jaw. They'd hit Stockton's city limits, but the drive had taken almost twice as long thanks to rush hour traffic and two separate accidents on the I-5.

"Mmm. Woke myself up grinding my teeth last night." She reached for the coffee she'd finished over a half hour ago, sighed and sat back. "You know that nightmare where your teeth turn to dust?"

"Yes."

"That dream really stinks."

Especially when there were so many better ones to have. He might have physically shut Simone down last night, but his rejection hadn't done much to quell the desire that had been building inside of him all day. He must have been nuts to have started what he did in her office. He hadn't thought she could look any more desirable than when she'd come apart in his arms, but seeing her in action in the courtroom ran a close second.

That his brother's case had "slipped her mind" felt like a festering splinter under his skin. How many times did he have to be reminded that when it came to Simone and her career, he would always come in a distant second? His anger wasn't directed at her. Not completely anyway. He was more furious with himself for daring to believe. "Any idea what Kyla and Eden are up to today?"

"Kyla mentioned something about diving deep into Cal Hobard's history. Eden's good at that kind of thing, so she won't let her do anything reckless." No, Eden would be the reckless one and for once, Simone would choose to turn a blind eye.

"Eden's good at a lot of things." Vince glanced into the rearview mirror. He'd spotted the same dark sedan three times. Were they being followed? The car didn't have any issue speeding around other vehicles, but it had yet to pass them, despite Vince varying his speed. "What about Allie?"

"She's convinced Mara was leading some kind of secret life."

"You don't agree?"

"I don't know what to believe anymore. I swear ever since this case started, things have gone topsy-turvy. If Mara isn't or wasn't who she said she was then what was her endgame? Why bring our office this case against Denton? Why start this ball rolling if she was only going to try to stop it?"

"Hopefully we'll find an answer at the motel."

"Come on, Vince, can't you at least brainstorm some ideas here?" She turned in her seat and looked at him. "I know I'm not real high up on your likability list at the moment, but this case—"

"This case will turn out to be whatever it turns out to be." He hit the turn signal and merged over to the right to turn off for the airport. The sedan followed. "What good is guessing going to do? And your likability factor is fine, don't worry. It's your trustworthiness I'm having issues with."

"You don't trust me?"

"Should I?"

"Yes. I told you I would look into Jason's case and I'm going to."

"No offense, but I'll believe it when I see you sitting in that visitor's room having an actual discussion with him."

"You said you made an appointment, right? Get the details to Kyla and she'll put it on my calendar. Best make it after Thursday."

Vince gnashed his teeth. Nothing said priority than

having your assistant put it on your to-do list. "If you still have a job."

"Job or not, I gave my word." She stared straight ahead with laser beam focus. "I'll be there." When he didn't respond she muttered, "You don't believe me."

"Let's just say you've got some work to do in convincing me. Grab hold of something. I want to try something here." He took a sharp turn, tires squealing, horns blaring, brakes screeching.

"What are you doing?" She fisted the seat belt and sat back as he pulled a sharp left into a parking lot, slipped into a space and turned to see behind them.

"Testing a theory." He waited, counting the seconds until the sedan passed down the street at a semi-crawl. "We've picked up a tail."

"A what?" She twisted to look out the back window. "Someone's following us?"

"You're the lead prosecutor on a case someone doesn't want going to trial. It's not out of the realm of possibilities. Hang on."

"Again?" She squeezed her eyes shut as he went into reverse and backed all the way out before following their tail. "That them?" She pointed to the car slowing down for speed bumps.

"Sure is. Get your phone out and snap a pic of the plate." One of the advantages to her never letting it out of her hand. "Got it?"

"Yes."

"Great." He veered off and slipped into an empty side street. "Get it to Cole or Jack and have them run the plate."

"But won't that put the search in the system?"

"Yes, it will." He circled the block and then headed back to the main road. "Let's see who cares."

They reached the Sleep and Snooze Motel, but Vince didn't see any sign of the tail. To be safe, he pulled into the parking lot behind the main office. The roar of airplane engines ripped the air as they got out of the car. The smell of gas and exhaust hung heavy, and so thick he thought he could probably chew it.

"This place is as unsettling as we thought." Simone walked beside him in her unusually practical attire of white slacks and a pink-and-white shirt. The odd splash of color reminded him of paintings he'd seen in some of his clients' art collections. "I need a shower already."

"Seems even more incongruous that Mara would frequent this place." He pushed through the office door, using his arm to avoid the crusty film of dirt coating the handle. One clang of the desk bell had a middle-aged platinum blonde emerging from a back room, the sour expression on her craggy face surely a sign of things to come. "Morning, ma'am. My name is Vince Sutton. I'm an investigator from Sacramento." Her gaze barely flickered to the ID he flashed. "We're wondering if you've seen this young woman here before?" He pulled out a picture of Mara.

She squinted, moved in. His eyes burned against the stench of tobacco. "Pretty thing. What did she do?"

"I'm afraid she was killed a few days ago," Vince said in his most sympathetic voice before Simone could open her mouth. "I was really hoping you might be able to help us. We were just at the diner over a few blocks and they said they thought she'd been staying here. Used to come in regularly for their milkshakes," he lied. "I'm sure you know the one I'm talking about."

"Corney's, sure. She really dead?" Dull gray eyes dimmed. "Ah, maybe I can have another look?"

"Certainly." He set the picture on the sticky registration desk and she leaned in again. An old-fashioned guest book was wedged under her ample chest. "Her family's asked us to look into her death."

"There's some speculation she was murdered," Simone added as if following his script. "Can you imagine?"

The woman's mouth worked as if she were chewing on her tongue. "Might have seen her here and about. There was a man, too. Tall, thin-haired guy. Rat-like eyes. Thinner than a weed. Wore one of those, what do you call them?" She motioned from her shoulders to her feet. "Long jacket things?"

"A trench coat?" Vince asked. Cal Hobard.

"Yeah. I figured maybe it was a little something on the side, you know. Even though she didn't seem the type."

"She wasn't here very often then?" Simone sighed.

"No, she was regular, just odd hours," the woman said. "Three, four times a week she'd come in, he'd meet her, then they'd leave separate. Poor thing probably wasn't getting much out of it, if you know what I mean?"

"What room would that be?" Vince asked.

"Twelve. The private cottage in the back. Said they wanted to be out of the way. Look, it's paid up through the month. Always cash. First time she paid, rest of the time, I'd get money left in the slot at the start of every month."

"I don't suppose you'd let us take a look inside her room, would you?" Vince asked. "We want to be able to tell her family we explored every possibility. Give them some closure."

"Don't have no key." Her brows went up. "They paid extra for a special lock. Not that you'd see that as a deterrent, I'm guessing. But what I don't see, I don't know. You know?"

"We do. Appreciate your help." Vince pocketed the picture, gave the woman a smile and pushed the door open for Simone.

"Butter wouldn't melt in that mouth of yours," Simone said. "See? You can be charming with more folks than just me."

"How else do you think I get what I want?" They walked past the weather-beaten doors, rickety, rusted-out cars parked in front, numbers hanging crooked from barely there nails. "Number twelve. Must be… Yeah, this is it." He pointed to the freestanding building at the far end of the lot. "Definitely out of sight." He walked backward for a while, getting the lay of the land. Good line of sight. Easy to pick out cars and people who didn't belong. "Looks like you'd have to know it was here to know it was here."

"Not a place someone comes to for a good time."

Vince bent down, pulled out his lock picks and set to work on the warped green door. There were bars on the two windows on either side, one of the frames sagging.

"Don't suppose you'd be willing to teach me how to do that." Simone dipped down to observe.

His hand slipped. "I'm sorry?"

"Well, since you've taken an interest in my work, it seems only fitting I should do the same. Besides, who knows when I might need to pick a lock to gain access?"

"You do know these picks don't come with a warrant or subpoena, right?" And that the set happened to be illegal in most states.

"Ha-ha. You want to speed it up there? I'm covered in a layer of ick." She slicked a hand down her arm.

The lock popped. "Wait." He held out his arm to stop her before she barreled in. To be safe, he pulled out his gun and pushed her behind him. "Let me clear it first."

"My knight in shining leather. I can take care of myself, you know."

"Take those shooting lessons I gave you and then we can talk. Until then, you follow me."

"Someone had an extra serving of testosterone in his bran flakes this morning." Simone hugged her arms around her chest as he stepped inside the tiny cabin-like structure. When she heard the safety on his gun click, she took that as a sign and entered.

Her brain went numb. Her eyes took a second to adjust to the odd lighting as a dull mechanical buzz echoed in her ears. "What is this place?" A sleazy hookup spot or grungy getaway it was not. Until now she hadn't even ruled out a drug den. Instead, she'd walked into some kind of headquarters that might have put NASA to shame.

Vince motioned her forward so he could close the door. The deep hum of computers filled the room. HD screens, CPUs and printers lined the far wall. The bed was piled high with files and paper. The mirrored closet doors had been papered with what looked like a family tree, except where there should be branches of cousins and aunts and uncles, there were criminal mug shots, inmate numbers, surveillance photos. Some names and faces she knew; she'd seen the federal case alerts cross her desk. Others were local, like the Stark twins who had taken to robbing downtown liquor stores two years ago.

"Congressman Nate Fulton's on here." Simone dropped her bag and bent down, tracing her fingers over the local politician's photo taken at a fundraising event. "He was just elected last year. And Representative Rebecca Railston from San Francisco. There are rumors she's going to run for mayor in the next election. Vince, there are businesspeople and politicians from all over the state on this map. Big names from…" She broke off, her eyes landing on a familiar face dead center of everyone else's, with green lines leading to him: Paul Denton. "Do you see this? I was right. Denton is part of something bigger. This is some kind of crime syndicate that—" She stopped and noticed as Vince moved in, his eyes pinned to the grainy black-and-white photo at the top of the tree, the name Alik Babin written beneath it. "Who is that?" she asked.

"The head of the snake. And here're his fangs." Vince stabbed a finger into the face below Babin's, the gnarled nose settling into her nightmares. "Isaac Kruse."

"Kruse?" Simone searched her memory. "The man who murdered Sabrina Walker? The man you—" She couldn't bring herself to finish the thought.

"Kruse never said a word after he was arrested." She heard the rage simmering in his voice. "The detectives couldn't prove he was working for someone despite what they believed. Babin isn't someone you squeal on."

"And I'm sure Kruse's broken jaw didn't help." She placed a hand on Vince's back, noting the taut muscles.

"Babin's one of those myths in law enforcement," Vince said. "Every agency's had him on their radar at one point or another. Back when I was working security, his name came up a few times as a possible threat to clients. He's international, got his hands in everything from illegal arms to drugs to murder for hire." He stopped, swallowed. "Human trafficking."

Why hadn't she ever heard of this guy? "Is that why Kruse had Sabrina Walker?"

"Could never prove it. As if proving it would have made any difference," Vince said. "She still would have been dead."

This was not a door she needed him walking back through at the moment. "I wonder what this had to do with Mara."

"Yeah. I'll search here. You start in the bathroom."

She followed his instructions and stepped into the midsized bath. She really hoped the dark beige tile was a decorating choice and not the result of a lack of cleaning. "I should remember to keep gloves in my bag." She rummaged through the cabinets, finding nothing more than a bottle of painkillers and a stash of feminine hygiene products.

Simone wiped sweat off her forehead and lifted her hair off the back of her neck. The humidity in this room felt stifling. She looked up at the long narrow window along the top of the shower. She stood on the edge of the tub and searched the ledge, popped the window latch and pushed it open. Stale air blew in. Outside she could hear someone throwing a bucket of water against a building. At least she hoped it was water. "Gah. I'm going to need a tetanus shot after this." She turned, grabbed the shower rod and put a hand on her hip as he pushed the door open. "Hey, you're wearing gloves."

He dug into his jacket pocket and handed her a pair of black latex gloves.

"Thanks, but I've finished. Consider your knighthood relinquished. I'm not finding anything in here." She climbed down and snapped the gloves on.

"Did you check the toilet?"

"Strangely enough it did not occur to me."

"The tank, Simone." He hefted the lid off the tank, set it on the seat. "Well, here's a start." He pulled out a plastic bag containing what looked like copies of phone records. He grabbed a towel and wiped off the bag, then shoved it into the inside pocket of his jacket and put everything back.

"You can't take that, it's evidence," Simone whispered as if someone could hear them. "Honestly, Vince, is there anything you won't do—"

"You have your monsters, I have mine."

"This isn't a contest. We can do this within the confines of the law."

"Men like Babin are rarely held responsible for their crimes." The loathing in his eyes as he looked at her made her shiver. "I would have thought recent events would have proven that to you. Your system doesn't work."

She tried not to take offense. "All that's been proven to me is that we have to work harder. Smarter. And stand in their way."

"Mara was standing in their way, Simone." That pinprick stare of his may as well have been a knife in her heart. "How'd that work out for her?"

He walked out of the room and left stony silence in his wake. She couldn't argue with him, not now and not about this. But his animosity toward everything she'd put her faith in these last two decades only reminded her of how far apart they truly were. For her, the law, the system, was a guideline. For him? A challenge. And Vince Sutton never met a challenge he didn't like.

"Are we any closer to figuring out exactly what this place is?" she asked when she joined him.

"Some kind of information-clearing station." He motioned to the open drawers of the desk. "Found a stack of fake IDs in a drawer in the nightstand, some with Mara's picture on them."

"If Mara's even her real name," she said as the front door opened. Vince moved in front of her, blocking her from whoever had entered.

"It's not," a male voice said.

Simone grabbed Vince's arm and pushed him aside so she could look directly in Cal Hobard's shifty eyes. "Her name was Natalie Subrov." He stared at Vince, and then Simone, his expression easing into exhaustion. "She was one of my agents."

Chapter 16

"One of your agents?" Vince asked as Simone attempted to worm her way around him. "Exactly what agency would that be?" He kept his arms out, unconvinced Cal Hobard was anything other than an adversary. "And what was with the cat-and-mouse chase this morning?"

"Relax, Sutton." Cal closed the door and shoved his hands in his pockets. Vince's hand immediately went to the butt of his gun. "After the week I've had, I don't have the energy to tackle anyone, not even you. And don't flatter yourself. I didn't need to follow anyone."

He gestured to the blinking red light on the top of one of the monitors Vince, in his distraction over Kruse and Babin, hadn't noticed.

"Take a seat." Hobard motioned to the chairs at the computer bank. "You, too, Simone. It's time we had an honest conversation."

"You didn't answer his question." Simone followed Vince's lead and sat. "What agency are you with?"

He pulled out his wallet and flashed his badge. "FBI. I'm head of a special task force on organized crime and political corruption." He moved a stack of files out of the way and sat on the edge of the bed. "We've been building a case against Alik Babin for the better part of three years, placing agents in various pockets of his operation. Mara, Natalie," he corrected with a slight wince, "was our ticket to Denton. I owe you an apology, Simone. You were never supposed to be involved in this."

"Yet here I am." Simone crossed her legs.

"Track the money, take down the boss, is that it?" Vince covered her hands with his and squeezed as a sign of unity. "What went wrong?"

"The DA's gall bladder," Simone said. "That's when this all went sideways, right? He was supposed to be the one Mara approached with her so-called evidence, but Ward ended up with sepsis."

"We'd planned to wait until he was back in the office," Hobard confirmed. "But then we got word Babin was going to skip the country for Venezuela. Filing the charges against his money man was the only way to freeze connected accounts and keep Babin where we could get to him."

"Because there's no extradition with Venezuela," Simone clarified for Vince. "So, what? I became the patsy in the office dangling false evidence in front of the judiciary?"

"There's nothing false in the evidence you were given, Simone." Cal's resigned voice knocked a dent in Vince's anger. "Yes, it was meant to be used against

Denton privately, but if anything, your dedication to the case gave it an authenticity we couldn't have predicted. Lawson was supposed to offer Denton a deal to testify against Babin and end it before it got very far. Your refusal to do so—"

"I got in the way," she interrupted.

"We readjusted because you got us the one thing we couldn't, extra time. Thanks to you we were able to gather even more information from the inside. As of now, all but three of my agents are in the clear with enough intel on Babin and his operation to bring him down for good. All we have to do is tilt that first domino." He flicked a finger.

"That domino being Denton," Vince said. His head began to throb. The smell of gasoline was beginning to get to him. "Is there still a deal to be made?"

"So Mar—Natalie was a decoy," Simone said. "She never had any intention of testifying against Denton. How could she? She'd have been lying under oath the second she uttered her name." Simone raked her hands through her hair. "That's why you were so determined I make a deal with Denton. You didn't want Mara on the stand."

Cal leaned back and stared at the ceiling. "Ward couldn't push for a dismissal or a deal any harder without looking suspicious, but he also didn't want you taking the fall for suborning perjury."

"Simone didn't know," Vince cut in.

"It wouldn't matter." Simone retook his hand and squeezed. "It would have all come out at some point and given how adamant I was about not cutting a deal with Denton, no one would believe I wasn't in on it."

Vince balked. "Some system you believe in."

"We argued about it that night," Cal said. "Natalie was sure there was something more to the case. She'd picked up on something we couldn't get a lock on, but was determined to figure it out before court convened that morning. She didn't want to let you down, Simone." Cal gave her a weak smile. "She admired you quite a bit."

"So what happened that night?" Simone asked. "What changed?"

"Near as we can tell, she was tailed when she left Sacramento. We thought we'd taken care of it a few weeks before, but clearly we missed something or someone. Babin's got people everywhere, in law enforcement, prisons, DA's offices." He cringed. "Senate offices."

Simone's expression went cold. "We've been through everyone's records," she said. "The only person who raised a red flag in my office was you. Can you believe this?" She gaped at Vince.

Vince hesitated. "I haven't decided," he admitted. He considered himself a pretty good lie detector and while he might think Cal Hobard wasn't the most aboveboard person he'd ever met, he wasn't ready to dismiss what Hobard had said. Whether any of it was true remained to be seen.

"I have to agree with you, Simone." Cal's comment surprised Vince. "We've run extensive background checks on everyone at your office since you unexpectedly took the case. We needed to make sure nothing got in your way from the inside."

"Then what have you found?" Vince asked. "Aside from a couple of crooked politicians connected to Denton and Babin?" He pointed to the photographs and

Congressman Fulton in particular. "Personally, I'd like to know. I voted for that guy."

"You mean Nate?" Hobard got to his feet and approached the wall. "He's not the one we had eyes on. In fact, Nate's been part of the secret committee overseeing the investigation. No, this is who we suspect." He tapped his fingers against the elegant, silver-haired woman in the background.

"You have got to be kidding me." Simone's feet hit the floor. "That's Senator Beverly Wakeman. She's one of the biggest anti-crime voices in Congress."

"She also has a son who can't seem to find anything but trouble. That's him, there." Cal motioned to the young man standing beside the senator. "Drugs, gambling, prostitutes. She's spent most of her life trying to protect him."

"He get in deep with Babin?" Vince asked not really needing an answer.

"That's the evidence Natalie was looking for. About a week before she was killed, Natalie was convinced she'd cracked the encryption code on Babin's server. When I left her that night, she'd started downloading dozens of files. Maybe if I'd stayed she'd still be alive."

"Or both of you would be dead." Simone got to her feet and started to pace. "You don't have those files, do you?"

"I do not." He drew his gaze slowly around the room. "We've looked here, searched her apartment—"

"So that was you who cleaned her place?" Simone accused.

"What?" Cal blinked. "No. We searched, but left it as we found it. If there was one thing Natalie excelled at it was living in chaos. She thrived on it."

"Someone gave that place a thorough once-over," Vince said. "Didn't leave a print in sight. Not hers, not anyone's that the lab techs found."

"I read the report. I also read the lab results that came in this morning. The blood on the crystal fragment you found in her trash came back as male, no relation to Natalie."

"Our cleaner?" Simone asked.

"Makes as much sense as anything else does right now. So what now?" Vince asked Hobard. "Where does the case stand?"

Cal shook his head. "It doesn't. Unless Simone's found some other evidence to present in court that doesn't involve anything Natalie provided."

"Not yet, I haven't." Simone tapped her foot. She looked at Vince, something flashing in her eyes as she slipped her hand into her pocket. The key. "But I'm not done looking. I still have forty-eight hours."

"Get in touch if you come up with any way that I or my agents can be of assistance." Cal's phone beeped. He looked at the screen, sighed and shook his head. "I swear they put a homing beacon on me. I need to take this." He headed for and pulled open the door. "I'll be back in a—"

He stumbled back, gripped the doorknob so hard his knuckles went white.

"Cal?" Simone moved toward him as Cal turned and looked down at his chest. He let out a wheeze Vince recognized all too well.

A bright red patch spread across Cal's shirt. The bemused, dazed expression on his face faded as his eyes went glassy. He jerked as a second bullet blasted through his torso and plowed into the wall inches from Vince's head.

Vince dived off his chair and grabbed Simone around the knees, knocking her to the ground as bullets continued to stream in. He looked over his shoulder as Cal's body fell in a heap. Instinct kicked in. Vince rolled, grasped the door and slammed it shut as bullets plowed into the wood.

Simone looked at him from across the room, eyes wide with terror. "What do we do?" She sniffed, eyes shifting around the room. "Wait. Do you smell that?"

"Smoke," Vince confirmed over the sound of his pounding heart. Black smoke plumed through the open bathroom window. "Someone's set the place on fire."

Chapter 17

Simone did the only thing she could think of. She dug out her phone and started taking pictures.

"You've got to be kidding me." Vince coughed and reached for her as she angled her lens toward the evidence. "9-1-1 would have been my first choice."

"Then you do it." She took shallow breaths, blinking back tears as the smoke thickened. The tiny space was filling up fast. She would have to work quickly. As if from a faraway distance, she heard Vince shouting into the phone.

The stench of gasoline grew thicker. She choked, unable to clear her airway. She dipped down, covered her mouth and nose with her arm, glanced to the door. She went around him and lunged for the handle.

"Simone!" Vince's shout accompanied a new round of bullets as she pulled open the door. He tackled her to the ground, losing hold of his phone as he landed on top of her. "They aren't going anywhere until they're sure we're dead."

"Then we'd better figure another way out! I'm not dying in this hole." She shoved at him.

"Stay down!" Vince leaped up onto the bed and slammed his elbow through the barred window to let some of the smoke out. More shots rang out as cool air swept in and was swallowed by the heat slipping through from the bathroom. He flattened himself on the mattress and rolled off.

Simone crawled into the bathroom. The heat alone was enough to burn her skin. Flames licked the window ledge. She felt around for the towels she remembered hanging behind the door. She found the sink and turned the water on, dousing the towels before she pressed one to her mouth and raced out. She stumbled to Vince, pushed the other towel into his hands. He nodded in approval.

"Try not to hyperventilate," he ordered.

She coughed, looked down at her phone as Eden's face appeared on the caller ID. Bracing herself, she answered, but the pain in her lungs was too much. She gasped, choked, bent double and dropped to the ground. Simone could hear Eden's faint voice calling out to her, but the sudden roar of flames from behind her took over. Simone tried to focus, but could only see a frayed line in the soiled carpet. Odd. Inhaling what was left of the damp towel, she reached out with her other hand and slipped her fingers into the rip. Smooth edges. Not worn. Cut.

She dug her fingers in, pulled back and the carpet gave way to the floorboards beneath. One of which had a large notch in the corner. "Vince!" Her voice was muffled by the now useless towel. She shimmied on the floor, peering through the smoke as she heard sirens in the distance. She banged her hand flat on the floor as hard as she could to get his attention, wherever he was.

Vince dropped down beside her. "Look under here," she croaked.

Simone used her last bit of strength to pry up the floor board. She looked down at a metal box. Hands locked around the handle, she pulled it free. She heard the inferno in the bathroom. Tiles exploded off the walls.

Vince threw himself against the door to buy them more time. He pulled the box free from her grasp and pushed her to safety behind the upturned mattress, using it as cover to look out the window. "They're leaving. Sirens must have gotten their attention."

She wanted to ask if he saw who it was, how many there were? Did he see a license—she felt herself sway.

"Don't you dare pass out on me!"

Vince's order snapped her back to life as the bathroom door blasted off its hinges and slammed full force into the floor. Seductive flames slipped into the room, caught the electronics instantly.

"Another couple of seconds." Vince took her hand. She grabbed hold, determined never to let go again. "Okay. Let's go."

He wrenched the motel room door open, tugged her forward, but as she moved, she saw her cell phone lying on the floor by her bag. The pictures! She dived for it, reaching her cell moments before the flames, but not soon enough. She screamed as fire scorched her palm, still she held on. She felt an arm lock around her waist and haul her up. The room spun. Then she was flying.

Then…

Nothing.

"Stop worrying about me! Take care of her."

Simone couldn't help but smile at the distant, yet familiar, bellow. She felt as if she were floating, suspended, in blessedly cool air tainted with the hint of ozone and tinder. Someone was having a barbecue around here. She took a long, deep breath and crashed to earth.

Shoving onto her side, she retched. Air. She needed… she gasped, her chest tightening as if someone had slipped bands of steel around her ribs. Someone pushed something weird over her face. Soft, sweaty, stale smelling plastic. She grabbed at it, struggled against it, until she felt Vince's hand on her leg, on her arm and then in her hair. She blinked open her teary eyes. Vince. Relief surged through her.

She said something. Or tried to. He frowned, shook his head. She finally saw it was a mask over her face and pushed it off, much to Vince's obvious displeasure. "I said you look like—" She didn't get the last word out as Vince kissed her.

Simone sobbed against his lips, touched his soot-covered face to prove to herself he was okay. Only now did she realize she'd thought she was going to die in that fire. She held on to him, determined not to let the moment pass as if it meant nothing to her.

When he pulled back, he looked into her eyes. "Now leave it on." He replaced the mask and helped her sit up. She was on a gurney outside the back of an ambulance. The medic in charge of her oxygen examined her blistered hand.

"Looks like second-degree burns," the young man said, turning critical eyes on her. "I hope the cell phone was worth it."

"What?" Her voice was garbled under the mask.

He turned her palm up so she could see the outline of her phone on her palm. "You're going to have a scar."

"Oh."

"Scars mean you survived," Vince said as if he thought she'd be upset at the idea. She'd never had a scar before. Never broken a bone or been in the hospital. At the rate she was going she'd be breaking all those records by the time this case was over. "Don't go wearing it as a badge of honor," he continued. "Those pictures you were worried about?"

She nodded. The idea of losing everything Mara—Natalie—had worked on had been unacceptable.

"Two words." Vince caught her chin and shook his head. "Cloud storage."

Her laugh sounded a tad hysterical even to her own ears. She leaned against him as he sat behind her, slipped his arm around her waist as if he, too, needed reminding she was okay. Together they watched the firefighters and first responders put the blaze out. She lost track of time, feeling sleepy and dazed as the noise drifted around her. With her hand bandaged and her breathing no longer so painful, she passed the mask to her caregiver. "I'm okay," she croaked. Her throat ached, but for the most part, she'd survive.

The squeal of tires behind her made her jump. Vince got to his feet as Simone saw a streak of strawberry blond hair headed for her. "Eden," she whispered. "She called when we were inside."

"Simone!" Eden barreled through the blockade and scene tape, Cole, Allie and Jack hot on her heels.

"Sac PD." Jack flipped his badge to the local officers and gestured to Simone and Vince. "They're with us."

"As if they could have stopped her," Vince muttered as Eden dived at Simone, who found herself on the receiving end of the strongest hug of her life. "I'm fine, too, if you were wondering," he said.

Simone reached for his hand, but she didn't let go of her friend. How could she given the tremors coursing through Eden's body? Having been on the other end not so long ago when Eden had been the one in danger, she couldn't blame her. "I'm okay," she whispered in her best comforting-sister tone. "Vince got me out. I'm okay."

"I thought you were dying." Eden sobbed, seemed to be horrified about it and swiped a hand under her eyes. "When you answered your phone and all I heard was you choking and then the fire—"

"You could hear the fire?" Simone blinked. Huh. She hadn't considered that.

"My turn." Allie pushed in to get her own confirmation Simone was all right. She didn't need as long to verify Simone was indeed alive and kicking. Within seconds Allie shifted into doctor mode as she examined Simone's bandaged hand. "What am I going to do with you two?" She touched Simone's face, that mixture of sympathy and frustration mingling on her fairy-princess features before she turned her attention to Vince.

And locked him in an equally fierce hug.

Vince's eyes went wide over her head, a silent plea to

Simone who realized being hugged by a friend scared him more than flying bullets and ravenous flames. Her heart constricted as reality hit hard. She'd done it again. She pressed a hand against her chest. Fallen in love with him. Again.

Or maybe she'd never fallen out of love. But this time…she blinked back a new rush of tears. This time was different. This time she understood what she had to lose.

"One of you want to tell us what's going on?" Cole's calm demeanor didn't fool Simone as she forced herself to pick up the conversation. She knew that tone. He was mad.

"Allie's suspicions were right." Vince still looked unnerved as Allie shifted her hold and kept her arm around his waist. "Mara Orlov wasn't who she said she was. She was an FBI agent working a case."

"My case," Simone clarified. "Cal Hobard was her superior."

"Hobard? The politico guy working for your boss?" Eden frowned. "The one that was acting like a class-A chump—wait. You said was."

"He's dead." She'd have to deal with the guilt of her incorrect suspicions about Cal at another time. "They, whoever *they* are, killed him. Then lit the place up." She looked at the heap of charred, smoking rubble that could have served as her funeral pyre. She saw the hotel manager standing to the side with the fire chief, wildly gesticulating as she pointed at Simone and Vince.

"All this is tied to the Denton case?" Jack asked. "But why?"

Simone looked at Vince, then down at the box by his feet. "Hopefully we'll find some answers in there.

If Vince hadn't called 9-1-1 and gotten emergency services here, they'd have waited until we were toast."

"And you call me tactless." Eden sat on the gurney beside her and took her uninjured hand. "They were that determined to see you dead, huh?"

"I caught a glimpse of them out the window," Vince confirmed. "They were professionals. Hired guns. The kind of team I might have run when I worked security."

"Ex-military, you think?" Cole asked.

"Hope not, but yeah. That's my guess."

"See enough to give a description?" Jack asked.

"Of their faces? Not sure. But the main shooter had a tattoo on his forearm. I can draw it for you."

"You can draw?" Simone frowned. Did she know that?

"News crews are going to be here anytime," Cole said. "We need to decide what we're going to do about all this."

"Nothing to decide." Eden earned interested stares from everyone. "They wanted Simone and Vince dead. I say we give them exactly what they want."

Chapter 18

"A source within the police department has confirmed as many as three potential fatalities in the arson-suspected fire at the I-5 motel." The harried reporter tapped a finger against his ear as he spoke into the camera. "While we've been unable to confirm the identity of the victims, I can report that Sacramento Deputy District Attorney Simone Armstrong was on scene just prior to the explosion. Along with Miss Armstrong, witnesses have identified Sacramento private investigator Vince Sutton, who also happens to be Miss Armstrong's former husband. There has been no information regarding the third victim. We're still awaiting a statement of confirmation from the DA's office, but one has to wonder if this is yet another twist in the Paul Denton case in which the local businessman is accused—"

Simone clicked the TV off and sagged deeper into the sofa in the basement of Eden's townhouse. "Exactly how long do we have to stay dead?"

She folded her arms around her knees as her friends filed in and out of the home Eden planned to vacate in favor of Cole's 1960s' gentleman's cruiser. A boat. Simone dropped her head back. Her best friend was going to live on a boat.

"Longer than a few hours." Cole angled an open bag of tortilla chips in her direction. She snagged one, nibbled on the edge because there didn't seem to be anything else to do. Great. Now she wanted a margarita the size of Mexico. "We don't want to run out of provisions."

"I'd say we can survive the apocalypse." Vince took a seat on the arm of the leather sofa and dropped a reassuring hand on Simone's shoulder. "You sure you don't want them to contact your parents and tell them what's really going on?"

Simone shook her head. "By the time anyone tracks them down wherever they are, this whole thing will be over." Honestly, she wasn't convinced her "death" would be little more than an inconvenience to her globe-trotting progenitors. It had been years since she'd shared more than a cursory phone call with either of them. What a sad realization to come to.

She looked at the small round table that had, until recently, displayed a photograph of the four of them— Eden, Allie, Simone and Chloe. If she closed her eyes, she could remember that day so clearly, taken a few months before Chloe's murder.

Chloe.

A new anger simmered inside Simone; an anger she

suspected she'd finally opened herself up to. All these years she'd pushed aside any idea of bringing Chloe's murderer to justice. She hadn't wanted to get her hopes up, to let herself believe it was possible to close that chapter of their lives once and for all. But in those horrifying minutes trapped in that fire, it wasn't Mara Orlov or the Denton case that had crossed her mind. It was the idea she'd be leaving her two best friends alone to deal with whatever Chloe's killer had planned for them.

She wasn't leaving this earth with Chloe's murderer still out there. He thought he had the power? He thought he could stalk them into submission and frighten them? Then he truly had no idea what he'd created the day he'd taken their friend.

"What about you?" Simone asked Vince, trying to compartmentalize.

"What about me?"

"Anyone we should notify?"

"No one cares about me." The casual, dismissive response had her tugging Vince down beside her.

"I care." She wedged herself under his arm, feeling safer than she had in days. He smelled clean, with barely a hint of smoke after his shower, which he'd taken in the tiny guest bathroom on the first floor so she could use the master. "They care." She gestured to her friends as they bounced from downstairs to upstairs, mumbling and muttering to themselves. "And there are plenty of other people who do, too."

"I suppose there'll be a bit of chaos at the bar when word hits." Vince drew her even closer, pressed his lips against the top of her head.

"Word's already hit." Jack descended the stairs, and, after a brief hesitation when he looked at the two of them curled up on the sofa, shifted his expression to neutral. Simone squirmed in her seat. "When we're done here," Jack continued, "I'll take a run over and try to put some minds at ease. Get a feel for what's going on with your employees. We'll keep things together for you, don't worry."

"Do I look worried?" Vince asked.

"You don't," Jack said. "But Simone's going to need Botox if she keeps frowning like that."

She managed a weak laugh, grateful he'd returned to teasing her. She rubbed her fingers across her forehead. "I don't do botulism, but thanks for the warning. Ow." She sucked in a breath as the burns on her hand throbbed. Pain was good. Pain meant she was alive. Didn't mean it didn't hurt, though.

"Acclimating to the dungeon?" Cole directed at Vince from where he was sorting through photographs.

"You know so much has happened that I'm not even going to question that description," Vince said.

Simone could count on one hand the number of times she'd ventured into this place. Eden had turned her office into her own private incident room for the past three years. Her friend's obsession with bringing cold-case criminals to justice had manifested into this space dedicated to her hunt. Multiple computer screens and CPUs, laptops and printers, file cabinets overflowing with information that could—when applied properly—bring peace of mind to victims' families and friends. The oversize desk in the center of the room had been reorganized to reflect the Denton case. Eden took the photos from Cole and tacked them onto one of the four magnetic whiteboards. The photos had been downloaded from Simone's phone.

"I know you're probably wiped out." Eden tucked her long hair into a knot, anchored with pencils, her feet bare as she paced the thick ornamental rug that gave the dank space some color. "We need to get things rolling if we're going to avoid having to plan your funerals."

Simone swore even as her eyes drooped. She knew faking their deaths was the best way to reassure whoever was responsible for Mara's, and now Cal Hobard's, murder. With all of them, herself and Vince included, now "dead," the DA would have no choice but to drop the charges against Denton and ease the minds of those he was covering for. If the bad guys thought they were in the clear, they'd be more likely to make mistakes. She'd bet Senator Wakeman and Alik Babin were about to make some life-changing ones. But her funeral? She tasted bile in the back of her throat. She hadn't even thought of that. "Aren't we waiting for Allie?"

"She said she had an errand to run," Cole said.

"Looks like you've got just about everything we saw in that room." Vince relinquished his hold on Simone to examine the pictures more closely. Simone followed, mainly to keep herself from falling asleep, and perched on the edge of the desk. "From what Hobard told us, Mara—"

"Natalie," Simone corrected.

Vince nodded. "Sorry. She's Mara in here." He tapped a finger against his temple. "Mara believed there was a connection between Alik Babin and Senator Wakeman." He pulled a key from his pocket. "Hopefully there's something inside that lockbox that we've been missing, because I'm not seeing it here."

"I've met Senator Wakeman." Simone thought back on their encounter earlier in the week at the DA's office. "I might not have Allie's nose for deduction, but she doesn't come across as anything more than your typical superstar politician. She's been a proponent for criminal justice her entire career."

"I can't believe you said that with a straight face." Vince shook his head. "'Politician' says it all if you ask me. Most are capable of anything, especially when it comes to holding on to their jobs."

Simone's spine stiffened. "Now hold on—"

"A discussion for another time," Cole cut her off. "Or maybe never. How about we open this thing and see what we've got before we go making assumptions that could destroy any one of our careers in a microsecond."

"That's my cop." Eden wrapped her arms around Cole, aiming a silly grin at Simone. "Always the peace-maker."

"It's more like I'd prefer to stop lying to my boss and the DA sooner than later about these two being dead. Pass me the key."

Vince handed it over.

Simone's belly tightened as Cole opened the lock-box. Inside was a stack of files and scribbled-on sticky notes that reminded Simone so much of Eden's system she felt a new pang of grief.

"This file says Lance Wakeman." Cole divided up the items. "Senator Wakeman's only son. My, my. He's certainly not the kind soul his mother's claimed all these years. He's what? Twenty-five?"

"Twenty-six." Vince let out a low whistle. "Mara was good. She got hold of his sealed juvenile records. Busted for pot when he was twelve and went downhill from there. There are at least a dozen school transcripts, all of which end when he got booted."

"No wonder she can hold her own in Senate hearings," Simone observed. "Look what she's been having to deal with at home."

"I've got newspaper clippings from the society pages in Los Angeles and New York going back at least ten years." Eden started tacking them up on another of her boards. "Parties, art gallery openings, nightclubbing. She dug up everything."

"Maybe one too many things." Jack set his file down and held up a solitary piece of paper. "I've got a redacted arrest report from six years ago." He held it up under a light. "This isn't a copy. It's the original document from the Los Angeles Police Department."

"This one's a copy." Simone lifted another report. "But it's not about Lance Wakeman. This is about Tandi Crawford." Simone frowned. Where had she heard that name before?

"Hang on." Eden snapped her fingers. "She's that high school senior who went missing about eight years ago." She dived toward one of her cabinets. "I have a file on her. Seventeen years old, went to a frat party on a nearby campus. They found her car abandoned in a parking lot a few days later, but never any trace of her. She just vanished." Eden riffled through her records. "Her parents tried to keep the case in the public eye, but after a couple of days, no one would touch it. Her mother died a few years later. Father said it was from a broken heart."

"One of Eden's cold cases," Simone explained to Vince. "She has a bit of trouble letting go."

"Must run in the family."

"Yeah, well, my obsession is about to pay off for you big-time." Eden slapped her inch-thick file onto the table. "Vince, check your papers. Eight years ago, what school did Lance Wakeman attend?"

Vince looked through his notes, then at Eden's. "The same college." He pointed to the fraternity name. "The same frat house."

"This is it. This is what Mara found. We need to do some more research here." Simone almost cheered. "It's time we called—oh, no." She covered her mouth, the horror of what she'd done—or hadn't done—seeping through her. "Kyla." She looked at Eden who seemed as dumbstruck as she felt. "We forgot to call Kyla."

"Yes, you did."

Everyone spun toward the voice coming from the staircase. Kyla descended, her lithe form taut and tight, her arms wrapped around her torso as she pinned red-rimmed eyes on Simone. "I thought you were dead."

"Kyla." Simone raced forward, catching her in a hug before she'd stepped off the last stair. "I am so sorry. I should have realized, should have remembered." She'd never felt anyone so stone-stiff before. So unyielding. She held on, silently willing Kyla to forgive her. Finally, she felt the young woman shudder as she slipped her arms around Simone and held on. "I'm okay. We're okay."

"I thought you were dead," Kyla whispered. "It's been hours. Hour after hour and I couldn't stop thinking there was something I could have done, something I should have known or found out that would have prevented…and then Allie showed up at the office—"

"Shhhh." Simone smoothed a hand over her curls, rocked her slightly. "This was our fault. I'm so sorry." She leaned back, caught Kyla's tear-stained face in her hands. "Never you. Not about you. I should have had someone contact you immediately. Please forgive me. Forgive us."

Kyla sniffled, quirked her head, stepped back and wiped her eyes. "Can I hold off on that until we find out who killed Mara and Cal?"

Simone nodded, disappointment welling. "Of course we can. I'll make this up to you, I promise."

"Well." Kyla set her bag down and tugged on the bright orange scarf in her hair. "I have been thinking about asking for a raise." The teasing glint in her eye assured Simone that all would be forgiven. Eventually. "Did I hear you had some research that needs doing?" She approached the table, sending Vince a sly, accusing look as she slipped into the group.

Simone caught Allie's arm when she passed into the basement. "Thank you."

Allie patted her hand. "That's what friends are for. You and Eden with your tunnel vision." She shook her head. "It's like there's no room in your brain except for what you see and what you want. Never what you need." She angled a pointed look at Vince before joining Eden. "Work on that, would you?"

"Okay, back to business," Jack called out, bringing the room to attention. "Somehow we need to connect the dots between Senator Wakeman, her son and Alik Babin. Mara did it, or at least came close. What are we missing?"

"You've all been busy." Kyla glanced through the folders on the table then shifted her attention to the boards. "Who's this Babin guy?"

"Organized crime lord," Eden said and earned a bit of a groan from her friends. "What? You have a better name for him?"

"How about guilty?" Simone suggested. "Denton was the money man for someone. Now we know who and Babin's pretty big if what Cal Hobard believed is true. But that doesn't tell us who killed Mara or Hobard or even why. Kyla, can you pull up the name of that fraternity Lance Wakeman belonged to? Maybe we can talk to some other members and see what they might remember about any possible connections."

"Sure." Kyla looked to Eden for guidance on which computer to use and a few seconds later was tapping on one. "Bad news," she said. "That fraternity lost its charter seven years ago when Wakeman was still a member."

"After Tandi Crawford went missing," Jack said. "That can't be a coincidence."

"Still doesn't explain how he connects to Babin." Vince ran his hands through his hair.

"This might." Kyla gestured at the screen. "There's a fraternity archive behind this secured…" She scrunched her face, worked some of her computer magic. "Here we go. Photographs from the fraternity's last year. The dates match. This was taken the night Tandi Crawford disappeared." She clicked a picture on her screen, copied and opened it in a photography program, edited and printed. "Here." She brought it to the table where everyone examined it. "This looks like Tandi. She had a small heart tattoo on her upper right shoulder, right? Purple dress, gold hoop earrings."

"Did you take up speed reading when I wasn't looking?" Simone asked.

"I don't have a choice, working for you," Kyla said. "And right in this corner over here, who does that look like to you?"

"That's Lance Wakeman," Cole said.

"And he's talking to Alik Babin," Simone said.

"That's not all." Vince picked up the picture and brought it over to the whiteboard and aimed the light on it. "Kyla, can you blow up this section right here?" He circled the area in shadow behind Tandi Crawford.

"Yes, but I might lose some resolution."

"I just want his arm."

"What do you see?" Simone rose up on her toes to peer at the photograph.

"Not sure yet. Might be wrong."

"I doubt it," Simone mumbled as Kyla popped the other photo onto the board.

"How's this?"

"Cole?" Vince held out his hand. "You got that sketch of the shooter's tattoo that I gave you?"

"Right here." Cole handed it over.

"It's the same shape. What is it? A coat of arms?" Simone asked.

"Whatever it is, it's distinctive enough to recognize even from a distance. Good catch, Kyla. General description works, too. We have a face to run through databases now." ·

Eden slapped her own papers on the desk and made everyone jump. "Kyla, I'll double your salary if you come work for me."

"Wha-huh?" Kyla blinked.

"Where are you going to get the money to pay her even a fraction of what I do?" Simone waved aside her friend's pouting.

"Maybe we should prove a United States senator complicit in at least two murders before we all make employment changes?" Cole suggested. "So you've connected Babin to *Lance* Wakeman. It's circumstantial at best. Two young guys at a college frat party? Nothing about that is enough to file any charges on anyone let alone someone like Alik Babin. Or even Wakeman."

"Oh, come on," Vince spat. "You've got a missing girl at a party with a known human trafficker and a spoiled rich kid who never met a crime he didn't like. Add in a guy who looks like a classic thug standing only feet away from all of them and you say you can't even bring them in for questioning?"

"That's what I'm saying." Cole's voice turned cool. "The law is the law, Vince. Doesn't matter how much it smells, this doesn't get us anywhere."

"Then your law really does smell." Vince's jaw tensed.

"Cole's right." Simone smoothed a hand down Vince's arm that was so tight she wondered how his bones didn't break. She knew how personally he'd take a case like Tandi Crawford. Another young girl he couldn't save. Another young girl he wanted to avenge. As much as she understood, she couldn't let herself think the same way. "All of this is nothing more than coincidence. We know what it is, but until we can prove it—"

"Or until we can get someone to admit it," Allie interrupted. "All of you stop and step back. How did Mara approach this? She didn't look at the top and work her way down. She started at the bottom." She tapped Lance Wakeman's picture. "We need to do the same. Denton might have been the main thread connecting everyone, but Lance Wakeman's the common denominator. If he's in this as deep as we all suspect, how far has his mother gone to protect him?"

"So, a senator of the United States killed two FBI

agents because she thought they were getting too close to her baby boy?" Jack asked. "Seems far-fetched and I've seen and heard plenty."

"Whatever else Senator Wakeman is, she's your key to unlocking this entire case," Allie said. "If there's one thing I've learned in my years as a therapist, it's that there is little on this earth more dangerous than a mother protecting her offspring. You want to break this case open? You start with her."

"You all right?" Simone stepped into the backyard and slid the screen door closed behind her. "You've been out here a long time."

The sight of her intimidating ex-marine of an ex-husband sitting like a giant among the garden gnomes brought a small smile to her face.

"Needed a break." He tossed away the daisy he'd been plucking the petals off and crossed his arms over his chest. "Truthfully, I wanted a drink, but figured maybe silence would be as effective."

She crouched down beside him, rested her hands on his leg. "I know this isn't easy for you."

"What? Playing dead? Funnily enough it's not that much different for me." He reached out and tucked an errant curl behind her ear. "I'd imagine it's a lot more difficult for a social butterfly like yourself."

"The people I truly care about know the truth. The rest?" She shrugged. "We're going to get them, Vince. All of them. Babin included."

She saw his jaw clench, as if resisting the urge to argue with her. He was such a solitary man, a man not prone to let anyone in. A few years ago she'd come close, but not nearly as close as she could get now. Not because the door was open any wider, but because she'd found a different way in.

"Those phone records you found stashed in the toilet at the motel? They link one of the senator's security officers to Babin. It's evidence, Vince. Solid evidence. And now we've got a plan," she assured him. "By this time tomorrow, it should all be over."

"And then what?" he asked. His sharp tone made her heart hurt.

"And then we'll see what comes next." She slipped her hand up his chest, around to the back of his neck and drew his face to hers. His breath brushed across her cheeks as she anticipated what she'd been wanting ever since she'd walked back into his life. "But how about for tonight we do our best to forget?"

He kissed her. A gentle brush of lips, contrary to the tough facade he displayed every moment of the day. "I'd prefer not to do so with an audience."

She smiled. "They're gone. Cole and Jack needed to put in an appearance at the police station to keep matters rolling." His chest felt firm under her seeking fingers. "Allie, Kyla and Eden have left, too." She bit at his upper lip, caught it between her teeth and drew him to his feet. "Hours and hours and nothing to do."

"I can think of a few things," he murmured and his hands plunged into her hair.

He stared into her eyes, his determined, heated look erasing all that had come before, the years that stood between them. "Let's go inside." She slipped her fingers between his and drew him back to the house.

He paused long enough to lock up then let her lead him through the living room to the stairs. "What's this?" He plucked the small gift bag off the banister hook.

"Good question." Simone flipped the tiny name tag over, laughed and dipped her hand inside. She pulled out a box of condoms. "From Eden."

"Have I mentioned how much I like your friends?"

How she loved the sound of his laughter. "I might have picked up on it. You can thank her tomorrow. Tonight, you're all mine." This time, when she kissed him, she held nothing back. She took what she wanted, demanded, devoured. Her lips moved over his in a way that gave him no choice other than to match her stroke for stroke, touch for touch. They stumbled up the stairs, her unwilling to relinquish his mouth, him sneaking his hands under the hem of her shirt, his fingers skimming her bare back as he guided her up and up. His tongue danced with hers as he angled his head and drew her deeper into him.

For the second time that day, she could barely breathe. Her blood pounded in her ears, her thighs trembling, anticipating what would come next. She felt him hard and ready against her. She gasped as he drew her shirt up and over her head. She had the fleeting image of the white T-shirt floating down the stairs before he slid his palms flat down her sides.

She gripped the back of his head as he went to his knees and pressed his lips against her navel. She groaned. He unzipped her pants, looking up at her as he pulled the fabric over her hips. Down her thighs.

Her knees went weak. She held on to him as she lifted one foot, then the other. The lace panties now had his attention. "Vince." She quivered as he kissed the heat of her through the thin fabric. She bit her lip and rested her head against the wall, seeking solace as the pressure built inside her.

He touched her, teasing the elastic aside. She whimpered, as memories of these feelings in her office came back to her. She was already climbing, could already feel herself ready to fall into bliss, but this time she wasn't going alone. Not until she got what she wanted.

Not until she had him inside her.

"Stand." She gripped his shoulders, encouraging him to get up. "Vince, stand."

The primal sound he made against her ears was one she'd never forget. She pressed her lips to his, wanting to taste him. "This time, my way," she whispered. The sight of him fully clothed while she wore nothing other than lace did something to her she couldn't explain. Something she didn't want to explain. All she wanted to do was feel. Feel him. Touch him. Envelop him.

Steps away from the bedroom, she saw him toss the box of condoms ahead of them. Steps away from the bed, she stopped again. Let her hand drop and claim the box. She slipped her fingers up and then down his sides, much the way he'd done to her moments before. She felt his muscles tighten beneath her touch. His arms flexed. His breathing echoed in her ears as she took hold of his shirt. Without breaking eye contact she pulled it up, unable to hide her smile as he ripped it over his head. That his hands went immediately to the snap of his jeans proved he was as anxious as she was.

She covered his hands with hers, pushing them aside as she did the job herself, luxuriating in another kiss. Having unzipped him, she reached in and cupped him in her palm.

He groaned and deepened their kiss. She stroked him, loving the steely length of him, the desire he had for her. It didn't matter what had come before, didn't matter what had come between them. What had driven them apart. She couldn't let herself think beyond now, beyond what she wanted. What she needed. And right now, what she needed, all she needed, was Vince.

"Enough," he said.

"Not nearly." She laughed out loud as he leaned over and ripped the sheets off the bed. When he reached for her, she darted away, waving the box at him. She pointed to him and then to the mattress. He obliged her and lay on his back, bracing on his elbows. In return, she shimmied out of her underwear, exposing herself to him for the first time in years.

The cool air of the ceiling fan prickled her skin, her nipples peaked, igniting long-dormant embers of desire within her. She tore open the box and tossed him one of the foil packets.

"Looks like Eden planned a big night for us," she teased as he covered himself.

"Far be it from me to let her down." He held out his hand, the arousal in his eyes matching that of his body. She moved over him, straddled him, felt the heat of him pressing against her. His hips began to move, inching him closer to where she wanted him, but she shook her head. She leaned over. Her mouth hovering over his, she lifted and sank onto him.

Vince arched his back and exposed his throat to her. His hands gripped her hips. She wanted to kiss him, to feel him everywhere as she surrounded him, but she waited. He pulsed hard inside of her, stretched her as she set the pace, slowly, as deliberately as she could. His hands covered and caressed her breasts, slowly to match their rhythm.

Tiny explosions went off inside her. Wherever he

touched her was all that mattered. She could feel herself climbing so fast, so overwhelmingly, she had to close her eyes to keep control.

"Simone." Her name on his lips only increased her desire. "Simone, look at me."

She didn't want to let go. Didn't want this to end. She wanted to stay here, in this perfect moment, with him, for the rest of her life.

"Simone." The whispered plea broke through and she dropped forward. She opened her eyes, cried out as he sat up, rolled her under him and drove himself more deeply inside of her.

She locked her legs around him as she matched his kiss. She couldn't get enough of him, urging him faster until she couldn't resist the pull any longer. Her orgasm triggered his as she and Vince rid themselves of the past and soared into the future, however uncertain, but together.

"I might actually be dead after all." Vince pulled Simone's naked, lax body over his and settled his hands into that favorite place of his in the dip of her spine. He wasn't entirely sure if he could feel every cell in his body or if he'd short-circuited and gone numb. The way she cuddled against him, her thick hair draping over his arm, her delicate fingers tracing the outline of his tattoos, he honestly couldn't recall ever feeling more at peace.

"I'm pretty sure you'll be back to life in no time." Her voice soothed him. "This one's new."

"Hmmm?" He tucked his chin in as she shifted to look at him. "The phoenix?"

"It's pretty."

"Oh, good, because that's what I was going for." He grinned. "Try...trial by fire."

"Is that what I was? A trial?"

His heart skipped a beat. "What makes you think it has anything to do with you?"

She drew her arms in and rested her chin so she could meet his gaze. "We did have some conversations the first go-around. I remember you telling me each tattoo was a symbol of a rite of passage; something meaningful that happened in your life. Good or bad." Her passion-dazed eyes glimmered. "So was I good or bad?"

He remained silent, unable to choose between flippancy and honesty. One would irritate her. The other?

"I really did a number on you, didn't I?" The empathy in her voice wasn't something he was used to and didn't particularly like. She reached out, stroked her hand down the side of his face.

"I wasn't exactly a paragon of communication myself, Simone. I survived." He drew his fingers up and down her spine, reveling in how she shivered under his touch. If they could stay here, only had this, then life could very well remain perfect. "So did you. We both came out stronger on the other side. The question is—" he took a deep breath "—what do we do now?"

She sighed and closed her eyes. "I don't know."

"How about we start with you telling me what's going on with Chloe's case." He stopped when her entire body went stiff. "And her killer."

"How did you—" She blinked up at him.

"Aside from the fact that I'm a detective and I know you far better than you realize?" He continued to touch her, to stroke her. "I saw your reactions to those photos that maniac left on your car, Simone. You really didn't think I'd let it go."

"You should be angry." Her eyes narrowed. "Why aren't you angry?"

"I'm disappointed you didn't trust me enough to tell me."

"It wasn't about trust—"

"No. It was about not wanting to let me into that part of your life. But I am in that part of your life, Simone. And I'm not letting some killer stalk you and make you relive the horror without doing something about it. So I did." Her brow knit hard enough for him to tap a finger against her forehead. "Botox, remember? I made sure those pictures got to where they needed to go."

"Oh, wow." She slid off him and rolled onto her back. "That's why Jack and Lieutenant Santos weren't surprised when I gave them the pictures. They already had them."

"Yeah, guilty. Not apologizing, either."

"So this whole staying over thing, sleeping on my couch and midnight conversations—"

"All part of my evil plan to keep you safe." He looked over at her. "Came with some nice perks, though. You okay? What are you thinking?"

"That I seem to have lost whatever control I had over my life." She sat up, turned her back on him. "As far as the world is concerned, I'm dead. My job, the case, everything I've worked for my whole life is hanging over my head like a guillotine and I don't have any idea who's holding the rope."

"It's not me." He remained where he was, thrown back into that uncertainty from three years ago. Other than enthusiastic bed partner, what role did he play?

Her life was in flux? Given the situation, he wasn't entirely sure he'd ever dragged himself out of flux. "I want what's best for you, Simone. I want you to succeed. But I learned enough last time to know if we're giving this a serious go, then I need an equal partnership this time around. I want to participate in your life. I want you to be a part of mine."

"So maybe we have this talk about what comes next after I've put the Denton case to rest and things settle down."

He felt his heart shrink. "Things will never settle down enough for you to be comfortable with this conversation, Simone. We both know that. You're still wearing those blinders for justice you put on that day in the field." All the things he wished he'd said three years ago, all the arguments he'd come up with after the fact hovered, but didn't manifest. Nothing had changed. He loved her. More than he had before. And yet…everything had changed. "Until you're willing to make room for me, for anyone, you're going to find yourself alone in all the ways that matter." He got to his feet, retrieved his pants and tugged them on. When he saw she hadn't moved, he picked up his shirt, sat beside her and pressed it into her hands. "I love you, Simone. I've always loved you. From the moment I saw you at that fundraising event to the day I walked out. But me loving you isn't enough. At least it isn't for me. I want to be let in."

A solitary tear trickled down her cheek when she squeezed her eyes shut. "I don't know that I know what love is." She wiped the tear away. "I don't know how to do this, Vince. I didn't last time, so I focused on work. Because that I could control. This?" She waved her hand between the two of them. "These feelings I can't define? They scare me. And I do the only thing I can think of when I get scared. I switch off. But then I wonder about this and how much I've missed you and then I worry about when I'm going to mess it up and drive you away. Or…" She let out a shuddering breath. "Or what if something happens to you? If I don't let you in all the way, I don't have to hurt when something happens. I can't control any of it. And that terrifies me."

He cupped her chin in his hand and stared into her eyes. If he hadn't loved her before, that she would finally admit these fears to him showed him they'd already moved far beyond where they were three years ago. "Then maybe you stop trying to." He pressed his mouth to hers, tasted the saltiness of her tears. She clung to him, opened to him, breathed life into him as he lowered her back on the mattress and gave himself over to her. Again.

Chapter 19

Simone tugged Vince's shirt over her head and slipped out of bed. She looked back at him, both grateful and jealous that he'd found enough peace to sleep. She, on the other hand, couldn't find any.

His carnal prowess might have settled her body, but her mind? That was another story. Cookies. Yeah, maybe cookies would help.

She went downstairs, popped open the cookie jar from on top of the fridge where Cole had added a fresh supply of lemon sandwich cookies earlier that day. She held two in her palm, considered, added a third. "Oh, the heck with it." She grabbed the entire jar and took a seat at the breakfast bar where she found the disposable phone Jack had set up for her until her miraculous resurrection occurred.

She saw a voice mail message from Eden, noted the time and took a chance. She called her back.

"Mmm, yeah?" The sleepy voice caught Simone off guard. "Who is this?"

"It's me." Simone bit into a cookie and instantly wished for milk. Or coffee. "I wasn't sure if I'd wake you or not."

"News flash, I was asleep." A rustling of blankets and murmurs echoed through the phone. "Hang on a second."

Simone took that second to turn on the coffeepot.

"Clearly my little gift didn't have the intended effect," Eden said with a yawn. "What'd you do? Put Prince Charming into a coma?"

Simone smiled a little and retook her seat. "Not quite. Why did you call?"

"Why did I what?"

If only she could throw coffee through the phone. "There's a message here from you. I didn't listen to it."

"Oh, yeah, okay. Sorry. It was about Jason's case." Her sleepy voice gradually gave way to alertness. "I did a lot of digging in some of those areas you can't exactly access."

"If there's a felony involved, please refrain from sharing."

"Hey, you're the one who called me and no, there was no felony committed. I think. No, yeah, I'm good. I took a look at the other defendants Jason was accused of working with. They're a bad crew, Simone. Like seriously bad. But here's what caught my attention. Did you know Jason fired his original lawyer and went with one provided by his so-called partners in crime?"

"He fired the one who worked out the plea agreement? Elliot something? Yes. I knew, but after the fact."

Simone mumbled around a cookie. "I don't know the circumstances."

"Well, I do now. While you were almost getting yourself flambéed yesterday, I had an informal meeting with Elliot. Good guy, actually. Has a reputation for being a real proponent for his clients. If Jason had stuck with him, he'd have been out ages ago."

"So what happened?" Simone wasn't entirely sure she liked where this was heading. "Better yet, how did you get him to talk to you?"

"You mean how did I get around that pesky attorney-client privilege thing? Please. I told him I was looking into Jason's case in connection with another. And then I asked if there was something in particular we should be looking into where Jason was concerned."

"And?"

"Elliot said he visited Jason three times after his arrest. Once to prepare for a plea bargain—"

"Which he eventually turned down," Simone said.

"But again, that happened later. Jason was on board as far as Elliot knew. The second time he talked to Jason, Jason admitted he was being threatened by other members of the crew who were already on the inside. And, here's where things get interesting. Jason wasn't the only one being threatened. Turns out someone got hold of his brother's wedding photos that ran in the local paper. That same someone got creative and left them stabbed into his mattress. Next thing Elliot knows, he's visiting Jason in the medical ward where his client fires him and announces he's turning down any plea bargain that will reduce a full sentence. He put a stop to it, pled guilty and has been sitting in prison ever since."

Simone couldn't swallow. She couldn't talk. Vince's

wedding photo? Her stomach churned as her entire body went cold. "Hold on."

She dropped the phone and dived for the sink, gagging and washing her mouth out. When she picked the phone up, Eden was calling her name. "I'm fine. You're telling me Jason Sutton took almost a ten-year sentence to protect his brother?"

"Mostly."

"That's your hedging voice, Eden. Spit it out before the sun comes up." Which would be in… Simone glanced at the clock. In another four hours.

"Before he signed off Jason's case, Elliot asked for copies of everything in Jason's cell. He might have left his office for a few minutes so I could look through them. There were some pretty graphic notes and letters explaining exactly what would happen to Vince." She hesitated. "And you, if Jason didn't keep his mouth shut and do his time."

"Oh, no." Simone sank onto the stool. What was going on in her office? Who had missed this? Jason had been railroaded and now the Denton case was fracturing. None of this had been in the file she'd seen, that she'd been shown. How many other cases, how many other defendants were paying a political price in a game she hadn't even known was being played? "I want this to be some kind of joke."

"This kid didn't have a chance from the moment he was arrested, Simone. His record, his past worked against him. I know you saw his file, but that doesn't tell half the real story. He went from being willing to take a plea in exchange for testimony to taking the full blame for a robbery he couldn't have planned in a million years. Every other person involved in that armed robbery went free. Even worse, I'm betting Vince doesn't know anything about it."

If Vince had any idea this had gone down, he wouldn't have stopped until his brother was out. "As far as Vince knows the system had it out for his kid brother and I was complicit." Simone rubbed her fingers over her forehead. "Turns out he was right."

"He's not right. You didn't know."

"Not knowing isn't a valid defense." Guilt piled on top of regret on top of fear. "I need to fix this."

"Because you promised Vince?"

"Because it's the right thing to do," Simone countered. "And yes, because I promised Vince. But I can't be seen to be involved." And that was going to be the trick, wasn't it? "I've got a conflict of interest and can't make any attempt to get Jason out legitimately." There was so much at stake over the next few days with the Denton case, how did she add Jason Sutton to the mix?

Not only that, she needed to put some distance between herself and Vince. And fast. She needed to come across as completely impartial where Jason's case was concerned. If getting his brother out of prison meant she had to sacrifice her future with Vince, it was the least she owed him after all he'd done for her.

"Okay." She took a deep breath as an idea formed. "Okay, I think I know how to get the ball rolling, but I'm going to need your help, Eden. You'll have to be my eyes and ears on this. My go-between." The system, her system, had failed Jason Sutton, just as Vince had always believed. That she was in any sense culpable tarnished anything and everything she'd done before and since. She wouldn't—she couldn't—let this stand. "I can't guarantee all of this is going to be aboveboard, but it might be the only shot we have. You good with that?"

"What do you want me to do?"

"You're awfully quiet." Vince reached over and took her hand, the midmorning traffic busy enough to keep them distracted as Cole and Jack drove them in Cole's SUV. "Everything okay?"

"There's a lot at stake." She looked down at the signed affidavit in her lap. "I can't help but think that meeting with Paul Denton went too easily."

"Element of surprise. The last thing he expected was for you to show up with a plea offer. WITSEC for him and his family in the town of their choice?" Vince said. "Then you almost gave Poltanic a heart attack when he saw you standing there? Come on. That had to give you a little satisfaction."

"It wasn't the worst way to spend a few hours at county." She squeezed his hand before pulling free. "They'll keep him in solitary until I get things sorted with the marshal's office. Turning Denton over to the Feds should help break whatever hold Babin believes he has on our office through Wakeman. Cole? Are we good with the FBI?"

"Oh, they're thrilled." Cole's voice dripped sarcasm. "Nothing like finding out two of your undercover agents were killed by a state senator. They're planning on throwing a party. We're not invited."

"As long as they do it in the DA's office, should be fine," Jack said as his phone rang. "McTavish. Yeah. Sure. We're en route now." He handed his phone to Simone. "Your boss."

Simone winced as she accepted the call. "Hello."

"I didn't know what to say when the Feds called me last night. You're okay? You're really okay?" She knew Ward well enough to recognize he wasn't faking his relief or concern.

"A little crispier than I was a few days ago." She looked down at her bandaged hand and flexed her fingers with a bit more effort than she liked. "But I'm good. Is everything in place?"

"I'm reading over the deal you cut with Denton before I sign off on it. And we just received confirmation that the Los Angeles police have taken Lance Wakeman into custody. They'll be transporting him up to us in the next few days depending on how our meeting with the senator goes. You sure about all this, Simone? You know what this can cost you if you're wrong."

"I'm not wrong." But yes, she knew. If it cost her her career, so be it. She just needed to hang on long enough to finish what she and Eden had begun early this morning. "Going over all the evidence Mara collected along with the statement from Denton, we have a definitive connection between Alik Babin and Senator Wakeman through her son, who appears to have been one of Babin's top dealers in both illegal drugs and in his prostitution businesses. Whether we can get her for Mara and Cal's death will remain to be seen."

"I have every faith in you, Simone," Ward said. "You'll make it happen."

"I appreciate you letting me take the lead on this." As if she'd expected anything less. If this backfired, someone was going to pay and he wasn't about to take the hit for her. "We should be in the office in a few minutes."

"Senator Wakeman is on her way up as we speak,"

Ward said. "I'll keep her in my office until you're ready. And Simone?"

"Yes, sir?"

"It's good to hear your voice." He clicked off before she could respond.

"Thanks, Jack." She handed the phone back to him. "I don't suppose we've got any solid forensics linking the senator to Mara's crash or Cal's shooting."

"No," Cole said. "The blood found on the crystal shards in Mara's apartment belong to a male of Mediterranean decent. We've run the sample through all known US databases but haven't gotten a hit. Tammy's working on international as we speak."

"The blood we found on the chain of her necklace matches the blood from her apartment," Jack added. "So there's a bit of good news."

Good news. Simone managed a shaky smile. Right now she couldn't imagine any news being good.

"Before I forget." Vince leaned over so he could keep his voice low. "I managed to get our meeting with Jason changed to tomorrow afternoon. Figured you might be up for a break by then."

"What?" Her ears rang as she turned alarmed eyes on him. "Oh, sure. Yeah." Her throat tightened as she lied to him. She couldn't step foot in that prison now. And she couldn't tell him why. Not if her plan was going to work. "Sounds good to me."

Vince's eyes narrowed. "What's going on?"

"Nothing." She collected her bag and papers as Cole turned into the DA's office parking lot. "Tomorrow. Should be fine."

"Text from Lawson," Jack called over his shoulder. "He says we're clear to the conference room."

"Last chance to change your mind and let the Feds take the lead, Simone." Cole looked at her in the rear-view mirror. "Say the word and I'll turn around now."

As rational a choice as that might be, she'd promised Mara. She owed it to Hobard to end this herself. "Park in the far west corner, Cole. We'll take the stairs."

Granted Vince understood Simone had a lot going on, but he'd never known her to flat-out lie to his face. Sure his brother's situation might seem like a side note at this point, but she'd better keep her word. The pressure she was under would ease as soon as the meeting with the senator was behind them. After that, there wasn't anything in her way where Jason was concerned. A ball of unease began spinning low in his gut. Was there?

Cole and Jack stopped at the door as he and Simone climbed the last stair. "Looks like it's pretty clear." Cole looked over his shoulder. "You good?"

"Ready." She tugged on the hem of the short, white belted jacket and matching skirt Kyla had retrieved from her loft, shifted in the bright red heels that fed into his fantasies from last night. "Let's do this."

Cole opened the door and Jack took the lead to the conference room. Keeping a hand on her back, Vince steered her clear of her gasping coworkers who went into instant gossip mode. Kyla, a beacon of support in her brilliant pink dress, nodded to them as they passed.

Doors opened and slammed. He could hear running and pounding and distinct cries of "You'll never guess" and "Simone's alive!" echoing through the halls.

Simone didn't balk. She didn't hesitate. She looked straight ahead and, as always, kept her eyes on the goal.

Because nothing ever got between Simone Armstrong and what she wanted. And right now Vince knew all she wanted was Senator Wakeman's confession.

They were greeted by four men in the conference room, their dark suits identifying them as FBI faster than their voices could.

"Agent Fitzhugh, ma'am." One of the men, the youngest as far as Vince could tell, stepped forward to offer his hand. "Cal Hobard was my immediate superior and Natalie was…" He cleared his throat and in a flash Vince understood. "She was very special. I want to thank you for helping us close this case against Alik Babin once and for all."

"We haven't closed anything yet," Simone said. "I'm very sorry for your loss. She was an extraordinary young woman."

"Thank you, ma'am." He gave a short nod. "We've already started the process of getting Paul Denton and his family into witness protection. We should have them locked down in the next forty-eight to seventy-two hours. Meanwhile, we've moved all of them to a safe house well out of the city limits."

"Preparing for the worst?" Vince asked.

"Better to prepare than not, sir." Fitzhugh turned slightly amused eyes to him. "From one marine to another."

Vince grinned. "Good to know, Special Agent."

"That's code for something, I'm sure," Simone mumbled. "What about Babin himself?"

"Alik Babin's been under constant surveillance for the past two years, ma'am. We know where he is and we know where and when we plan to take him. All our agents are waiting for is our go."

"That means it's all on you, honey," Vince translated.

"Yeah, thanks." Simone squeezed his hand. "That I got. Okay. Let's get this over with. Jack?"

"Let me pop my head in and see how the senator and the DA are doing." He left the room as Simone took a seat, Vince on one side of her, Cole on the other.

"Eden said to tell you she's here in spirit," Cole said as the FBI agents lined up behind them.

"Thanks. That helps."

Vince wasn't so sure. Aside from the night she'd walked into his bar last week, he'd never seen her look this nervous. "This should help, too." He reached into his pocket and pulled out Mara's—Natalie's—photograph from her file. "She's one of yours. You'll do her proud."

"Here they come." Cole sat back.

Vince did the same.

Simone inched forward to the edge of her seat, set Natalie's picture on top of Paul Denton's signed affidavit and waited.

When the door opened, not even three decades as a stalwart politician could prepare the senator for the sight of the two people who had uncovered her dirty secrets and those of her son. The two people she'd believed to be dead. But Vince had to give her credit for a quick recovery. She appeared to pull herself together and moved into the room.

"Miss Armstrong." The slight tremble in her voice was all that gave her away. "I'm so happy to see you're alive and well. Ward, why didn't you tell me?"

"I suppose I wanted to see the look on your face when you saw her for yourself." He nodded at her and pulled out a chair. "And that would be the one. Please."

He motioned for her two body men to join them. "May I introduce Vince Sutton, a private investigator who's been invaluable in breaking open the Denton case for us."

Vince got to his feet, stretched his arm across the table, not to the senator, as she seemed to assume, but to the larger man to her left. A man with an olive complexion, jet-black hair, equally dark eyes and... Vince looked down before shaking the man's hand. A large angry red welt slicing across his palm. "I didn't get your name."

"This is Dimitri Soukis," Senator Wakeman said as she tried to size Vince up. "He's in private security."

"Former Greek Army?" Vince asked.

Soukis gave a sharp nod.

"Bet you have some interesting tattoos." Vince looked over his shoulder at Jack. "Apologies," Vince said to the senator. "It's a military thing. We can identify one another from vast distances."

Ward closed the door.

"Am I to assume that since you're back at the office there've been some developments in the Paul Denton case?" Senator Wakeman sat in much the same position as Simone, poised, and ready to pounce.

"The Paul Denton case is officially closed," Simone said. "We offered him a plea deal early this morning in exchange for his testimony."

"That's wonderful news." Even beneath her carefully applied makeup, Vince could see the senator's face pale. "I look forward to hearing about the results."

"I'd be happy to share his statement with you right now if you like." Simone opened the file in front of her, turned it around and pushed it across the table. "Please.

Take your time. Read it carefully. While you do, however, allow me to bring everyone else up to speed. Eight years ago your son Lance attended a party at his fraternity house, a party, it turns out, where a high school senior named Tandi Crawford was last seen. We have photographic evidence that places your son at that party, Senator, so please don't waste anyone's time by denying it."

The senator lifted her eyes from the file and then closed it. She sat back and peered at Simone for a good few seconds. "I wasn't going to. My son attends a lot of parties."

"What that photograph also shows is that your son was in the company of a man named Alik Babin. Now I'm not going to waste anyone's time by explaining who that is because everyone in this room, yourself included, Senator, knows already. Since that night, your son has been arrested at least seven times for various crimes including possession with intent to sell, soliciting of prostitution, illegal gambling and statutory rape. All these charges, as you well know, have never made it past an initial arrest."

"My son has problems," Senator Wakeman said, the pulsing in her jaw her only giveaway that Simone was getting to her. "I've tried to help him when I could."

"Except he wasn't helping you very much, was he? Because Alik Babin knows something about your son. Something not even you could protect him from. And it's my belief Mr. Babin has been using that information ever since to make certain his criminal operations across this country have gone unchecked for the most part."

"I'd like to see evidence of these accusations, please."

Senator Wakeman shifted her stoic attention to Ward. "Or do you let your lackeys run with wild accusations all the time?"

"Personally, I'm finding this story fascinating," Ward said. "Please, Simone, go on."

"It must have frustrated you to no end," Simone said, "when I wouldn't cut a deal with Babin's money man. A man who had full knowledge of your son's illegal dealings with Babin. A man who could literally identify the money trail. Maybe if I had, maybe if I hadn't let the press pressure me, Mara—Natalie—would still be alive. You couldn't let that trial go ahead, could you? Once those books went into evidence and your son's name, the sole owner of LW, Inc., became part of the public record, there'd be no stopping the avalanche of trouble that was going to land on your head. So Mara had to go. And you had Dimitri there take care of her for you." Jack reentered the room, nodded once and stood with his back against the door.

Dimitri went stone-still.

"Looks like a painful scratch on your hand," Simone said to him. "About the size of a gold chain around a young woman's neck. Never mind. Now that we know where to look for you, we'll deal with you later."

No reaction.

"Ever the good soldier, right?" Simone's voice conveyed her annoyance. "Mara was good, too. Senator, she had your son dead to rights. And she was onto you. She found out about all of your, what was it you called me? Oh, right. Lackeys. You've got them everywhere, don't you? Even this office. Yes, we know about our intern who, until five minutes ago, worked as your spy. You had ears everywhere so you'd know when someone was getting close to Babin's operation, close to your son. And as the chairwoman of the committee on law enforcement, you had an open door to all the information you needed. What you didn't count on were those agents and officers with integrity, who would consider it an affront that a sitting senator would be in bed with a scumbag like Babin."

"As I said, my son has problems." The senator was shaking now. She lifted a trembling hand to smooth her already perfect hair. "One does…what one must to protect one's family."

Was the senator slurring her words?

"If that's an admission of guilt, it's not enough," Simone said.

"It's the opening salvo to a conversation, young lady," Senator Wakeman said. "What is it you want?"

"What I want." Simone's knuckles went white as she clenched her fists. Vince reached over, touched her arm and, in an instant, felt her relax. "What I want is for Mara Orlov to walk through those doors and live the life she'd planned. What I want is for Cal Hobard to be the one to lock Alik Babin away for life. What I want is for the woman I've spent most of my life looking up to, to tell me I'm completely wrong and that you haven't betrayed a lifetime of work. But I can't have any of that." Whatever despair had been in Simone's voice disappeared as she turned cold eyes on her one-time idol. "So I'll settle for your son."

"Given what I've already done to protect Lance," Senator Wakeman said with a snort that belied her reputation, "do you really think I'm going to allow that to happen? Lance is already out of your reach. I've made certain of it."

"Have you?" Simone smiled. "Because as of forty-five minutes ago the Los Angeles Police Department detained Lance while he was boarding a flight to Venezuela. He's in custody and is being brought here even as we speak. But I can tell you one thing with absolute certainty, Senator, that as much pleasure as this conversation we've been having has given me, I can't wait to talk to your boy."

Senator Wakeman licked her lips, her pallor slightly gray as she touched a hand to her throat. "I, um. I'm afraid I'm not feeling very well. Perhaps we could continue this at another—" She pushed herself up from her chair and wobbled, but even before she reached for the edge of the table, Vince shot to his feet.

The senator's eyes rolled back. She slid to the floor.

"Call 9-1-1!" Vince bellowed as her other body man dropped beside her and started CPR. "Simone?" He looked over the table at her. She stood and stared down at the scene as if from some great height. Cole slipped an arm around her shoulders.

She looked back at Vince with what he could only describe as dead eyes. "I guess there's no ridding myself of that stupid avenging angel moniker now, is there?"

She turned and walked out the door.

Chapter 20

Simone glanced away from her office window when the knock sounded on her door.

"Simone?" Kyla poked her head in. "Can I get you anything?"

"No, thanks." She rubbed her hands down her bare arms. "Are they gone?"

"The police and EMTs? Yes. Simone—"

"If you're about to tell me that you quit so you can work for Eden, please, can we discuss it another time?" She tried to smile as she walked over to her desk. A desk that she couldn't find any purpose for. The awards on her shelves, the evidence of her success, pictures with political stars and up-and-coming movers and shakers. She picked up the pen her father had given her. Clenched it in her fist. None of it seemed real.

"You're not getting rid of me that easily," Kyla said as

she entered the office. "This wasn't your fault. No one knew about her condition. You couldn't predict she'd—"

"That she'd die during questioning? Not even my overworked imagination could come up with that one." She sat behind her desk. There was something she needed to do. Something she was forgetting. But all she could see was the image of Senator Beverly Wakeman, a woman she'd admired, modeled herself after, dying right in front of her. "I'm fine, Kyla. Why don't you go home. Take the week off. With pay, of course."

"Not a chance. I'm sticking with you." Kyla moved closer, but Simone held up her hand.

"Kyla, I love you and I appreciate what you're saying, but believe me, there's nothing anyone can do right now for me except leave me be." She turned tear-filled eyes on her assistant. "Please. I'll call you when I'm ready for you to come back, okay?"

"Yeah, okay." Kyla nodded and backed out of the room.

Simone sagged in her chair, waiting for the door to click, but it didn't. Instead, it opened again and Vince walked in, looking every bit as determined as she'd expected him to. "If you're here to talk about Jason, not now."

He stopped, his hand still on the doorknob, a flash of anger crossing his stony features. "I'm not here about Jason. I'm here for you."

"I'd rather be alone." She gripped the edge of her desk, trying to find something, anything, to concentrate on. If she didn't, she was afraid she'd shatter.

"I'm not going to give you the 'this wasn't your fault' speech if that's what you're thinking."

"Good, because Ward, Agent Fitzhugh, Cole, Jack and Kyla beat you to it."

"That's because I thought you'd take it better from them than me." He walked over and sat on the edge of her desk, inches away from her. Warming her. Making her want nothing more than to bury herself in his arms even as she wanted him to leave. "Life stinks, Simone. The two of us know that better than most people. I'm not going to cry over that woman's death. Nor should you."

"Then maybe you should have been the one lobbing verbal threats in her direction."

"Her dying does mean Lance Wakeman won't have any choice but to testify against Babin. He'll get a deal, sure, and he'll serve some time, but we'll get what we were after—Alik Babin. Fitzhugh said his men have already taken him into custody. And you know what? First thing he did was confess to Tandi Crawford's murder. They've got agents out looking for her body as we speak. You did it, Simone. You got him."

"And it didn't cost me a thing."

"It didn't, actually," Vince said. "Sitting around here feeling sorry for yourself isn't going to get you anywhere."

"What would you like me to do, Vince?" She rose and stared at him, jaw set. "Maybe we should take that little jaunt down to the prison to talk with your brother? See what bits of useless information I can pry loose in the lost hope I can get him out of there? Does that work for you?" She jerked open her desk drawer and yanked out her purse. She needed him gone, out of her life if she had any hope of being seen as impartial and getting his brother out. "Well, let's go. I haven't got anything pressing on me anymore. I'm free and clear, got to make sure I live up to my end of my bargain."

He was quiet for a long time, but she wasn't going to give in. She couldn't. Not when this had to be done.

"Is this how you want to end things between us, Simone? On this note? By going back on your word to me?" He crossed his arms and looked at her. His pin-point gaze had her squirming, and not in that mind-blowing way he had last night.

He'd opened the door she'd needed. Now all she had to do was walk through it. "How could you have been so blind? I never had any intention of talking to your brother. How could I when he's part of the reason I'm sitting in this chair? I needed your help, Vince. I did what I had to in order to get it. I used Jason. I used you."

"I know."

She barely hid the gasp. "What do you mean you know?"

"Correction. I suspected." And there, right in front of her eyes, she saw the man who had walked out on her three years ago. The hurt. The betrayal. The disap-pointment. "I wanted to believe you could put me and what I needed ahead of your career, your desires, but I didn't quite manage it. Now I know why. You just con-firmed it." He walked to the door. "Did you ever do what I asked and think back on the night I left you?"

"No. I haven't had—"

"Time, yeah, I figured. I asked you to come home, to help me celebrate."

"Celebrate what?"

"That was the day I bought the bar. I wanted to sur-prise you with it, to share it with you because it was something you told me to go for. And I did. But you got caught up in a case and didn't call. And when you finally got home at around midnight, you didn't even ask me about the dinner or the wine or the key to the custom glass doors I planned to have made. You just forgot."

Simone couldn't move. She couldn't breathe. She didn't remember. Even now, she had no recollection of his call, of his invitation. Of the excitement he must have been feeling.

"I'm glad you've closed the Denton case, Simone. Glad for whatever else will come of it." He gave her a smile, dipped his head and opened the door. "Have a good life."

And then he was gone.

"You're not even going to offer to go kick his butt this time, are you?" Simone asked Allie and Eden as they poured generous glasses of wine and joined her on her sofa.

"Nope." Eden shoved her feet against Simone's thighs. "But I might kick yours. You're a class-A fool, you know that?"

"I did what I had to do." Simone wondered when the tears would stop threatening to spill. It had been almost two weeks since the Denton case had been officially closed. Alik Babin had been charged on numerous federal counts, Lance Wakeman was being sequestered by the FBI, US Marshals and at least a half dozen California police departments in regard to several missing persons cases, including Tandi Crawford's.

And last week, Washington had paid homage to Senator Beverly Wakeman, who, as far as anyone else knew, had died of shock after learning of her son's lifetime of misdeeds.

That the senator's bodyguard and hit man had pled guilty to the deaths of Natalie Subrov, aka Mara Orlov, and Special Agent Cal Hobard and was going to a penitentiary for at least two lifetimes should have been the icing on Simone's professional cake.

"You two are always taking things to the extremes." Allie sighed and grabbed a handful of the tortilla chips Simone had become addicted to. "Eden filled me in on how you managed to get Jason Sutton an early release. There wasn't any reason you had to cut ties with Vince to make it happen. You could have figured a way around that if you'd really wanted to."

Could she? Or had she just been too scared to take the chance? "I didn't want any of the favors I had to call in coming back on him." Simone tugged at a loose thread on her yoga pants. Her black yoga pants. Her days as the DA's Avenging Angel were over. Oh, she still had her job, as did Kyla, but she had yet to find anything remotely appealing about returning to work. Everything felt different now. Tainted. Painful. "Jason was wrongfully convicted by the system I represent. He got cheated partly because of me."

"And that means you needed to sacrifice your own personal happiness? And you call me egotistical." Eden leaned over and hauled out her bag. "And honest to Pete, could you please start stocking some chocolate in this place? My daily venture into the store that must not be named is costing me a fortune." She revealed a white candy box familiar in the valley and popped open the lid. "Considering we've got a murderous stalker breathing down our necks, I'd think you'd want to grab a little happiness where you can."

"That sounds like the perfect way to top off the day." Simone glared at her friend. "Let's talk about Chloe."

"Maybe we should." Allie stunned them into silence. "We never have. We never do. We tiptoe around her like we're walking on her grave. We lost a friend whose murderer was never caught. He's celebrating that, reveling in it, and I can't go another day without dealing with it. Now we have a chance to find him, to make him pay for what he did and instead we've been trying to find something, anything else to focus on as we just hope it'll all go away."

"Allie," Eden whispered. "That's not what we've—"

"Of course it is. You with your super-dangerous investigations and Simone with her avenging angel thing and then there's me, who's spent more than half her life trying to figure out why that psychopath killed our friend."

"Allie, what's going on?" Simone shifted out of her self-imposed melancholy and took her friend's hand. "This doesn't sound like you at all."

Allie blinked big dark eyes at them. "I'm tired. I'm so tired of thinking and worrying and analyzing. I want all of this to be over and know he's been ended, to know that Chloe can finally rest in peace because we got him." She sobbed. "I want to sleep through the night, just once, and not wake up in the morning to realize the nightmare's still happening. And above all, I want what you two have. Eden with Cole, and you, you big dummy, if you don't understand and see how much Vince loves you, you're even more of a blockhead than I thought you were."

"He has done a lot for you, you know," Eden said.

"Yes, I know." Simone sighed. "Coming to work for me even when he didn't believe I'd help Jason—"

"That's not what I'm talking about." Eden glanced across Simone to Allie, who shrugged.

"No reason not to tell her now. Not if she doesn't care about him."

"I never said I didn't care about him. And tell me what?" Simone demanded.

"Sounds a little like she cares to me." Eden tapped her fingers along the chocolates. "Which one is the coconut again? I always forget."

"It's the one I'm going to cram into your face if you don't tell me what you're talking about," Simone snapped. "What did Vince do?"

"Aside from falling even harder for you than the first time around?" Eden rolled her eyes. "Come on, Simone. You don't really think you got that continuance from Judge Buford by your arguments, do you?"

"Settle in." Allie patted Simone's leg. "This is going to be good."

"We're not open until five!" Vince bellowed through the door of the bar when the knock sounded for the second time. "Come back then."

Or don't. Whatever. Vince slapped the dishtowel against his leg and rounded the counter. He noticed Travis and his manager giving him a wide berth these days. Not that he could blame them. Watching the tributes to Senator Wakeman pour in over the last few weeks was enough to turn him into a giant green rage monster.

"They're not going away." Travis stepped back as if getting out of the line of fire. "Maybe we should make an exception?"

"I'll make an exception all right." Grateful for someone to yell at that wouldn't end with him being sued for abusive behavior, he ripped open the lock and pulled on the door. "Can't you—" He blinked, staring at the young man in front of him. He was taller than Vince remembered, hunched, but that pretty-boy face of his hadn't changed save for the feather-thin scars on his left cheek. "Jason?"

"Hey." A sheepish smile crept over his brother's mouth and lit his blue eyes almost to the point of brilliance. "Sorry about the time. I was afraid I might lose my courage—"

"Oh, Jason." Vince stepped forward and wrapped his arms around his brother. He held on, remembering all the times he'd held this frightened little boy as his father had raged, protected him as best he could even when he'd feared for himself. He didn't want to let go for fear his brother would disappear again. Only when Jason returned the embrace did he force himself to do so. "How are you here? When did you get out?" He gripped Jason's face in his hands. "Are you okay?"

"I'm good." Jason nodded. "Better than good. I wasn't sure if you wanted to see me, but I thought I'd take a chance." He beamed. "I guess I'm glad I did."

"Get in here." Vince slung his arm around Jason's shoulder and dragged him inside. "Travis, this is my kid brother, Jason."

"Hey." Jason's trademark shyness seemed even more intense than before, something Vince should have expected given how he'd spent the last few years.

"You hungry? You want something to eat? I want to hear everything, beginning with how long you've been out."

"Ah, a burger would be great and I'm happy to fill you in. I got out this morning."

"This morning? Why didn't you call me? Wait." Vince frowned as he pushed Jason into the booth Simone had sat in only weeks before. *Simone...*"I thought your parole hearing wasn't for another few years."

"Me, too. My new lawyer has some major pull, I guess. Some bigwig out of Los Angeles. Two weeks ago I went into a meeting room and there he was. Knew more about my situation than anyone else and told me he was getting me out."

Suspicion grabbed Vince around the throat. "How is that even possible?"

"He wouldn't give me any details, except to say none of it would have happened without someone pulling strings on the other side. And he mentioned some reporter woman, Evelyn, Elaine—"

Vince's breath caught in his chest. "Eden?"

"That's it. Eden." Jason grinned. "Should have remembered that. Pretty name. Why? You know her?"

"Oh, I know her. I also know she doesn't work alone. Let me get you that burger." He pulled out his phone as he headed into the kitchen. "Eden? Vince. I'd like to speak to you. In person. Come to the bar. Tonight. You know why."

"Are you sure about this leave of absence, Simone?" Ward looked across his desk at her as if he expected her to explode. "That's a pretty big decision to make after everything that's happened. You could ride this publicity straight through to the election."

"I'm sure." Other than her decision to go to law school and become a prosecutor, she'd never been more sure of anything in her life. "The job isn't for me. It's not what I want."

"Maybe I haven't made being DA appear as glamorous as I should."

Simone smiled. "Not sure that's possible."

"You have to know the job's yours if you want it, election aside. You've got some of the best approval ratings they've seen in decades. The FBI and police department have heaped enough praise on you that you can write your own ticket from here on."

"I'm happy where I am." But that didn't mean she didn't need a break. "A few more rungs up the ladder might be nice someday…"

"Consider it done."

"But District Attorney?" She considered her options once again. "No. I want my freedom, Ward. I want to have a life." And she'd have one, of some kind at least, once they finally brought Chloe's killer to justice. Something she couldn't do while under the active employ of the DA's office. "And there are some things I want to do when I get back. I've got some vacation time I want to take."

"Ah." Ward referenced what was showing on his computer. "All at once?"

Was that a gasp she heard? "How about I take a month and you give the other month to Kyla. She's got the bar coming up and I'd like her to be able to focus on it completely."

"You two make quite the team. I heard she was instrumental in puzzling together Mara's, um, Natalie's evidence."

"If she hadn't thought to look through the old fraternity pictures, we wouldn't have connected Wakeman to

Babin." And none of this would have happened. "You might keep that in mind if and when she applies for a position in this office."

"I will. You heading out today?"

"Yeah. Just need to clean a few things up first. I'll give you a call and let you know when I'll be back." She headed to the door.

"Whatever else you might think, Simone, you did extraordinary work on this case. You've made a real difference."

"Thanks." She only wished his compliments mattered as much as they used to. "Have a good day."

"Oh, hey, Simone." Kyla jumped up from her desk looking as if she'd been bitten by something. "Everything go okay?"

"Mmm-hmm. You're officially off for a month with pay. So get to studying. Don't let me down by failing the bar your first time out. Messages?" She held out her hand for the stack she'd come to expect. Requests for interviews, consults, old so-called friends reaching out, she'd been inundated by them ever since she'd become a front-page headline thanks to Benedict Russell and his new syndicated national column.

"Not too many today. You should get through them quickly." She handed over the pile. "And one more thing?"

Simone stopped at her door. "What's that?"

"You have a visitor." She bent down to retrieve her things.

"You leaving already? I thought maybe we could get lunch." She tried to hide her disappointment as Kyla headed down the hall.

"I think you'll be too busy rattling windows. I'll call you!"

"Rattling windows?" Simone mumbled, shaking her head. "Sometimes I don't know what gets into that girl's—Vince!" She stopped short inside her office where she found him sitting behind her desk. "What are you doing here?"

Part of her braced herself for whatever verbal assault he'd returned to lob at her, but the other part, the part that was in love with him, had never been so happy to see anyone in her life. Two weeks had felt like a lifetime. She sagged, tried to stiffen her spine, but she was exhausted. Given everything she'd been through recently, she knew two weeks could very well be a lifetime.

"I don't know if you're aware." He kicked his feet up on her desk, probably in an effort to annoy her. It worked. She stalked over and smacked her hand against his boots. "But I really hate being lied to."

"Too bad." She tossed her messages onto her desk. "I repeat, what are you doing here?"

"You got Jason out of prison." He leaned back, folded his hands behind his head and stared at her. "You didn't want anything getting in the way, including your relationship with me, so you led me to believe you weren't doing anything to keep up your end of the bargain."

He was here out of gratitude? Pride shifted between them. "I don't know what you're—"

"Don't!" He shot to his feet and grabbed hold of her arms. "No more lies, Simone." He kissed her, a brief pressing of lips, almost gentle, but she leaned into him, caught hold of him and a soft sob escaped. "You put him first," he murmured against her lips. "You put me first."

"Not in the beginning." He deserved the truth. And she didn't want any more lies between them. "I couldn't see any way to do it, but then Eden offered to help."

"I talked to Eden last night. She told me everything."

"She's been doing a lot of sharing recently. You had her run a game on Denton's lawyer to make him late for court."

He grinned. "You play things your way, I'll play things mine. What do you say? You want to give us another shot? A real shot this time? An equal shot?"

"Yes." Her whispered response was doused by the disappointment crashing through her. "Yes, I do, but I can't, Vince. Not now. The timing." She broke off, wondering how to tell him what was coming down the road. "It wouldn't be fair… I can't focus on you, on us until…"

"Until Chloe's killer is caught?" He kissed her again and drew her into the circle of his arms. She slipped her arms around him, clung to him, afraid to let him go again. "Eden told me that, too. Maybe you all could use some help with that? Seeing as I've got a new assistant manager at the bar now, I'm reopening my investigation business. Helping to close a twenty-year-old murder case sounds like a good place to start."

She squeezed her eyes shut. Of course he'd offer her everything she needed. "I love you. I promise, I've learned from the past. I won't—"

"We aren't going to make promises neither of us can keep," he said. "But what we can do is promise to always talk. To communicate. To be honest with each other."

"And maybe set strict office hours so as not to interfere with our personal time?" She smiled against his chest. "I can make that work if you can."

"Sounds like an arrangement I can live with. What do you say?" He leaned back and looked into her eyes. "Wanna take another chance and marry me again?"

"I do." She lifted her head and kissed him. "I really, really do."

* * * * *

Be sure to check out the first book in
Anna J. Stewart's HONOR BOUND *miniseries*
MORE THAN A LAWMAN
available now from Harlequin Romantic Suspense.

And look for the next HONOR BOUND *story from*
Anna J. Stewart, coming in October 2017!

⊕ HARLEQUIN®

ROMANTIC suspense

Available June 6, 2017

#1947 KILLER COWBOY
Cowboys of Holiday Ranch • by Carla Cassidy

When a serial killer sets his sights on ranch owner Cassie Peterson, it's up to Chief of Police Dillon Bowie to keep her safe...and keep his own heart from getting broken!

#1948 COLD CASE COLTON
The Coltons of Shadow Creek • by Addison Fox

Claudia Colton never thought returning to Shadow Creek would unlock the secrets of her past, but when PI Hawk Huntley shows up on her doorstep, he brings more than answers. Danger—and love—is hot on his heels!

#1949 ESCORTED BY THE RANGER
by C.J. Miller

Supermodel Marissa Walker's best frenemy is found murdered backstage, and everyone is convinced Marissa did it. When the attacker targets her as well, Jack Larson, a former army ranger, is called in to protect her. But as the attraction sizzles between them, the killer is trying to get closer than they ever imagined...

#1950 SILENT RESCUE
by Melinda Di Lorenzo

Detective Brooks Small is on forced vacation in Quebec. He's cold, miserable and wants to go home. Until he spots a frightened woman held at gunpoint. Soon, he's convincing the woman—Maryse LePrieur—to let him help her save her kidnapped daughter. It doesn't take long for the attraction he feels to ignite, and the rescue mission quickly becomes personal.

_____

HRSCNM0517

Tears she hadn't even realized were so close to the surface
spilled over with little prompting.

"Hey. Hey there." Hawk was gentle as he reached out,
his hands resting on her shoulders. "What's wrong?"

"It's just that—" Her breath caught and she hiccuped
around another thick layer of tears. "It's Cody. Something
could have happened to him. I mean, I understood it. But
until I saw him before and realized—"

The large, gentle hands that gripped her shoulders
tugged, pulling her close so that she was flush against his
chest. Before she could check the impulse, she wrapped
her arms around his waist as he pulled her close.

"It's going to be okay." The words were whispered
against her head, a promise she tried desperately to cling
to through her tears.

"But what if it isn't? She's—" Another tearful hiccup
gripped her. "My mother's still out there. My family is
still at risk."

Her fears raced faster than she could keep up with them.
The questions that whispered late at night through her
mind, wondering where her mother was since escaping

from prison. The continued fears that Ben wasn't done with her, determined to wend his way to Shadow Creek to come after her. And now the possible news about her own birth.

When had it all gone so wrong?

And would any of them ever be free from the diabolical influences of Livia Colton?

The tears that had pushed her into Hawk's arms faded as the rush of adrenaline and emotion worked its way through her system. In its place was the haunting realization of just how good it felt to stand in the circle of Hawk's arms and lean on him. She was a tall woman, and she'd always had a figure her mother had kindly—and not so kindly, pending her mood—dubbed big-boned.

How humbling, then, to realize he still had several inches on her and his big, strong arms were more than long enough to wrap around her soundly.

She felt protected.

Safe.

And for the moment, she was fighting an increasing attraction to a man she had no business wanting. Aside from the fact they didn't know each other, Hawk had plenty of baggage of his own and a life he likely wanted to get back to. His visit to Shadow Creek had a purpose.

A goal.

And once he reached that goal, he'd leave Shadow Creek and all its depravity and deceit in his dust.

Don't miss
COLD CASE COLTON
by Addison Fox, available June 2017 wherever
Harlequin® Romantic Suspense books
and ebooks are sold.

www.Harlequin.com

HRSEXP0517

JUST CAN'T GET ENOUGH?

Join our social communities
and talk to us online.

You will have access to the latest
news on upcoming titles and special
promotions, but most importantly,
you can talk to other fans about your
favorite Harlequin reads.

Harlequin.com/Community

 Facebook.com/HarlequinBooks

Twitter.com/HarlequinBooks

 Pinterest.com/HarlequinBooks

THE WORLD IS BETTER WITH

Romance

Harlequin has everything from contemporary, passionate and heartwarming to suspenseful and inspirational stories.

Whatever your mood,
we have a romance just for you!

Connect with us to find your next great read, special offers and more.

 /HarlequinBooks

@HarlequinBooks

www.HarlequinBlog.com

www.Harlequin.com/Newsletters

◆ HARLEQUIN®

 A *Romance* FOR EVERY MOOD™

www.Harlequin.com